The Caging at Deadwater Manor

SANDIE WILL

Disclaimer: *The Caging at Deadwater Manor* is a work of fiction. Names, characters, places and incidents either are the products of the author's imagination or are used fictitiously. Any resemblance to actual persons, living or dead, events or locales is entirely coincidental.

DEDICATION

For my wonderful dad.
Thanks for the insight on the story.
I miss you.

ACKNOWLEDGMENTS

Thank you to my husband, Charlie, two sons, Tom and Michael, and Aunt Lesley for the endless support and encouragement throughout this process, especially the hours of listening and reading my story as it evolved.

Thank you to my sister, Jill Celeste, and promotions director, Suzanne Moore, for the social media help, marketing guidance, and your patience while I asked a thousand questions.

Thanks also to Trisha Stucker and Beth Seletos for your editing and insight and Shirley Burnett for the perfect cover.

Special thanks to my virtual promotions team for your support in helping me make this book a success. I can't express how thankful I am to all of you for your many words of encouragement and sharing promotions on the day of the book release. You all rock!

1

Standing outside my bedroom, I take a deep breath before tiptoeing across the dark, creaky hardwood floors that lead down the hallway. The last thing I want is to draw attention. I've practiced the same pattern almost every day since I was a kid, just to be prepared for days like this. If I hit the boards carefully, odds are, they won't tell on me.

I'm feeling nervous, though. He's right around the corner. One creak and I'll be back in my room, stuck in my cell, wishing I could get the hell out.

I hate him, really.

When I was a kid, I would have never thought it possible. I used to look at him with adoring eyes like any daughter would. In time, though, especially without my mom around, he's become more and more distant and—well, I guess there's no other way to say it—mean. I know every kid at one time in his or her life says this about a parent or two, but this thought is not fleeting for me like it is for others. They get over their anger and feel the bond again with their parent. I've never had that opportunity with him. Just talking to me sets him off, and his irritable mood always ends with another insult, especially if he's drinking. So, I decided years ago to avoid him as much as possible.

The best way to do this is to leave, and tonight is the same as every other night. I want to get out. I want to ride my bike along Baillie's Bluff Drive and the winding roads that lead me to River

Park and my friends. It isn't the best beach along the West Coast of Florida, but it feels like *ours*. My friends and I have gone there since before the park opened to the public, when the beach was pristine and the smell of boat exhaust was non-existent.

I miss those days.

Unfortunately, my dad came home before I could leave to meet my friends. He must have finished with his "victims" early. He's usually still at his office torturing someone in his dental chair at this time of night. Being the only dentist open late—useful for patients who work nine-to-five jobs—means he has an easier time stealing their money with his overcharged fees. I never understood how a person by the name of Doctor Kynde could end up such a douche.

I begin down the hallway, my muscles aching with each exaggerated step, and reach for the quietest spot while steadying myself against the wall. As I make my way, I curse him for forcing me to take the bedroom on the second floor, leaving me no exit route but the front door. That is the door to my freedom—freedom that only comes when I feel the warm summer breeze sweep past my skin and witness the envelope of a pink and blue sky that's about to fold into its own darkness until revealed again in the early morning hours. It's only during this time that I can fathom escaping this hell.

"Hey, Jeannie weenie! Happy birthday, you old lady, you!" my brother calls, as he runs across every creaky board on his way toward me.

I spin around to see his smiling face, which quickly freezes into an awkward stare when he sees me mouth "shut the fuck up!" I quickly glance down the hallway for our dad.

"What, you turn eighteen and hostile all in the same day? What's up?"

That's all it takes. I soon hear the clunk of his recliner and feel the vibrations from his heavy footsteps, which are now heading my way. In all of thirty seconds, my hopes of escape will be gone.

"You absolutely suck, you know?" I spout back. "Now, I'm stuck having to deal with Dad on my birthday. Thanks."

"Aw, come on! I haven't seen you all day and this is all I get?

I'm your favorite brother. Remember that, or has senility set in?"

I glare at him to be quiet but know it's too late. I will soon hear the boisterous voice of my dad bellowing at the back of my head, wishing me an insincere "happy birthday." I close my eyes, preparing myself. My heart begins its exaggerated thumping as soon as I hear his raspy breathing.

"Rick, you talking in her good ear, or what? I'd like to wish Miss Handicapped a happy birthday, too," he shouts, making his way closer to me. "Maybe she's not really handicapped. Maybe she's just faking it. We know how she likes to lie and keep secrets." He belches. The stench of beer suddenly permeates the air around me.

I glance over to Rick, who is staring sharply at Dad, and then bow my head in hurt. My breathing grows shallower, and I move toward my room, knowing I'll cry as soon as I close the door.

I hate my hearing problem, but I hate him more. It's not like I can't hear anything at all. My left ear is deaf, but my right ear is fine. Even if I were fully deaf, I'm not sure why he has to attack me over it. I can't help it that I was struck in the head with a baseball. Besides, why would I lie about something like that? Why is he questioning it now?

"What's the matter, my little sweetheart? Where's the happiness that you used to have, huh? Why the hell are you so miserable all the time? Could it be related to being a liar? Perhaps if you hold your nose and blow out your ears hard, you'll be able to hear again, huh? What do you think about that idea?" He snorts in my good ear, holding my arm so I can't get away from him. "If you think that I'm wasting my money on some ear doctor that's going to tell me my daughter can function just fine, you can forget it!"

Now he's enraged, looking at me with disgust in his eyes. "Did you hear any of that, or are you just too stupid? Huh? Can you hear me? Huh? Huh? All I ever hear is 'huh' from you. It gets annoying, doesn't it?"

I pull away as hard as I can, not wanting him to see the pain in my eyes, but he has too tight of a grip for me to escape. He then comes closer, slowly, resting his mouth near my good ear. I brace for words that a child should never have to hear—words engrained in my psyche since Mom died.

"You're nothing but an embarrassment to this family. We might as well lock you up and throw away the key—forever. Lord knows, your mother must have regretted having had you."

I don't respond, knowing I can never get back at him through the sobs. It's bad enough he's seeing the tears flowing down my cheeks and onto the floor, dotting the wood grain in no particular pattern.

He pushes himself in closer, pinning me against the wall. "What do you think, Jeannie? Should I lock you up for the rest of your life? Mom's gone, so you should be gone too. You need to pay for what you've done."

I stretch as far away from him as possible, pulling myself toward my room.

"I know what you did to her," he growls.

I reach for the doorknob, until he finally retreats and lets go of me at just the right moment to make me slam into the door. I glance over to my brother. He looks horrified. It's the same look as always. My brother is no match for my dad. He has tried several times to come to my rescue, but he's not as big as my dad. Besides, it only fuels my dad's tongue into even worse offenses toward me. All my brother can do is watch and help me recover later.

I fumble around until I finally find the doorknob and throw myself into my bedroom, slamming the door behind me and bracing myself up against it breathlessly. I can taste the salt of tears on my lips, as I wait for further character slaying.

Please leave. Oh God, please make him leave!

I rest my good ear against the door to hear him better. He's right outside my door. I can hear his breathing—a loud, erratic gurgling sound that echoes through my room.

"You can't hide in there forever, Jeannie. We need to talk. So, let me in!" The door thuds against my back, sliding me forward until I dig my heels into the carpet and push back with all my strength.

I don't care if he breaks me in two. I'm not budging. He'll have to break down the door to get to me.

A couple of thuds later, he finally stops, clears his throat and heads back down the hallway. As he leaves, I whisper desperately, "One of these days I'll leave you forever, you bastard."

His footsteps stop abruptly after my last word. My heart leaps. Panic sears through my limbs, making me push harder against the door again. I listen quietly for his return. After a few moments, however, he finally continues down the hall. I start to relax, but this gives way to the jerking and shaking of panic attacks, which I suffer from on a daily basis now.

Panic attacks caused by my own dad.

They're not mild, either. As usual, my heart pounds uncontrollably in an erratic rhythm, as though it will launch out of my chest. I lean forward over my thighs. My breathing is short and shallow, which panics me more than anything else. I start breathing heavily, gasping for air.

There's nothing like the feeling of not being able to breathe. I guess I can relate to how my mom felt just before she died.

I keep telling myself that it will pass. This helps me calm down bit by bit, until eventually my breathing becomes less labored. I lean back against the door again, fatigued from it all.

Crawling over to my bed, I hoist myself up onto it with the help of the dresser. My limbs are weak with exhaustion. It usually takes me a couple hours to finally gain control of my body.

My mother's picture is staring back at me on the nightstand. Hopefully she's been watching over me all these years somehow. I'm not sure if it's possible, but this is the only place I feel safe. It's the only place where I still feel near her, but away from him. In some ways though, he's getting his way. I *am* locked away, hiding from him and his drunken tirades. I'm afraid that one of these days, he'll make sure it's permanent.

I throw myself onto the bed and grab her picture. "I miss you, Mom. I wish you were here. Dad's gone insane, and we're all not functioning very well without you. I don't know what to do. I need you, goddamnit! The past four years have been hell. You know how uncomfortable he is with my hearing thing? Well, now it's worse than ever, and he thinks I'm faking it. I'm not! On top of that he's constantly drinking and telling me I should be locked away. That I've done wrong by you. I don't know what he's talking about. He just goes ballistic when he's drunk. If you can hear me somehow, someway, can you make him stop?" I plead. I try to have faith that she can hear me, but every day, it fades, because she probably would have reached out to me by now. There are plenty of people who claim they've reconnected with their departed loved ones, but I'm not sure if it's true. I have yet to experience anything from her.

No matter how much I try to block it out, her death is fresh in my mind. It might be because it was so unexpected or perhaps it was the way it happened. I don't know. All I know is that my mind is jumbled from the shock, because I can't remember much about the days leading up to her death. I can't even remember our last conversation. If only I had the opportunity to talk with her one last time.

* * * *

The call came in about nine o'clock on a Thursday night in January. Mom wasn't home yet, which was unusual. We assumed it was her calling, but it wasn't. My dad's expression grew tense, and he suddenly became still, listening intently to the doctor from the hospital. After he assured them he'd be in, he dropped the phone and walked out of the kitchen to the front foyer. Looking for his car keys, he yelled at us to hurry and find them for him. He didn't tell us what was wrong at first, only that he was taking us to see Mom, since she wasn't feeling well.

For all his rush, when we pulled up to the hospital, my dad didn't immediately get out of the car. I grew impatient and grabbed his shoulder, demanding to know what was going on. He could only sob into his hands. Rick and I just looked at each other, not knowing what to do. So, we dragged Dad out of the car and into the hospital lobby. I remember wanting to cry but couldn't, since I truly believed she'd be okay. At that point, I still thought she was just "not feeling well."

The hospital attendant guided us down a hallway. I peered into every room searching for her, wanting to see her sitting up in bed slurping down soup like the rest of the patients I observed on the way. I remember wondering if she'd have the full getup like all the others with their oxygen tubes and intravenous lines.

We stopped at the doorway of one of the rooms. I assumed this was my mom's, and it took everything in me to keep from rushing in. The nurse looked over to me with pity in her eyes, as she ushered my dad into the room. "You're May Kynde's husband, right?" she asked.

He nodded.

"I think you should go in alone first."

At that point, I knew my mom was in there. My worst fear was confirmed.

I couldn't think about the possibility of her dying though, and I don't think Rick could either. Instead, we both watched the ongoing nursing activity, as the streams of traffic passed back and forth. I tried to keep my focus more on the nurse's family interactions in the other rooms rather than my mom's. I couldn't bear the reality. I kept thinking how the other patients' families looked pretty happy, with no sign of death or gloom. The only ones who looked even winded were the nurses who scurried around, attached to their computer stands as they rolled them by, complaining about the immense time it was taking to finish their data entry. All I could think was that this was a good sign. Maybe these families were past the initial panic and scare of serious conditions. Maybe these families weren't losing their moms. If this section of the hospital was for patients like them, it only made sense that I wouldn't lose my mom either.

As I watched my dad walking toward us with a lost expression, though, I knew immediately that I would never talk with my mom again. I'd never hear her voice or sit chatting on our porch over her coffee and my hot chocolate on Sunday mornings. What would I do without my anchor? She was the one that knew me better than anybody—the one who made me feel safe.

What would my dad do without her? He had his issues, but when it came to Mom, he loved her deeply, completely. How would he manage without her?

My thoughts raced through all the things I would miss and all the things she would miss too. How was a fourteen-year-old supposed to handle this?

"You want to see her?" asked my dad, whose eyes were now red and puffy. His voice was crackly as he explained that she drowned in a car accident. She was under water for at least forty-five minutes before anyone found her—way too long for her to maintain brain function without oxygen. He had to stop the machines that were keeping her alive. She was basically a vegetable: lifeless.

I searched his face for a better answer than that. I just kept thinking that somehow he had to fix this. When he didn't acknowledge me any further, I looked away, refusing to accept the unacceptable.

Then, all of a sudden, I knew I had to see her—somehow I could save her.

I pushed past my dad and the nurse and entered her room. My heart was pounding when I reached the curtain that was separating me from my mom. I quickly slid it open to reveal the image that has haunted me every night since.

I'll never forget her face. It was bloated and distorted and looked nothing like my mom's. She didn't look peaceful either. Her gray hands were clenched, as if they were still holding onto the seatbelt. I think her hands have bothered me more than her face all these years.

I stood there watching her for some miracle of a movement. Finally, I softly whispered, "Mom?" to see if she would turn to look at me. The realization that she had died didn't take long to set in after her motionless body didn't respond.

I cried then, thinking of how she must have screamed as her car filled with water; she must have struggled with her seatbelt as she desperately tried to free herself; she must have suffered as she drew in water with every breath; she must have been scared as she suffocated in the dark—alone and cold. Goose bumps raised on my arms as I wondered if she thought of us before going unconscious.

What was *I* doing while she was struggling in the car? I can't remember exactly, but I'm sure it was something stupid and meaningless. This crushed me, because I should have known—should have felt *something* or sensed something was wrong. If I had, could I have helped her in some way?

"I'm sorry, Mom," I said between sobs. "I'm sorry I didn't sense it."

She still didn't move. I leaned in then and whispered, "I love you."

* * * *

Now, all I can do is stare at her picture until I can't think about it anymore. These spells of self-doubt and anguish are becoming a pattern after my dad's attacks. I know on some level I'm still mourning her and need him for comfort, but he continually pushes me away.

Before the accident, he was a different person. We'd go hiking and kayaking. We'd camp in tents and sing songs under a full moon. Sure, Rick and I would go to Mom to talk about our problems, but Dad was always there with a quiet, steady hand. He was my hero.

When Mom died, we lost Dad. At first I thought the stress of being a single dad and dealing with our grief didn't give him a chance to deal with his own. As time has gone on, though, he continued his career, but he never continued our relationship. All he finds comfort in is his beer. His anger toward me has become unbearable and I don't know what to do. All I know is that I miss my dad—the quiet, caring man who loved me.

I try to block the pain with my music, but the deafening hissing sound in my left ear is louder than usual tonight, causing me to rethink that idea. As I try to ignore the never-ending noise in my head, I hate myself again and wish I were "normal" in my dad's eyes. If only we were the happy family we used to be.

Unfortunately, tonight's no different than any other night, even though it's Thursday, June 2, 2016.

Happy eighteenth birthday to me.

2

"Jean! You okay, Jean?"

Someone pushes me on the shoulder, startling me. I swipe at the person who owns the jabbing fingers, half-pissed that I was woken up and half-afraid that they might belong to my dad.

Yeah, right. Like he'd ever ask if I was okay.

"Jeannie, don't listen to him. He's an ass, and a fat ass at that."

I grin slightly at my brother's voice. Always trying to make me feel better after the storm.

"I hate him for hating me so much," I moan, stretching and waking up. "Mom would never let him treat me like this."

"What happened to your hearing and Mom's accident is not your fault. I don't know what his problem is and why he's always accusing you of being a liar and a faker. I wish I could tear his head off when he attacks you like that, but I know I'll only make it worse for you," Rick says, sounding frustrated. "I'm sorry, Jeannie."

"I need to get out of here."

"Now? I can take you over to River Park if you want. Dad left after his tirade two hours ago, so we probably should leave before he gets back."

"No, I mean forever," I say, slowly lifting my head off the pillow to look for my green Keds on the floor. My hair is matted to my face with the dried tears that streamed onto my pillow earlier. I push my hair back.

"Jeannie, just let me take you out for your birthday dinner. We can go anywhere you want."

Rick looks frazzled and nervous, shaking his leg as he talks to me. His layers of blonde hair are lying across his forehead. It looks like he just styled it. Rick is perfect. He is just what Dad wants. He's smart, driven, fit—and easily controlled. He also has the added bonus of having nothing wrong with him to embarrass the family. For that, Rick is rewarded with lavish gifts at every occasion and all the love my dad can muster. I want to hate Rick, but I can't. We've been through this for years together.

"I think my birthday was over when Dad screamed at me in the hallway. I need some time to think—and plan."

"Well," Rick says, studying me, "okay. I understand. You're not going to go do something stupid like kill yourself or run away though, are you?"

"I'm calculating leaving this house, not life," I say, getting up from the bed. "Oh, and it isn't 'running away' anymore, because I'm an adult. I'm going to do what adults are supposed to do, and leave. Plus, I'm not stupid, you idiot."

Rick looks at me with remorse. "Point taken, Jeannie. About leaving, though. Adults usually have a plan and a little money. If not, they end up homeless. But that's enough preaching from your older brother, though. Let me know if you change your mind about dinner."

I leave Rick behind and head to the garage to pull out my only wheels–my road bike. My brother got a BMW for his sixteenth birthday, and all I got was a little cash to buy myself "something safe." Dad was convinced that I'd kill myself with a car, because I "can't hear anything." So, between the cash and some neighborhood window washing, I bought myself my form of escape.

I pedal down Baillie's Bluff Drive like always. It's later than usual, though. I wish I had a cell phone to check the status of my friends, but my dad won't allow me to have that, either. I made plans to meet up with them at River Park earlier, so hopefully they've kept themselves amused enough to stay put.

Today's attack by Dad starts creeping back into my mind, even though all I want to do is forget it. Luckily, I'm easily sidetracked while on my bike, since I have to watch for traffic. My bike is an escape not just from *him* but also from my emotions. It's almost as if I'm addicted to the feel of biking. Without this freedom, I doubt I'd be sane.

After a few minutes, I finally calm down and start to appreciate my surroundings. To my right, I can hear the loud chorus of cricket melodies coming in and out as I pass by each area of brush. The air is moist with humidity, making me breathe harder as I pedal. Up ahead is the first sharp turn of many. I maneuver quickly, making my way along the rows of mangroves that border the coast. On the opposite side are continuous fields of mature oaks. Their cloaks of heavy vine and moss almost extinguish the existence of their weary branches. Seagulls and cranes are bountiful, hovering around some sort of food delight. This glorious view is inherently dependent upon the sun, which is my daily timer.

The sun's up, but I can tell it will be starting its descent soon. This makes me rush even more to reach my friends.

I hope they're still waiting for me.

I pedal furiously along the roadway. The power plant smokestack comes into view, egging me on. I'm getting closer. The wind is whipping through my ears, masking my torturous ear noise and helping me forget its existence. I fly past the small convenience store near the park entrance, the park ranger's house, and straight down to the sand at South Beach—we started calling it this before it was a fad diet.

As I round through the parking lot into the picnic areas, I see some heads bobbing in the water.

They're still here.

I drop my bike where the sand meets the asphalt. Excitement runs through my legs, and I struggle to rush through the sand to greet them. My friends are my support system—and they waited. It's nice to smile again.

"Hey, girl!" I hear off in the distance. "Where the hell have you been?"

"Oh, just being insulted by my drunk dad. Nothing new," I call back. The waves are making it hard for me to hear, smashing along the gray sand. My legs ache with every step, slowing me down. Derrick yells back to the others, who are throwing each other around in the water. Then, he turns his attention back to me as I reach him at the shoreline.

"You made it! How does it feel to be eighteen? Get anything good?" Derrick asks.

"Nah, just heartache."

"He couldn't even leave you alone on your birthday?"

"That would have been enough in the way of a gift, but not even that. Guess he just wanted to make me feel oh-so-welcome in my own home." I roll my eyes. Wet sand engulfs my feet, making it hard to walk.

Derrick stands shivering a little with his colorful, wet board shorts dripping water down his legs and onto his wrinkly white feet. The wind pushes his black hair into his face, layering it every which way. He's a nice guy. We've known each other since the early days before we moved here, when I used to visit Florida to see my grandparents on Calvary Road not far from South Beach. I used to take my grandmother's bike out even back then and ride beside the shoreline down near a fish camp owned by Derrick's parents, which included a few docks and a bait shop adjacent to their trailer. They later sold the camp, and now it's a mega boating storage yard with elevated rows of endless slots for every variety of boats.

Back then my great-aunt lived near my grandmother, and she did her best to keep me entertained during my sleepover visits. Aunt Lesley would set me up with the various kids in the neighborhood, each of them stopping by to meet "the new girl." It was mostly uncomfortable with the boys, since we barely spoke, but we always kept in touch as the years went by. It was handy when we eventually moved to Florida. I was twelve years old and started middle school mid-year, so it was nice to have a few friends to hang with whom I already knew.

Behind Derrick, I see Todd and Melissa heading toward us.

"Well, at least you're with us now," states Derrick, becoming distracted when Melissa comes up behind him. It's funny how he can sense her presence.

"Your dad acting like an ass again, Jeannie?" she asks. She nudges at Derrick's knees to try to make him falter, and her long brunette hair whacks him in the face when he reaches to tickle her. Her short stature is an advantage, though, as she dodges most of his attempts.

"Yeah, but what else is new? I just need to stop letting him get to me."

"Well, forget that bastard, Jeannie. Soon you'll be on your own and away from that hellhole of a home. You'll be riding past it someday in your fancy red Corvette, spinning smoke in his face. He doesn't deserve you."

"Thanks, Melissa," I say with a grin as she hugs me.

"Happy birthday," Todd adds, shyly. Todd Cahill is my dream man. I'm not sure exactly what attracts me to him the most. Maybe it's his shyness or his warm, inviting demeanor. Maybe it's his smile, his hair, his muscles, or his tan. Maybe it's just the whole package. All I know is that he's my main reason for pedaling so fast. We've kissed a few times before but he's never actually asked me to go out with him. "We have a surprise for you, Babe."

I love it when he calls me that. These people care about me, support me, listen to me—and don't mind if they have to repeat themselves every once in a while.

I'm pretty good at lip reading now, so understanding what they're saying isn't a problem most of the time, if they're facing me. My dad didn't pay for any deaf services, of course. I just learned on my own. Most of the time, I keep conversations to my right side, so that even if they're not facing me, I can hear most of what is said.

Todd wraps his arm around my shoulder, and we make our way up to the picnic shelter. To my surprise, there's cake and presents waiting. I hug him close in return.

Is today the day you'll finally take a risk on asking me out? I wonder, as I look up at him, trying to read his expression. He isn't revealing much. His hazel eyes just keep looking forward as if he doesn't want to be tempted by my brown eyes. I notice his haircut for the occasion—perfectly straight cut lines around his ears and neck. Instead of shaving, he left a slight shadow along his jaw line, just the way I like it. His sandy-brown hair is severely parted as it flows with the wind above his eyes. I wrap my arm around his slender waist, feeling his smooth tanned skin under my fingertips. We move under the pavilion. Finally, I'm having a fun birthday party.

"In honor of the last of us to turn eighteen, we honor you, dear Jeannie. Your beauty knows no bounds," Derrick says. I giggle at his lame attempt at being proper. He almost falls into the cake when Todd smacks him on the back after calling me a beauty. Melissa doesn't seem too happy with him either.

"What? That's what Todd always says—" Derrick replies to Melissa. She glares at him and looks like she really wants to smack him. Todd probably wants to also. He glances back at me as if to see if I heard Derrick.

I did, and I can tell Todd knows it, since he's avoiding eye contact with me now.

"Well, let's just get to it," Todd says nervously, clearing his throat and wiping the sand off his hands. "You get the first piece, Jeannie."

"Thanks, guys. Thanks for making this birthday the best," I say. They break out into the worst rendition of "Happy Birthday" I've ever heard.

Within minutes, I'm sitting on the beach with cake in hand. Todd sits close, watching Melissa and Derrick chase each other in the water again. His arm rests up against mine while he gobbles down the cake in two gulps. It's kind of odd, but he's a guy. Guys eat fast.

"Good, huh?"

"Yeah, it is. Thanks again for all this. Sorry I was so late."

"No need to apologize. I'm just glad you made it. We would have all been disappointed if you didn't," Todd says, piercing his toes into the sand.

I can feel this moment is going to be good. Todd puts his arm around me and kisses me behind my ear. "You're beautiful, Jeannie."

I must be turning red.

"I'm glad you think so, Todd." I move my feet in the sand too, smiling. Wind moves across the water, sprinkling us with mist and fine crystals of sea salt. The breeze feels cool against my skin, causing me to shiver.

"Let's go for a walk," Todd says.

We make our way down the path that parallels the coast for a few minutes until we reach the lookout tower. The gray wood moans, as we climb the stairs to each level. I wonder if the boards are strong enough to hold us. We make it to the top, and Todd sits next to me. We both gaze out over the intercoastal waterway. An elongated island of trees has formed in the center of Deadwater River, and I can see the residential homes beyond it.

"Hey," Todd finally says.

"Hey."

We both are quiet during the awkward silence.

God, I'm an idiot.

"Um—shit—I suck at this. I'm sorry." Todd grimaces at his introduction to what I thought was asking me out. "I—well—you don't have to if you don't want to."

"What?"

"I want to give you your birthday presents."

Todd pulls out two little boxes. His expression is serious.

"What are they?"

"A little something for your birthday. Open them."

I open the first box to find a chocolate kiss. I grin and look up at him. He leans over and touches his lips to mine, hesitantly at first. Then he puts his arms around me and kisses me more passionately. Within seconds, I forget my name, my surroundings, and my troubles. It's just him and me on top of the world at the most beautiful place on earth. He squeezes me tight. When he finally pulls his lips from mine, I can see he's smiling.

"You know, I could take advantage of you right here and now."

"Can I open my other present first?"

"Oh yeah, that's right. You have another one. I suppose I can wait while you open that one."

This box contains a fortune cookie. I pull out the message and read it.

"You're always on my mind. Go out with me, Jeannie?"

His eyes are on mine, waiting for an answer.

I beam as I say, "Yes," and kiss him again.

"Oh boy. She must have said 'yes,'" Derrick cuts in, grinning from the top step.

Todd and I both jerk back in surprise.

"Christ, Derrick, do you mind?" Todd asks.

"Just was wondering where you guys were at. Making sure everything is okay."

"I think they're just fine, Derrick. Let's leave them alone. Are you happy, now?" Melissa asks Derrick, climbing up beside him with an irritated glare.

Todd glances over to me and reaches for my hand. I snuggle with him, taking in the moment. "You don't have to leave, and yes, we're fine," I say.

The sun is making its way past the clouds and onto the horizon. Tonight it's yellows, pinks, and blues. Boats hurry toward the coast, leaving wakes of white waves behind them. As I look into the distance, I wonder if anyone is watching us from the many homes across the way. I wonder, too, if they are happier homes than mine. I think about seeing my dad again, but quickly snap myself back into the moment.

"Hey, isn't that Deadwater Manor? Over there; the old mansion with the chimneys. I didn't know you could see it across the river from up here." says Derrick. "I heard all kinds of crazies live there and eat each other alive like zombies."

Todd scoffs. "You believe everything you hear, Derrick. No way they are eating each other alive. Just maybe eating the ones in the morgue."

"Eww. You guys are gross," complains Melissa. Derrick starts mimicking zombies by attacking her neck.

I just shake my head.

"People still live there?" asks Melissa, pushing Derrick away.

"Why? You want to go see?" Derrick asks.

I look over to Todd to see if he's thinking the same. He shakes his head at Derrick, acting as if he doesn't agree.

Thank God.

"No way you're going to see me anywhere near that place!" I chime in.

"You sure you don't want an adventure, Missy?" Todd asks.

"Todd, you're an asshole. Stop making Derrick want to go," Melissa demands.

"Okay, okay, no need to get testy."

"No worries, Miss," Derrick assures her. "I would never let anything happen to you."

I make eye contact with Todd again. Once Melissa and Derrick head back to the beach, Todd leans in for another kiss. I willingly accept. I love the feel of his hands against my skin as he explores me, taking in my waist, thighs, and knees at first. Then he makes his way up my back and onto my shoulders, kissing them. I can feel the pulse in my neck bulging, and he begins kissing me ever so gently around my ear, down my neck and eventually between my breasts.

Meeting my lips again, he pulls me out of sight from the waterway and gently tugs at my bikini top, loosening it and letting it drop down. Todd draws himself back to look at me. "Beautiful."

I should stop, but I can't. The desire is too strong. Besides, why should we stop? I have known and trusted him for years. We grew up together and there has always been that spark.

"I want you Jeannie, but only if you're okay with it," Todd asks breathlessly.

I pull his face close to mine, kiss him passionately and whisper, simply, "Yes."

Todd climbs on top of me and tugs at my bikini bottoms. He tries to pull them down, but they get snagged on a nail in the wood. It takes him a couple of attempts, but he finally removes them. The condom does not go on so easily, and the bench is not exactly comfortable. Eventually, though, we fall into a rhythmic pattern, our hearts pounding. The sun has started to set with vibrant colors decorating the sky. I watch him as I listen to the muffled sounds of the boats, wind, birds, and waves that make their way into this moment. The sounds are soon replaced by our moans as we bring each other to climax, our bodies shaking until

we relax into each other's arms.
Happy birthday to me!

3

It's dark when I arrive home. This is against the rules. I know I'm going to pay for it, but I don't care.

Todd insisted on seeing me home. He bends over and whispers, "Happy birthday, Babe." He kisses me.

I can't help myself from kissing him back. I want him again. If only I could sneak him into my room.

"I'll see you again tomorrow, right?" he asks, touching my cheek.

"Yes."

He smiles and then his expression grows serious. He looks toward my house. "You going to be okay with him? You want me to come in?"

"I'll be fine. No worries." If he comes in, it'll just cause more drama with Dad.

"So, what's the problem with him anyway? Why is he so hard on you?"

"Booze, probably. He drinks himself to oblivion sometimes. I think he misses my mom. I do, too."

"I hope I'm not stepping over the line here by asking you this, but he doesn't hit you, does he?"

"No," I reply. "He just likes to scream at me, although tonight he let me slam into the door as I tried to get away from him. He blames me for my mother being gone. I don't know why."

"Did you ask him?"

"No. I'm too afraid to."

"It's not your fault. You know that, right?"

"Yeah." I try to hold back a tear, but it streams down too quickly before I can wipe it away.

"Hey, Babe. Come here."

Todd holds me and kisses the top of my head. "You're beautiful inside and out. Don't let him tell you otherwise."

I wipe the tear with the back of my hand. "Thanks. I'll see you tomorrow."

"You don't want to talk about it anymore?"

"No, I better go."

"Call me if you need me, okay? It doesn't matter how late it is."

"I promise."

We exit and Todd drags my bike out of the bed of his truck. "See you, Babe."

My heart leaps at the thought of seeing him again. "Bye."

I leave my bike in the garage and walk to the front door. I feel like I'm floating. Before I go in, I turn to watch Todd as he backs out of the driveway, waving to him as he drives away. Taking a deep breath, I slowly open the door. I'm not sure what hell to expect from my dad, so I brace myself for his "cheery" disposition and enter into the living room.

The lights are low. I can see flashes of light from the television and his foot hanging off the recliner in the family room. I walk briskly through the kitchen, pass behind him, and run up the stairs, hoping to make it to my room.

"How was your night?"

It doesn't take much for panic to set in anymore, and I'm feeling it already. I try to relax my pulse by taking a deep breath before I answer.

"The best birthday ever."

I sigh when I hear the recliner move. This means he's not going to let it go.

"Really? It was better than if you were here?"

I turn around to face him, convinced that I will not let him ruin my day any further. His gray hair is a bit unruly from the finger combing he always does when sitting in front of the television and yelling at this or that sports team.

"You left."

"I came back. You weren't here," he says, plainly.

I'm becoming even more anxious at his calm demeanor. This is highly unusual, and it can only mean he's enjoying my nervousness, toying with me. Luckily, he doesn't seem to be drunk anymore.

He's about to say something else but is interrupted by Rick calling out over the balcony.

"What's going on? We ready yet?"

"Yeah, I think we are," my dad says, not taking his eyes from mine. "After you, kiddo." He gestures me back toward the kitchen.

I'm hopeful that this may not be so bad since Rick is involved. I glance back at Rick, and he smiles at me.

"Bring your wallet. You remember that little thing we worked on?" Rick whispers to me as we walk out through the front door.

I have no clue what he's talking about. I end up standing on the front lawn while they prepare it—whatever "it" is.

Out of the garage backs a new yellow Volkswagen Bug. I frown, unsure what all this means. Dad jerks his head for me to come over. I hesitantly walk toward him, unable to keep my eyes off the car.

"We'll work on your license. Here's the key," he says with half a grin.

I stand there looking at them both with the key in hand. I want to be excited but am afraid to trust him. More than anything, my dad loves to take things away from me. Is this some kind of demented trick on his part to take me down somehow? I look at my key, contemplating my next step.

"Is that it? Did you not hear Dad? The car is yours!" exclaims Rick with all the excitement I can't show. "Jeannie Beanie's got real wheels now!"

I look over at my dad, searching him for any hint of sarcasm, evilness or hesitation, but I sense none. I can almost smell it when he's setting me up, but tonight the air is clear. I half-smile at him to see his reaction, and he smiles back. All I can see are his teeth in the dark, though. I can't see his eyes.

I turn to Rick. He's tuning in the radio and opening the sunroof, enticing me to enjoy this moment. I slowly walk around the car to get a better look. Dad's watching me. It makes me self-conscious, wondering when he will drop some kind of mean line or laugh while taking away the keys.

Finally, I don't care. All the guards come down, and I jump into the passenger seat to take in the new car smell.

"You have it, right?" asks Rick, jumping out of the car.

I sprint over to the driver's seat, when I finally figure out what he's talking about.

He's talking about my wallet. Yes, my wallet—my driver's license!

I have my license already. Dad never knew. I smile at myself in the rearview mirror, adjusting it. Dad's reflection is in the mirror, his arms folded as he watches me.

Does he seriously have no idea that I could back right up into him at this moment?

Rick quickly puts on his seatbelt, looking at me all proud of himself.

"You ready to shove this car down that asshole's throat?" he says under his breath. "I can't wait to see the look on his face."

"Why, what do you mean? There's no way a stupid, half-deaf person like me could *possibly* drive. How could I ever pass a driver's license test?" I say in a mocking imitation of our dad.

"I don't see a deaf person here, do you?"

"Huh?"

We both bellow, as we laugh at each other's Dad impressions. Dad shifts his weight to each side behind me, and I can tell that he's getting restless. What I wouldn't give to take him out—just accidently back right up into him. I know I never would. The only way I am getting rid of him is simple. Just pack this beast up and leave when he least expects it.

I beep the horn lightly and wave for him to get the hell out of the way before I change my mind. Instead of going away, he walks toward the car, sending me into a panic that now the sledgehammer will drop. Now, he'll enjoy himself as he crushes me.

Before he can get too close, I flash my license at him. Smiling brightly, I throw the car in reverse and speed out of the driveway. His shocked expression is well worth the backlash I'll endure later. He yells "Wait!" and follows me down the road.

"What an idiot. Doesn't he know he's walking on the wrong side of the road?" I laugh.

Rick belly-laughs as he throws his hands up through the sunroof, waving goodbye. "Smell ya later!"

I drive down the winding roads toward River Park once again, reveling in how my life is about to change. I know Rick is waiting for me to scream in excitement, now that I'm away from Dad. All I can do, however, is think. Imagine. Take it all in.

What a moment.

Rick's mood grows weary of my silence. I can tell from his body language that he's getting antsy as he taps his fingers on the armrest. At this point, I'm not sure what to say.

I pull up into one of the parking spots at River Park to talk for a few minutes. "Is this real?" I ask, turning the radio down.

"Uh, yeah! Aren't you excited?"

"I am! I'm just worried it's a trick. Somehow Dad is going to take this away from me, isn't he?"

"No, I don't think so! You should have seen him when he bought it. He was more excited than me! He picked every feature out on it and even cleaned it again when we got home tonight. He wanted everything perfect. I've never seen him like that before. He was sincere."

"Wow, could it be he actually feels guilty for how he's been treating me?"

"Well, I wouldn't go *that* far, but maybe today's episode made him think."

"Or maybe he's just trying to guilt me into staying. Well, whatever it is, it's not going to work. I'll definitely enjoy this in the meantime, though. This is the only good thing our dad ever did for me."

Rick raises an eyebrow at me.

"Okay, okay," I say. "It is the only good thing since Mom

died."

"I'm sorry you've had to be the brunt of all his anger, Jeannie. It's probably a combination of Mom dying and loneliness. Maybe you could try to talk to him about it."

"Yeah, right. No thanks. I plan on getting the hell out before he has another chance at me. I'll come home late tonight and be gone early tomorrow."

"That soon? Where will you go? I think you should do more planning and be smart about it. Otherwise, you're going to end up homeless, begging for spare change."

"There you go again. You think I haven't thought about it? I've spent the last three years thinking about it—and saving."

"Wow. You're really going to do it, aren't you?" The sadness in his voice sent a stab of guilt to my gut.

"First chance I get."

"You're nuts. I plan on hanging around for a while. Maybe I'll go to dental school and share in the fortune Dad has always had. I want to live like he does. He has a good life, financially."

"Oh, yeah. Financially. Is that all that matters? You see him treat me the way he does and you want to be like him?"

"Not like him as a person. You know I don't agree with his outbursts. By the way, what does he mean when he says he knows what you did?"

"Hell if I know. He only says that when he's drunk. Maybe he just needs someone to blame it on." I glance at Rick's concerned expression. "You have fun with all of your riches. I'm out of here as soon as I can."

I stare at the tower for a few minutes, soaking in the cooler evening air. The sea salt reaches my tongue when the wind blows in. I can hear the waves roaring onto the shore, and some of the noises I heard earlier during my time on the tower, but less intense. Night has calmed the place.

I smile when I think of Todd and our first "encounter." It feels like a long time ago already. I've never felt so close to anyone and can't believe I have no regrets.

"What are you smiling about?"

"Ah, nothing. Just thinking about the future. Let's drive."

Happy birthday to me!

4

Dad's up waiting for me. He's not waiting for *us*, just *me*. He lets Rick go to bed as soon as we arrive, of course. This confirms that I'm in for a tongue-lashing. At least there aren't any beer bottles around his chair. He still seems lucid.

"So, you got your license behind my back. Was it something through school?"

"No."

"This was just something you did without telling me?"

"I didn't think it would matter that much to you, since I didn't think I would be getting a car anyway."

"That, or you were afraid I would revoke it."

"Maybe," I say, staring at the ground. There's no arguing with him, so I might as well just agree.

"Well, since you're driving now, you should go visit your aunt tomorrow."

"Aunt Lesley? Tomorrow? Why?"

"She wants to wish you a happy birthday," he says, heading for his bedroom. "We'll talk about it in the morning."

"Okay." Then I remember that I never thanked him for the car. I guess I better show him that I'm a better person than he thinks I am. "Oh, one more thing, Dad. Thank you for the car. I really love it."

I'm barely looking at him. Kind words between us are so rare, I don't know what to expect in response.

He stops, takes a deep breath, and turns around to look at me. "You're welcome, Jeannie. I'm—well, I'm trying to not be such a bastard."

Okay, so he heard me earlier today.

My mouth drops open. All I can do is stand there dumbfounded and wait for him to disappear into his room.

I quickly retreat to my room, closing the door behind me. Sitting on my bed, I think about the day I will finally be on my own—not just a legal adult, but living like an adult too. My thoughts wander.

I guess, in some ways, it's one of my best birthdays since Mom died—at least the latter part of the day.

My main goal for tomorrow will be to see Todd. Moving can wait a day.

* * * *

That's exactly what I'm doing the next morning—waiting. I sit, looking out the living room window at my new car. All I can do is wait for my dad to get out of bed. He's supposed to tell me more about my trip to see my aunt today. I, on the other hand, am up early and can't wait to take the "Vug" to see Todd. This is going to be a good day.

Impatient, I head out to at least sit in it.

My car. My ride. Wow!

It's beautiful, reflecting various sparkles of reds and orange as I move past it. The tires are clean and black. The rims are polished. There's even a smiley ball on the tip of the antenna. I can't believe my dad went all out on this car. He even thought of the smallest of extras. The whole thing seems crazy, but here I am, all because of him. I can see myself in the reflection of the tinted car windows, and for the first time in a long time, I'm smiling while at home.

I open the driver's door to check out the inside. The interior is black with chrome accents. There's a specialty-installed stereo with iPhone ports and electric sunroof, windows and doors. All the toys a girl could possibly want, not to mention the new car smell. It's a smell I thought I'd never experience this soon. I really can't believe this.

A knock on the window breaks my excitement. It's my dad. I'm not sure whether to be annoyed or elated to see him at this moment. I guess having any thoughts of the latter is an improvement.

"So, you're up already. I figured you would be," my dad says, as I slide the window down.

Then why the hell didn't you get up earlier?

I grin back, not wanting to say what's rolling around in my head.

"Is Aunt Lesley at home or am I supposed to meet her somewhere else?" I ask.

"She's in the hospital. She had another nervous breakdown, so they admitted her for a couple of weeks. That's why I think it would be a good idea for her favorite niece to pay her a visit. She sounded depressed when I talked to her last. You still up for it?"

"Sure," I say, masking my surprise. "Which hospital?"

"Deadwater Manor. Are you familiar with it? Do you know where it is?"

"You're not serious. Are you kidding me right now? I really don't want to go to that psych hospital. That place creeps me out. Besides, she's probably resting. I'll make sure to help her when she gets out."

My dad sighs. "Very nice of you, Jeannie. Mature, too. A family member is in need and you turn your back on her. Nice. Remind me not to count on your sorry ass when I'm debilitated." He pauses for my rebuttal, but getting none, he continues. "Speaking of debilitated, have you taken a good look at yourself lately? What if something worse happened with your hearing? Wouldn't you be upset if no one came to visit you?"

I roll my eyes at him and look forward at the garage, wishing I could ram through it and get out the other side. I don't want a scratch on the car, so I opt for the diplomatic approach.

"Okay. I'll go," I sigh. "Happy?"

"I'd be happier if I didn't have to guilt you into these things. Really, Jeannie, when are you going to start thinking of other people before yourself?"

I continue to stare at the garage door, feeling completely irritated at the guilt trip.

"Oh yeah," he adds, "and after you see her, I want you to introduce yourself to a doctor friend of mine. His name is Doctor Garrett Wiggins."

"Why the hell would I want to do that?"

"Watch your mouth, young lady. I didn't raise you to talk like trailer trash. He's a friend of mine. Just do it."

I don't answer, and I don't agree. Instead, I turn on the engine and put the car in reverse, my foot still on the brake.

"Jeannie, are you listening to me?"

Blah, blah, blah. That's all I hear. Besides, he's talking into my bad ear. He should know that. I inch backward during his nagging and smile as if to confirm everything he wants. If only he'd walk behind me, so I can run him over. That would shut him up. I couldn't get that lucky. Actually, with my luck, he'd survive and turn me in to the police, so he could be rid of me. Either that, or he'd hunt me down like a dog and chain me to my bed or something.

Again, I smile at him, trying not to say anything that could hold me here. "What time are visiting hours?"

"Ten to five."

I nod, and he seems satisfied that I will do as he says. I start backing out of the driveway again. He throws a stern look at me, as if to say, "be careful." I'll never hear those words from him, because that would sound like he cares.

Why didn't I just pack up and get out of here today?

The thought of going to Deadwater Manor spooks me. The name alone is creepy. I think I'll put off going there. Instead, I'll drive over to the park. On the way, I can't stop thinking about the stories I heard through all the years I've lived in Baillie's Bluff. These included a myriad of patients being held against their wills and others being tortured with all kinds of psych devices. The worst I heard was about some escaped patient who was running around in traffic, confused of her whereabouts, and the police had to close all four streets at some intersection in Tarpon Springs. She looked hideous in her hospital gown and frizzy hair as she approached each car, chanting some unknown language at the drivers. I heard the police scene was disturbing too with her cat-like screams while they dragged her to the back of a cop car and returned her to Deadwater. Who knows if it was true, but the rumor went around school for several weeks last year. It was also rumored that several students were caught trying to sneak into the place as part of a prank. The story went that they were caught, strapped into some sort of electric shock chair, and put into straitjackets to teach them a lesson.

These are sketchy stories, but the thought of any truth to them is disturbing, especially with my aunt there. Maybe I should make it my mission to make sure she's safe. She's elderly now at eighty-two years old with no one but us. I've never heard of her having emotional issues before, but perhaps losing Uncle Jim finally got to her. She probably just grew tired of the elderly care housing she was stuck in since he died. The reason really doesn't matter. All that matters is that she is my favorite aunt, and I'll go there—not for my dad, but to make sure the care is acceptable for her.

As I pull up to the park, I start feeling excited about showing my new car to my friends. I know they'll probably go crazy over it, and we'll ride around forever, taking in all the scenes at the better beaches like Howard Park and other favorites like the Sponge Docks in Tarpon.

I park and walk over to South Beach, but it's deserted. There are no friends in sight. It's disappointing, but I pull out my beach towel to sit and think—one of my favorite things to do. The waves roll in. Shells slosh back and forth, each shell unable to find its stronghold, moving around erratically. The sun is stinging the back of my neck and shoulders already, letting me know that the scorching hot summer is already here. I was hoping for a few more good weeks of cooler weather this year, but June is not cooperating. Luckily, there's a breeze coming off the shoreline, helping to make the air a little less stagnant.

As I sit thinking, I look out toward Deadwater Manor, wondering if there is any way Aunt Lesley can see me. I grin in that direction just in case, wanting to reassure her, but deep down my gut is telling me to avoid it all together.

There's something not quite right about the whole car thing with my dad. He knows she's my favorite aunt. Maybe he wants me to see her crazy, so I won't like her so much, or because it will pain me to see her like that.

An hour later, there's still no Todd. I drop my head toward the ground, partially due to the sun's intensity and partially due to my disappointment with not seeing him.

I wait a few minutes more, but decide to leave for Deadwater Manor and come back later. Before I go, I walk around the outskirts of the beach area and to the tower, just in case everyone is there, but this, too, is deserted. Though we didn't plan to meet, they are usually here this time of day. There's no way around it. My friends are not coming. I have to go to the Manor.

I drag myself to the car. With one more glance back to the beach, any hope of seeing my friends disappears. There are only the chimneys from the Manor taunting me.

On the way, I drive by some of my favorite places, so I can procrastinate my arrival at my destination all the longer. The fish camp is just around the corner from River Park, so I drive slowly past the scurrying of boaters and fishermen sharing laughs and beer under the shade of hundred-year-old oaks that cover the main office, which is basically still a trailer. Three boat docks sprawl out from the camp and into the water where more boaters are arriving. It's always a busy place. I wish I had more time to observe.

I search quickly for Derrick but there's no sign of him, so I follow the road, carefully dodging deep potholes in the asphalt. I pass by old cracker-type homes on the left and their associated wooden—and mostly decrepit—docks on the right. Waves and the occasional tropical storms haven't been kind to the long stretches of wooden planks that continue out beyond low tide. The second to the last house on the left is Melissa's.

I stop in front of her house for a minute, contemplating the idea of visiting her for a while. The screened front porch has always been a favorite viewing spot of mine. Melissa and I spent many afternoons sprawled out on canvas rocking chairs as we watched each vessel pass by. Her house is pretty much a typical

Florida home with peach exterior paint and a small, one-story layout. This isn't the area for staying inside, though, so it really didn't matter. As long as we could see the water, we were happy—well, sort of. It was always better when Todd and Derrick visited.

Despite my yearning for some quality chair time, and perhaps a Todd visit, I think better of it and continue on my way. I head down a dirt road that leads to an old, brick street that will take me to downtown Tarpon Springs.

In my rearview mirror, I see the waterfront area. I still wish I could be sidetracked from my chore of the day. A second later, I see a guy with wispy hair walking up the street. I pause to get a better look. He draws closer along the chalky dirt road, kicking up stones and dust. He pushes the hair from his eyes. It's a movement I know well. My heart skips a beat. It's Todd.

Excitedly, I pull the car over to the side of the road and fumble around to find the door handle, keeping an eye on him in the mirror. Before I spring out of the car, I stop myself for a moment to gain my composure.

Be cool you moron!

I laugh at myself, and slowly open the door, looking back toward him. He stops and looks my way.

Shit, I hope he doesn't think I'm stalking him.

I wait for him to recognize me before getting out of the car. Within seconds, I see the smile that I love.

God, he's hot.

I smile back and walk toward him with nothing on my mind but devouring him. I wonder if it would be too forward if I greet him with my tongue down his throat.

Before I can think about it more, he rushes toward me. Within seconds his arms are around me, pulling me close. A surge of energy runs through me. He kisses me hard with his eyes open. I push myself on him with everything I can, feeling I can't get close enough, aching. He cups my face now, and kisses me softly on the lips and nose, and we collapse into a hug.

"I thought I missed you, Jeannie. I didn't want you to get the idea that I stood you up. I had to work late last night and slept later than I wanted."

"Yeah, almost a snub already. I don't know if I can forgive you for that!" I tease.

He grins as he draws his arms around me again, pulling my chest against his and touching the side of my breasts. "Maybe I just need to make up for my misbehavior. Let's go back to our special spot."

Perfect.

"Well, I don't know. Once a snubber, always a snubber," I continue, pulling him toward my car. "You're going to really have to convince me. Guess what? This is mine!"

"What? Are you kidding me? Did your Dad buy you this?"

"Yeah, believe it or not."

"Wow, this is awesome!"

His arm muscles are flexing, as he leans in to check out the interior.

Dang.

"Well, what do you say, we squeeze in the back seat of your new car and try it out right now!"

"No way! It's too small. Besides, I need some scenery."

"Oh, I'll give you some scenery alright," he whispers, pulling me toward him, rubbing his hand along my thigh and brushing his thumb between my legs.

"Okay, mister, quit that or I won't be able to drive."

I back away before he can indulge himself.

"Get in."

The drive over to the tower is difficult, as he heads for my lap to play with me. I'm glad I'm taking the back road into the park. We barely make it up to the top of the tower without stripping each other's clothes off. Todd makes me wait at each level for a long drawn out kiss to torture me with anticipation. Even when we get to the top, he explores me with his tongue before taking me. He especially likes my breasts, spending time getting to know each one, driving me crazy while he's at it. I can't get enough of him.

* * * *

As I listen to the birds and watch the trees waving at me, I feel completely exhausted when we're done. The scenery did not disappoint.

He's tired too, lying next to me with his eyes shut. I gently touch my lips to his arm, and then I wrap the blanket around us, feeling completely satisfied and happy. He grins.

"So, everything went okay then, I take it."

"What do you mean?"

"You know. Last night with your dad."

"Oh, that. Yeah, surprisingly he hadn't been drinking and we had a civilized conversation. Nothing deep. And then, of course, he gave me the car. Not sure why. Other than, he wants me to visit my aunt this afternoon. She was admitted to the hospital."

"Maybe he's starting to see what he's doing to you."

I laugh. "Yeah, right. I doubt that, but it's a step in the right direction. Luckily, I have my brother. He's my rock and keeps me sane. You're lucky to have a good relationship with both of your parents. I envy you."

"Well, we haven't had much money during the years, but they do love each other. You can see it. I want that someday."

I watch his expression for a minute. "Me too."

There's an awkward pause until Todd asks, "What are you going to do next? Thinking about college?"

"Not now. My priority is to get out of my dad's house. Then college, maybe."

"You should. With your brains, you could do whatever you wanted. What would you study?"

"Well, I love to read. So, I'm thinking about majoring in English or creative writing. I just need to get my life together first."

"You will. A few years from now, you'll look back at all his antics and scoff at it."

"I hope so. How about you? What are your plans?"

"Coast Guard, I hope. I can't imagine not working along the coast. I grew up with it and I don't want to be anywhere else."

"I can see you doing that, for sure. You already know how to handle boats too, so you'd be perfect," I reply. After another pause, I say, "Well, I better get going soon. I don't want to miss visiting hours, and I'm sure my aunt will—"

"Mommy, Mommy! I bet I can beat you to the top of the tower!"

The words take a few seconds to register.

"Oh, shit!" I yelp. I push away from Todd, frantically grabbing for my clothes. "A kid's coming up!"

Todd jumps up too. He looks over the side to see their whereabouts. It doesn't matter, because before we know it, we can feel little feet thumping onto the bottom platform.

Todd's eyes grow wide. He snatches up his pants and maneuvers into them, glancing over to me too. Loud screeching echoes up from below, and the vibration of little footsteps is getting more intense. There's no way I'm going to be dressed in time. Frantically, I jump onto the bench and pull the blanket around me, braless. Todd shoves my bra up his shirt and sits down next to me.

"Mommy, I think there's people up there," the little boy says loudly, peeking around the corner before the last flight of stairs. I grow rigid, trying not to move the wrong way. I smile at the boy as if nothing is wrong. He sheepishly stomps up the stairs. His mom huffs, out of breath, behind him.

"I know what those two have been doing, Mommy," he assures her. She takes one look at me in my blanket and stops on the second step, almost losing her balance.

"They've been wrestling. Look at their hair, Mommy."

I want to die.

"Um, yes, well it is pretty windy today, right you two?"

"Yeah sure is," we both chime in chorus.

"Come on, Collin, let's go back down to the beach. I'm—um—afraid of heights. Come on," she insists, holding out her hand.

Collin marches over and carefully makes his way down the steps, waving goodbye to us. As he rounds the corner, I can hear him ask, "Mommy, it's an awful hot day to have a blanket on, isn't it?"

"Yes, Collin," she answers.

"Why would that girl with the messed up hair have a blanket on when it's hot?"

"Well, I don't know. Maybe she's sick or something. Let's go."

Todd and I look at each other and burst out laughing.

"You want this?" asks Todd, as he dangles my bra in front of me, moving it away from my grasp. "How about this?" he continues, as he pulls my top out from his shirt as well.

"Give them to me!" I squeal, trying to grab them.

"Only if I get another peek," he demands.

I smirk and briefly open the blanket for his viewing pleasure.

"Again?"

"Nope, that's it, for now anyways. Hurry up before someone else comes up here!"

"Aww, do I have to?"

"Yes, you three-year-old," I answer, giggling at his antics.

After getting dressed, we walk to the car, arm-in-arm. It feels good to have someone so close and who might even care. Hell, I know he cares. He's one of the good guys.

"See you later then?" he asks, putting his hands on the car on either side of me.

"It should only take a few hours. Like I was saying, my dad is forcing me to go see my Aunt Lesley. She's in a mental hospital. I'll be back before you know it!"

"Wow. You sure you don't want me to go with you? You might need protection from all those crazies in the mental ward."

I arch an eyebrow.

"Oops, sorry. I wasn't talking about your aunt, just all the other crazies."

I look down.

"Fuck, I'm sorry. I'll shut up now."

"No, it's okay. I know what you mean. I'll probably just be in the waiting room or something. I'm sure there won't be too many crazies in there."

"Good, because I don't want anything to happen to my Jeannie. Which hospital is she in?"

"Helen Ellis," I lie.

Todd takes my hand and opens the door for me. "Okay, meet you back here at six then?"

"Six it is! No snubbing this time."

"Will you punish me again, if I do?" Todd asks, looking like he's calculating the idea.

"Yeah. I'll punish you with abstinence."

"Ouch! In that case, I'll be here at five-thirty."

Todd leans in and kisses me goodbye. "Before you round the corner to the park on the way back, could you take off all of your clothes and drive in naked? That would be hot."

I shake my head at him and start the car.

"Topless then?"

"You're going to get me arrested. Quit."

"Bra only?"

"Would you quit?" I ask, laughing at his silliness.

"Okay, well, see you later. Don't get lost now."

I flash him the best smile I can and drive away, still dreading the mission at hand. I feel bad about lying to him about my aunt's location, but I'm too embarrassed to tell him and don't want him to think that I'm related to a lunatic in a hardcore mental hospital. I contemplate turning the car around to go back to him as I watch him in the rearview mirror. I don't want to leave him. If only he were holding me again.

I know the consequences from my dad, though. Besides, I'm on a mission to help her. This is bigger than my own fears.

I just need to get it over with.

5

Making my way toward the bridge that leads to the Sponge Docks, the strong smell of styrene, a chemical used on the boats, permeates the air. This is a common childhood memory for me. I'm not sure why, but it makes me feel at home. I associate the area with the smell. It's a combination of chemicals, seawater, and the stench of fish—not my normal choice of fragrance. However, there's something about the smell of this area that has its charm.

I pass by the Docks to the narrow side roads lined with mansion after mansion and start feeling even more apprehensive about my visit. I'm not sure if it's the thought of seeing my aunt in such a place or the stories I've heard about it since my childhood. The thought of being around crazy people is making me tense. As I come closer to the Manor, I can feel the blood tighten in my veins. I have to suppress everything inside of me to not turn around or lose my way through the mazes of subdivisions that are more prevalent on this side of town. Driving along the coast, I start recognizing the coastline across from the shore, including the numerous boat docks.

There's our tower.

Seeing it is somehow comforting. How I wish I were there with Todd right now, making love to him with no one the wiser, and nothing between.

Our place.

Further down to my left, three enormous red brick chimneys

are coming into view, as I drive along Deadwater Drive. They seem to be standing on their own, tall and strong, as if declaring youth despite their years.

The place was built in the early 1900s for movie stars who would come for rest and relaxation, so I'm surprised at the chimneys' enduring stature. How it changed from a resort to a mental hospital is beyond me, but at least it's looking as if my aunt may be enjoying her stay somewhat. Deadwater Manor doesn't appear as bad as I expected.

I pull into the split driveway and am pleasantly surprised at the well-manicured rows of trees cut into cone shapes. A row of black lamp posts line the entryway of the hospital. I slowly circle the car up to the overhang covered with a green tin roof that matches several other buildings. The overhang is attached to the main building. Glass double doors adorned with two round parlor lights to each side welcome guests at the top of the cement stairs. The exterior of the building is painted a pale pink and each window is accented in an inviting white.

I round the entryway and park in an angled spot in front of one of the coned trees. Sitting in my car for a moment, I check out the place. It's so much prettier than I expected, but procrastinating like this is only reawakening the old fears.

What am I going to do if one of the patients starts yelling at me? Or worse yet, starts yelling at my aunt?

As I exit my car, I whisper to myself, "Stop being a baby and just be brave. Oh yeah, and no panic attacks. You can do this."

Thanks for that last phrase, Mom. You always were such an inspiration to me.

I force myself to walk briskly up the sidewalk toward the entrance steps before I change my mind. My aunt is the only thing that's pulling me into the unknown behind the black glass doorway at the top of the stairs. I peer into each of the three stories of windows to see if any patients are watching me, but I only see the reflections of the trees, giving me no damn clue what hell might be happening behind the walls. The thought of facing it alone is daunting.

Aunt Lesley is facing this alone, I remind myself. *You're only here for a short visit, to make it less scary for her.*

A stale cigarette odor grabs me before I make it to the top of the stairs, causing me to clear my throat. I can see myself in the reflection of the double doors. I hesitantly pull one open to find a well-decorated waiting room inside. The temperature is cool despite the mugginess outside. The room is actually comforting, painted in typical peach with gray baseboards and tile floors with nothing out of the ordinary. The warm smell of coffee lingers in the air, drawing my attention to the beverage station nestled between upholstered seating arranged in varying u-shaped patterns. Overall, the place is somewhat appealing and well maintained. My limbs feel a little less tight.

Straight ahead, a receptionist sits behind an opening in the wall. Gaining more confidence, I walk straight up to her.

She greets me with a smile. "Good afternoon. How can I help you?"

"I'm looking for my aunt. Her name is Lesley Odell. She came here last week, I think."

"Hmm—the name doesn't sound familiar, but no problem. Let me look her up. Just have a seat for a second."

I walk over to the maroon-colored chairs, take a magazine off the end table and sit down, glancing up at the receptionist now and then, in case I don't hear her call for me. As I wait, I notice the wall coverings with their brilliant sunset colors and simple style. The clock says it's one-thirty in the afternoon. I should easily get back to the park tonight in time to meet Todd. To the right of the reception area, there's a curved hallway to the unknown—a place I still cannot see. I wonder if that is where new patients are being held. I stand up and walk over to the hallway to take a peak, trying not to draw attention. As I pretend to peruse through more reading material in the magazine rack, I peer down the hallway but can only see a closed, wooden door with a small, frosted window.

Still no clues.

I wonder what that area is used for?

Suddenly, with all my attention elsewhere, my purse falls to the floor, catapulting everything I own back toward the seating area. I quickly try to reach the lipstick and pens, but they roll out away from me.

So much for being a detective.

As quietly as I can, I bend over and grab all of my loose belongings and shove them back into my purse, looking toward the receptionist a few times to see if she noticed. It didn't seem to faze her.

Christ, you are an idiot, Jeannie.

I laugh a little to myself at the irony of the situation, until I see my car keys lying on the floor beneath the magazine rack.

Can anything else go wrong?

Again, I slowly and nonchalantly move toward the hallway to confiscate my keys before someone else does.

Wouldn't it have been awful if I didn't notice my keys were missing and was unable to get the hell out of this place?

I shudder.

"You said you were her niece, correct?" the receptionist's voice calls out from behind the desk, causing me to almost drop my keys again.

"Yes, that's right" I say, clutching my keys.

"Okay, well, come sign in, and we'll take you back."

I walk up to the window and the receptionist hands me a clipboard.

"Sign these. Don't forget to put your date of birth and social security number. We'll use your birthdate as your login identification for future visits. All you'll need to do is punch it in the keypad down the hall. We'll be ready for you in a minute."

The stack of forms is huge. I rush through them, because I'm afraid it could take forever. I don't want to miss Todd. After signing all the forms and handing them back to the receptionist, I look out the beautiful windows toward the entryway view that offers all the reasons to live in Florida including sunshine, water, and palm trees. I always seem to forget to appreciate my surroundings or the small details. Mom always reminded me to do so.

I smile as I think of her, until my concentration is interrupted by footsteps coming down the hallway. I quickly look over to see if it's my aunt.

It isn't.

Instead, a male attendant greets me. His name badge identifies him as Drake.

"You're Jean Kynde?" he inquires.

I nod.

"Follow me, then."

I follow him down the hallway to the wooden door I saw earlier and enter. This room is much larger than the reception area with pink walls and white accents. To the left is a glass office; a semi-circle nurses' station. A couple rows of tables with metal chairs are scattered about, and a steel water fountain is stationed at the other side of the room.

Drake pulls out a chair for me and assures me he'll be right back. As I wait for my aunt, I try to imagine how it would feel to be locked up with a guard on every corner.

I wonder if my aunt feels like a prisoner. Why in the world did she agree to come here?

My attention is soon drawn to a commotion outside the same door I entered. I listen, but all I can hear is some mumbling, perhaps arguing.

Eventually, another man comes through the door. He appears to be older, with gray hair and eyebrows and sagging skin on his neck. As he approaches, I can see the script writing on his lab coat.

Doctor Garrett Wiggins; this is Dad's friend. Okay, so I'm in the right spot.

"Jeannie, correct?"

"Uh, yes. I'm here to see my aunt. Have you talked to my dad?"

"Yes, he's been telling me about some issues."

"Yeah, well, I guess my aunt had a nervous breakdown."

"Aunt?"

"Yes, Lesley Odell. You have her chart there, right?"

He looks at me for a few seconds and then looks away, unable to find words. He pauses. I'm not sure what is going on, but I don't like the uneasiness I'm feeling right now. I'm getting that gut feeling that something is wrong.

Did she die?

He pulls his chair closer to me like a true friend would. In a caring voice, he says softly, "Your aunt is not here."

I stare at him blankly for a second and then ask, "What? What do you mean? She's gone already or—or worse?" The reality of the situation starts to take hold as racing thoughts of never seeing her again start scaring me.

He touches my arm for a second and says, "Jeannie, listen to me carefully." I try to focus more on his mouth, since my difficulty in hearing is worsened by the tall ceiling in the room. "Your aunt was never here."

The racing thoughts stop. I look at him dead seriously, trying to figure out what the hell he's telling me.

Is she dead or not?

I look toward the table for a minute, not sure what he's going to tell me next.

She's dead? She's alive? She's somewhere else? She's a fucking FBI agent? What's going on?

"What do you mean? Where is she?" I finally manage.

"I don't really know. There's no record of her here. What I want to concentrate on is you, now. How do you feel about this?"

I frown and mumble, "Confused."

He nods and says sincerely, "It's understandable especially with the recent loss of your mom." At least, I think that's what he said.

I watch him, trying to figure out why we're having this conversation. I don't know how my dad knows this doctor, but his fake sincerity is not calming me. I glance over to the wooden door, and there are now two guards standing in front of them, one of which I recognize as Drake. Another door on the opposite side of the room opens, and two more guards move in.

This definitely doesn't feel right.

"Hey, they're just here for your protection," the doctor says. I lean back in my chair, as he moves forward and whispers, "No worries." His breath puffs across my hair, leaving me with a gift of strong cigarette stench. I try to lean back more but feel pinned. This guy does not know his boundaries. He starts stroking my arm in what seems like an attempt to comfort me, but it only makes me panic more. I can feel my palms moistening with every word.

"Is it okay if we talk for a while? I'd like to get to know you a little more, Jeannie. I've always heard your dad's side of things, but the opportunity to hear your side is what's important now. Why don't we have you go relax in another room, and then you can come into my office a little later?"

I try hard not to show the panic that's now taking over, hiding what I can of my heaving chest. It feels difficult to breathe with the short, shallow breaths that are now uncontrollable.

I'm going to have a panic attack.

I'm so screwed.

I look over to the guards, begging them not to force me behind the walls that will separate me from the rest of the world. I frantically search for a way to get myself out of what I know is inevitable, but it's useless with all the guards.

I'm going to become the prisoner. I'm going to become the next rumor throughout the school.

It's all part of a calculated plot my dad would be proud of. This is his victory—a victory that includes my never leaving Deadwater or having a life, even if he won't be a part of it. As long as he knows where I am, he'll be happy. I close my eyes in disgust, concerned about what I'm about to endure. I hate the unknown, but this is way beyond what any eighteen-year-old should have to experience.

"Jeannie, you still with me?" the doctor asks.

I look up at the cohort who is now starting to tug at my forearm.

"I think we need to get you comfortable."

I frown between the doctor and the guards. They both come forward to "help" me. Gasping for air, I throw my chair backwards to try the only path of escape I can think of, but they're too fast and catch the chair before I hit the ground.

"No! I am not going anywhere with you! I'm not a minor and my dad can't institutionalize me without my consent. Let me out of here!"

"Well, Miss Kynde, you just signed all the consents. There's nothing illegal here."

What starts as a rational protest spirals out of control quickly. Panic sets in. I'm crying, screaming, and clawing at them. I try to kick their groins, but they predict that move and easily pin my legs to the chair.

I start breathing heavier now. Panic takes over, and I'm quickly losing control.

"Get the syringe!" orders Doctor Wiggins, pointing to the table next to the water fountain.

Drake holds out one of my arms and lunges backward for the syringe with his other arm, knocking the table over.

Oh, God! Get me out of here!

Drake is grasping for the syringe on the floor, so I take the opportunity to bite his forearm, causing him to bleed and withdraw his clutch. This does nothing but make things worse for me, though. Drake leaps toward me, pinning the back of my head against his stomach muscles. My free arm flails back and forth, as I try to reach something to use to hit him.

It's no use.

Frantically, the doctor kicks the syringe toward Drake, and I watch in horror when the needle roughly enters my vein.

I think of all the things I'm going to miss: my room, long rides along the back roads, my friends, Rick, and of course, Todd.

Oh God, Todd! He's going to think I snubbed him! He's not going to be able to help me! Why didn't I tell him where I was really going?

I know my life is about to end, at least the way that I know it. The medication takes effect and the guard lets me drop. I smack my head on the floor. I look back up toward the fading enemy faces that are taking my life away, pleading with them to let me go.

"I don't want to stay."

Then all is dark.

6

I've never wet a bed before—that I can remember anyway. The cool dampness below my waist, however, makes me wonder if I have now. Whatever it is, I'm lying in it. I sniff the air for the smell of urine, but there's no indication that I soiled myself. More than anything, it's just annoying.

I open my eyes slowly, trying to focus on my surroundings. I brace myself for more syringes, but I don't see any. All I see are the white ceiling tiles that are dimpled with texture, one of which is stained by a roof leak. The fluorescent lights are on, hanging over me.

I try to turn toward the window, but I can't. It feels like my head is in a vise. My wrists and ankles are immobilized too. I can feel the buckles on my wrists when I tug at them.

I'm strapped in, I realize.

I close my eyes in fear, trying not to lose it again.

Take a deep breath. Breathe slowly. Don't lose control. You have to maintain your composure if you want any hope of getting the hell out of this place.

It's too late. I cry in frustration and try helplessly to keep from choking on my own spit. My body convulses from my lack of freedom. Tears flow into my ears that I cannot wipe. I'm immobilized and probably a junkie now too. All those years of never trying any drugs were wasted.

God knows what the hell they injected me with.

I tug at each of the restraints again, trying to pull them loose, but to no avail. I'm stuck on a flatbed with no mattress or pillow. It's just the board and me. I fight back the tears and move my eyes around the room, trying to determine what time of day it is. I'm guessing it's evening by the dimness of the light outside. The room itself is bare as far as I can see. Just green walls with a window and a door. My breathing grows heavy again.

After a few minutes, I calm myself down and start self-coaching. I must gain my composure for the next encounter with the hospital staff who probably get off on poisoning people. I'm not sure if I want to start screaming for help or not, since that might bring company in the form of some clear liquid in a little syringe with attached needle. In my current state, I might as well have a neon sign strapped to my arm that says, "Insert here."

I don't have to wait long. Shadows walk by the frosted door window. When I see the door start to open, I instinctively close my eyes. I'm not sure if I want to reveal my consciousness, so I pretend to be asleep. I know they're probably not that stupid, but I just need a few more seconds. Something bumps against the board and the wisp of air rushes along my arm when someone walks by.

I grow agitated again, and shallow breathing interrupts my fake sleeping. This forces me to open my eyes in panic, causing the person that is practically in my face to lunge back on the wheels of the stool.

It's Drake.

I close my eyes again, trying to block him out.

"So, you bite me, and then don't have the decency to say you're sorry?" he says. "Maybe I should bite you back. Wouldn't pinch too much since you're all drugged up right now, would it? You made me bleed, you know."

I keep my eyes shut.

He touches my arm. I clench my jaw, grinding my teeth in worry of what is about to happen to me.

"You're going to need me one of these days, you know. Better to get me on your good side now while you can. We're going to have long days and nights to get to know each other real well, being that I'm one of your attendants. Oh yeah, just so you know, the next time you bite me, I'll take your lip off."

I open my eyes to meet his. He's too close for comfort, but I can't push him away. His dark eyes are piercing, almost glaring, and then soften a little as I meet his gaze. He backs up a bit when I start to try to speak.

"Sorry, I just don't want to be a prisoner," I finally croak, clearing my throat several times. "I only came here to see my aunt."

"So, it's all a big misunderstanding. Your dad hates you and put you here on purpose, right? How many times do you think we've heard that one?"

Another guard—one I didn't even know was there—grunts in agreement.

"You just need to learn to cooperate with the good ol' doc. He'll keep you happy during your stay. In a few weeks, you can get yourself an exit ticket. Until then, no biting."

"So, just a few weeks, then I'm out of here?"

"It's up to the doc, but given the normal routine, I would say so."

Fuck that. No way am I staying that long. Somehow I'll have to figure out how to get around all this. I better play it like I'm a good patient for now, though.

I try to nod my head, but can't. "Okay."

"I'm going to take off these restraints, but if you resist even a little, I'll strap you back in faster and harder than you experienced the first time. Understand?"

"Okay."

As he makes his way around the table, unbuckling the straps, I feel reborn–given a second chance at life. There is something incredibly wrong with your body being held against its will.

He frees my head last, and I'm still afraid to move. I'm not sure what to do, actually. I'm petrified that I'll make one wrong move, and they'll have an excuse to restrain me again.

No chance am I going to let that happen.

"You can move now. Just take it nice and slow, sweetheart," Drake says with half a smile. He moves his arm behind my back, helping me upward and bringing my legs off the table with the other. "You're going to stay calm now, right? I don't want a repeat episode from before."

"Yeah," I say, looking right through him toward the windows to see if they can be opened. All I can focus on is how to get out. He continues with his rules and regulations speech while I daydream about how I'll run for it the first chance I get. After all, my car is sitting out front.

At least, I hope it still is.

"Got it?" asks Drake, moving away from me and making the chair squeak loudly.

"Yeah," I say again. One thing I remember my mother telling me long ago is to 'Keep it simple stupid' if I ever got myself in a situation with lawyers. This guy isn't a lawyer, but I don't trust him. I don't trust anyone in this place. I'm basically alone, and no one really knows I'm even here—except my dad. I shiver despite the warmth in the room.

"You'll have to stay in here awhile until you get the grand tour of the place and find out your room assignment, so don't get any ideas on leaving. We're good at chasing escapees—especially young girls like you," he adds sarcastically and closes the door.

The room is silent. I take in my surroundings, trying to figure out what angle to use with the doctor to let me leave. He'll have to see that I'm sane at some point.

I comb my fingers through my hair and notice a knot on the back of my head where it hit the floor during the earlier scuffle. It hurts to touch. I walk over to the windows and examine their structure as if I were some smart engineer or something. I figure there'll be no way to open it, and unfortunately, I'm right.

Of course they would think of that.

My goal is to prove myself normal—or escape through some back door or a window. Only problem is my purse is missing, meaning my keys are missing also.

I take a deep breath and notice the putrid green colored gown I'm wearing. It's similar to a hospital gown. Apparently, they stripped me down and changed my clothes at some point.

Lovely.

I cringe as the thought crosses my mind that it might have

been Drake.

Sitting on the board, I contemplate my plan of action. I've practiced escape a lot with my dad. Why should this be anything different? They're keeping me here against my will and if I can somehow succeed in getting away, I'll not only be escaping them, but my dad as well.

Victory.

The sun is beating down on the floor as it streams in through the window blinds, indicating that I have to be on the west side. My car, however, is on the north side of the building. At this point, I have to miraculously find my keys and then use my stealth skills to find my way to my car on the opposite side of the building.

Fucking wonderful.

I pace back and forth next to the board, trying to figure out what I'm going to do. Suddenly, the door flings open and a heavy-set woman comes barreling at me, grabs my arm and plunges something into it before I can get a word out. I try to grab at her, but she jerks back away from me as I fall to the floor.

"My name is Dolores. Perhaps you should greet me with respect the next time."

I can feel her heavy steps leave the room, but I can say or do nothing. Eventually I can't see clearly and am coming in and out of consciousness. I can feel myself being lifted and moved but don't know where I am or where I am going. I'm just bobbing up and down as if I'm in water.

* * * *

After God knows how long, I'm finally resting on solid ground. The movements stop, and I can't help but give into the drugs and stress of the day. Figuring I'll just sleep it all off until I can function later, I stretch out on what feels like a bed with guard rails, my toes feeling their way between them. As I start to give in to rest, I enjoy the warmth of the sun shining on my face. I'm again on the west side.

Hopefully, I'll never wake up.

7

No such luck. As I start to gain consciousness, I feel vibrations from the movements in the room. My face is nestled between a guardrail and the hard bed, causing a slight pain from my left side. It seems silly that they have guardrails on the bed to make sure I don't fall off. I move backwards to readjust the kink in my neck and try focusing on the room. Through the bars, I see two nurses huddled around a desk straight ahead.

That wasn't in the last room. They've moved me.

One nurse is wearing a white uniform and the other is wearing scrubs. Both have elevated white sneakers. Certainly, there's too much sole to chase me down.

One glances my way. I quickly close my eyes, hoping she didn't see I'm awake. Since I'm lying on my left side, I'm able to listen to their conversation, but only hear mumblings about days off and travel reimbursements. I focus in on them more. One is Dolores; the one that punched a hole through my arm when she zeroed in with the needle that took away my body control.

I guess I'd better greet her nicely.

Opening one eye just the slightest, I see she's the rotund one. I want to giggle at the loosened stitches on the backside of her pants when she bends over to tuck in papers in the bottom drawer.

As I peek every few seconds, I see that I'm in a dark room with unfinished brick and mortar walls. I don't see any drywall, just various sizes of red brick and wood. The floor is comprised of unfinished wooden boards as well. I don't want to look up to verify, but I get the sense I'm in an attic based on the musty smell and warmth of the room. It's then that I notice the wetness throughout my gown. This time it's from sweat. My labored breathing isn't just panic-driven either. It's also from the uncomfortable temperature conditions in the room.

I hope they're not going to leave me here.

The nurses move around the desk to grab some charts and then eventually leave the room. I wait a few seconds to make sure they're gone and then open my eyes to fully take in my room—and my situation. I look through the rails in all directions.

Yes, it's the attic—no doubt about it.

Flipping over onto my back to verify it with the ceiling, I sure enough see only rafters. This is suddenly inconsequential, though, as I register what I'm looking through to see the rafters.

More bars.

I sit up to take it all in, my head spinning with the thought of it.

I'm in a cage—a blue cage. This is a human cage.

Springing to my feet, I grasp the bars, looking around in horror. There's space to stand, but it's only the width of the twin mattress. One panel of the steel bars is hinged on one end—a cage door with padlock. I notice extra steel loops and straps with buckles inside the cage too.

Are you fucking kidding me? I might be caged and strapped? What the hell kind of psychiatric care is this?

The cage is positioned in front of a long narrow window on one end of the attic. Above this window is a smaller one in the shape of a semi-circle.

Sliding down the back of the bars, I pull my legs up to my chest. A feeling of doom spreads over me. I don't know how I'll ever get out of this place.

Then I notice another cage. It sits in front of another long, narrow window on the opposite side of the attic. A body is lying in that one as well.

Surely they wouldn't keep people up here forever—would they? They probably just bring people up here to calm them down or something.

I focus on the other person. I can see a petite, malnourished body. The spine is protruding from the back of the gown. Dark, long hair is lying on the mattress, making me assume it's a girl. She's very still, sleeping. Perhaps she's drugged. Just looking at her makes me feel pain. I wonder what she's been through. How long has she been here in her pink cage? It's ridiculous how they try to make the cages seem calming or docile, as if we're in a baby nursery.

I touch one of the bars, wrapping my fingers around its curvature, and wonder what it will take to make them bend. I play with the lock for a bit. Bending the rods would be impossible, but breaking the lock might be plausible. I examine the bars for any signs of weakness. Besides some chipped paint, they are solid. I sit back down in case the nurses come in soon. My options are few and I feel helpless.

How could my dad hate me so much that he'd do this to me?

"Was the lock secure, darlin'?"

My eyes open wide while I contemplate the voice from behind me. I'm not sure if it's Dolores, the other inmate, or the other nurse, since I can't exactly tell the direction the sound is coming from. I quickly try to remember Dolores' voice, searching the fog.

"I mean, we wouldn't want you running around here getting lost or anything, right?"

I can feel the vibration of her footsteps coming around to the front of my cage, making me cringe.

"Open your eyes, bitch, and look at me when I'm about to stab you!"

I look at her before I hear the last part and bolt toward the back of the cage, searching Dolores for her weapon. Pain sears through my thigh. I see her pull the needle back out, watching me with a victorious grin.

"Just something to make you a little more comfortable, Jean," she reassures. "Are your accommodations to your liking?"

"Oh yeah, I just love being locked away in an attic cage. Are you planning to feed me some raw meat next?" I ask with a scowl.

"Oh, no, you'll love the food here. It's class A. Problem is, it's always piping hot. So, you might have a bit of a hard time swallowing it, since it's sweltering in here," she says. Suddenly, she looks past me. "Oh, Drake, you're right on time! We were just talking about food."

Drake is standing near my cage with a food tray.

He nods to Dolores. "She's the one that likes to bite. Watch out for her."

"Yeah, I heard. That's why I stabbed her when she wasn't lookin'." She laughs as she walks to the desk.

Drake opens up the cage and puts the tray down near my legs. I can barely move now. There's no way I'll be able to push past him and run. I do manage to remove the top of the tray to see what kind of slop she's talking about. Drake continues to watch me.

"Feeling pretty good, huh? Told you the drugs are good here. I'll be back tomorrow, so we can talk more then," says Drake. He moves back and locks the cage, smiling. Sweat is coating his armpits and neck.

Dolores is right. The food is hot, and I'm unable to eat it. I glance over to the other caged girl. Drake enters her cage, but she doesn't move when he puts the food beside her. He nudges her shoulder and suddenly turns back toward Dolores.

"Shit, Dolores! Are you keeping an eye on these girls or what?" Drake says in panic. "She's fucking dead!"

"What? She probably suffocated," Dolores says, unconcerned, while she walks over to evaluate her. She pulls the girl backwards by her hair. "Yup, she's a goner."

I try not to stare, but I can't look away. The girl's face is ashen, mouth drawn downward, sort of like the old "Scream" movies. Her eyes are open.

Dolores checks her pulse. The girl's head drops, and now her dead eyes are staring at me. I cover my eyes to try not to look, but I can't help it. She looks hideous, and how they are treating her—Dolores in particular—is even more disturbing. Drake glances back at me before covering her with a sheet.

"Drake, just go get a stretcher or restraining board, so we can get her out of here before she smells," Dolores orders.

Drake nods and leaves, thumping his way down the stairs.

I look at Dolores with horror, as she calmly returns to her desk, ignoring me.

I turn and stare out the window, partly because the medication is really kicking in and partly because I'm sickened by what just happened. All I can see is the sky—purples, golds, and pinks tonight. The stress is stronger than my will, though, and I succumb to the sleep that's beckoning me.

* * * *

I awake to being pulled from my cage and onto the floor. I can see Dolores' white shoes as I try to get up. She grabs one of my arms and Drake grabs the other, dragging me toward the other side of the room. The side where the girl just died—the cage where the girl just died.

Are they putting me in there?

Drake opens up the cage door—the pink cage door. I pull my feet forward, trying to break their momentum before they can throw me in. I pull back against their grasp, stopping them in surprise.

"No! I'm not going in there!" I scream.

"Oh, yes you are," Dolores shouts loud enough to hurt my ears. "I should already be off my shift, but I'm stuck doing overtime because of the dead girl. I'm not happy about having to stay here late tonight. So, cooperate. Pink is for girls."

I cringe for a second to protect my good ear and fight against their advance, but I'm no match. Before I know it, I'm sitting in the pink cage on the same mattress and sheets that recently held the dead girl. I draw myself to my feet and back into the corner of the cage, staring at the spot where she drew her last breath.

"Oh, what's your problem? At least she didn't shit the sheets when she died. You're staying in there, so get used to the idea," Dolores snorts as she slams the cage door shut.

I frantically try not to touch any part of the sheet the girl had been lying on. I close my eyes, wondering why I'm here—this hospital, this room, and this cage. Eventually, I turn toward the window. It's dark outside.

I missed the sunset. I missed Todd. He doesn't know where I am and neither does Rick. I hope they can find me somehow.

A cooler breeze comes through the window, making the room more bearable than earlier and I can breathe easier. I gaze at the stars, trying to keep my sanity, concentrating on how I will persuade the doctor to let me leave. I have to, or I'll end up like the former resident of this cage.

* * * *

Another nurse is now on duty for the night. She glances over at me occasionally from behind her newspaper. The fluorescent light over her desk sways with the wind marching through the two windows. It feels like a storm might be coming. I wish it would. Storms make me feel comfortable.

I squat in the corner of the cage. My legs are fatigued, and I'm tired and frustrated, but I'm still hesitant to lie where the girl died. Still feeling the effects of God-knows-what-medication, I fall slightly forward a few times, losing myself to brief moments of sleep.

Later, I jerk forward one more time, enough to wake up and see the nurse nodding off as well, her newspaper down on her chest now. I look down at the sheets, contemplating how I'm going to spend the night in the death cage. I stand up to give my thighs a break, holding onto the bars to make sure I don't fall forward. I have to hold myself up due to the fatigue. My body shakes from the weakness.

A part of me wants to just give in and lie down and forget the events that occurred earlier, but I can't, at least while I'm still conscious. The steel feels hard against my back, as I push myself against the bars, trying to steady my legs. I examine the cage for any other options other than the mattress to sleep on, not knowing what I could possibly expect to find.

A deep snore comes from the nurse, causing me to lunge forward to my knees. I yelp and quickly boost myself back up and off the mattress, clenching the bars. I try hard not to think about the girl and what could have happened to her. I try even harder to not remember my mom in the hospital bed. My jaw grows tired from clenching my teeth with the anxiety of it all, and I try to hold back the panic attack that's continuously threatening its eruption. I squeeze my eyes shut tight.

How do I deal with this? How can I get past the thought of the lifeless girl that probably slept in this cage last night?

My erratic thoughts continue. Then an idea occurs to me.

The straps!

Brown leather straps with holes and accompanying buckles are hanging in the cage. They look strong—strong enough to hold a person.

Strong enough to hold me up and off the mattress.

I slowly move over to the center of the bars, trying not to wake up the nurse. Luckily, the storm is strengthening, adding more noise to the attic. Keeping an eye on the nurse, I quickly bend over and buckle my ankles into the straps, securing them up from the mattress. Pushing one thigh between the bars to keep me steady, I twist the other two straps into a position comfortable for my wrists. I can buckle one, but not the other, so I twist it more until I can't move. I'm elevated, and in a way, elated, as I peer down at the mattress, knowing I have won this small battle. The breeze is now whirling through the back of my gown, comforting me like a mother's touch. I smile and think of my mom who's probably watching over me, letting me know she's here, shielding me from the pain I should be feeling from my position on the bars. Shifting more, I find the best spot. My head falls forward. I stare at the death mattress and listen to the melodic thunder booming through the room. White light shrieks through the window. I feel like an angel watching over a leftover spirit who can't find her way. My eyes grow dry and drool forms at the corner of my mouth. I continue to stare silently until I eventually remember no more.

Goodnight, Mom.

8

"What? Is she a crucifix now?"

I jerk awake from the sound of the voice I loathe almost as much as my dad's. My eyes are having a hard time adjusting with the painful light filling the attic. The mattress is below me. A long string of spit hangs from my bottom lip. It takes me a minute, but I slowly remember the darkness from the evening before and my "escape." I'm still strapped into position above the mattress. Not even a hair touches it. I feel relief more than anything at first, then searing pain from every part of my body.

I scream in agony, as I try to readjust my position and bring my head upwards. I can't.

Drake runs toward me, passing Dolores who is standing in front of my cage. Her hands are on her hips, scolding me with her stature.

The straps plunge deeper into the wounds they created overnight with every breath, making me sob. Drake throws open the cage door and hesitates at my hands and ankles, seeming unsure as to how to remove me from my pain.

I gasp after each word as I screech, "Get that fucking mattress out of here!"

Drake grabs for my legs, trying to pull them up, but I insist that he remove everything that reminds me of that girl—of death.

"First move the mattress, sheets, and pillow—all of it. Please! I can't touch what she died on!"

I scowl at Dolores, trying to remind her of the atrocities she conducted the previous night.

She scowls right back, but her words are directed to Drake. "I don't know why you're babying her like this. Since when do patients call the shots here?"

Drake ignores her, speaking only to me. "Okay, okay—just hold on, okay?"

I whimper with every sharp movement of the cage while he throws all signs of the girl's death toward Dolores, who steps back only to watch.

"This is crazy! How could you do this to yourself?" he shouts, slowly unbuckling my ankle straps.

My legs dangle toward the steel bars at the bottom of the cage. Drake angles each foot toward them, and I'm able to steady myself as he begins freeing my wrists. My head still drops forward. As he unbuckles the last strap, I feel a warm trickling sensation flowing down to my knees and quickly to my ankles.

I guess I couldn't hold it anymore.

Drake looks down at the puddle that is forming on the floor below the cage. Enraged, he throws his hands up in the air and jumps outside the cage.

"Dead girls don't piss on you," Dolores teases him cruelly, "but live ones do! Serves you right for listening to her."

"I can't fucking believe this," Drake mumbles, shaking his head, pacing back and forth in front of my cage.

I'm afraid to speak, so I silently stand inside the cage, shaking from the dampness and pain in my limbs.

"Listen, you little bitch," Dolores snarls, taking over now, obviously tired of Drake's brand of gentleness, "pissing yourself is no way to get out of your cage. Do you hear me? I should make you sleep on the bare bars now and teach you a lesson on keeping your place clean. You do this again, and I'll make sure the doctor gets a full report and never lets you the hell out of here."

My eyes widen, and Dolores sees it. It gives her power—now she knows my worst fear.

"Don't test me," she warns, a cruel smile spreading over her lips. "I know your kind. Prissy girls that always get their way—

Daddy's little girl, right? You probably had everything handed to you on a silver platter. I used to have to deal with girls like you way back in high school. Rich girls are cruel. Some of the guys too. I don't have to worry about that anymore, though, because now I have the upper hand."

"I had *nothing* handed to me. My life has been nothing but abuse from my father!" I hurl back at her. "I'm not what you think."

Dolores snorts. "Like I'm gonna believe that." She backs from the cage and turns around, heading for the desk.

I try to hold back. I try not to let out all the years of anguish I've endured—anguish I've kept mostly locked in the back of my mind for so long. The drugs, Dolores, and frustration of my situation get the better of me though.

Drake stops pacing and looks over at me.

I start shaking more, but this time with anger. I suddenly realize that this is an anger I'm not going to be able to control.

"You have no fucking idea what you're talking about, you fat bitch! You don't have any idea what it's been like to be me—no idea at all!" Streams of tears flood down my cheeks, as I continue. "This is all my father's doing. His dreams are coming true. He put me here and you both know it. I'm sane and you're both trying to sabotage me into looking like an uncontrollable patient. You are all in it together, and I'll be damned if I'm going to let you win. You want a battle? You've got one! In the end, I will win—not my dad and not you sadists."

Shut up, Jeannie! Just shut up! You're just hurting yourself.

I scowl at them angrily, breathing heavy from my words, ready to take on either of them. "I hate you all! There's nothing wrong with me. I never chose to be hit with that baseball and lose so much of my hearing! I never chose for my mom to die! I never chose all the abuse!"

Out of control now, I fling myself back and forth against the cage in all directions, not caring if I inflict more pain on myself.

Drake rushes toward the cage, pleading with me to stop. Finally, I mistakenly slam both wrists up against the steel bars and cry out in agony. He quickly hops into the cage, shielding me from falling backwards. I fall onto him, and he struggles to keep me from hitting the bottom of the cage with full force.

Dolores grunts. "You never learn, do you Drake. You're just going to keep babying that whiny brat."

He doesn't acknowledge her.

She snorts now. "Well, clean up the mess. Don't you dare leave me with it."

Drake drags me onto the floor, holding my head in his arms, as he gently scolds me. "Do not do this, you hear me? Do not inflict your own pain. There's plenty here without you adding to it."

I look up at him, still unable to move my head from the stiffness of the night.

"Then, don't leave me in a cage with leftover souls."

* * * *

When I awake again, I feel softness below me. The smell of freshly washed sheets floats around me, reminding me of my bedroom. For a moment, I think I've dreamt my imprisonment. The excitement lasts only until I open my eyes and see the steel bars surrounding me.

I'm in the pink cage still. At least, I'm not on used linens. My neck, ankles, and wrists are sore. The pain is bearable now, though. I draw one of my wrists up so I can see the damage. It isn't as bad as it feels. There's some raw skin, but no bone is exposed, so I figure I'll survive. I examine all of my wounds. They are pretty much flesh burns—battle scars against this God-forsaken place.

Dolores is in and out of the room every few minutes, ignoring me and focusing on several tasks at once. I study her, watching her routine and mannerisms. As she flutters around the desk, her auburn hair bobs back and forth along her neckline. She isn't much for style, with her 1980s poodle-look hairstyle and puffy bangs above her forehead with some of the longer pieces drawn back into a bow. I wonder if she thinks she's in style or if she just doesn't care.

Probably the latter, but why take the time in making a nice little bow?

She seems to have bounds of energy during her work, checking things off a list and delegating them to another nurse who shadows her. If nothing else, she seems knowledgeable. She simply doesn't like patients.

I look over at my old cage. It's empty. In some weird way, I kind of miss it even though I was only in it briefly. It seems like it was mine and then it was taken away from me. This thought scares me, and I put my head in my hands, disgusted with myself.

Get back on focus. There's no way you belong in a cage, Jeannie, no matter what the circumstance.

I can't figure out why they had to move me to this specific cage, since the other one remains empty, but I'm not going to ask. It can't be just because it's pink, can it? Doesn't matter, I guess. My only way out is going to be through the doctor. He mentioned he would see me today before my "admission" procedures yesterday, so I'm hoping for the opportunity to convince him that I am saner than anyone else here. I hope it will be soon.

I'm not sure what time it is but the breakfast tray is in my cage, so it has to be later than eight o'clock in the morning. One thing is certain: it's late enough to bring enough heat and humidity in the room and make it hot already. My gown is dripping wet and my hair is sticking to my arms.

I wonder if a shower in this place means a fire hose.

"You going to take all day with those eggs, Jesus? Now that you're one with God, maybe you could finish that, so we can move on with our day. The doctor wants to see you pronto," says Dolores. She hovers around my cage.

"What time is it?"

"Don't worry about that. Just give me your tray, so you can get cleaned up before you see the doc."

I hand her the tray, though I would rather throw it at her. She grabs it from me and slams the cage door shut with a jerk from her elbow, turning around to lock it. I slump back into the cage, wondering what will happen next. Will I be able to realistically persuade the doctor? The guy locked me in this hellhole in the first place.

Maybe I *am* fucking mad.

"If you're looking for your savior, he's not here, sweetheart," Dolores says from across the attic.

I frown, trying to figure out if she means the doctor or God.

She realizes I don't know what she's talking about. "You know, Drake. Don't get any ideas like trying to seduce him. He doesn't have your back and never will. He does what I say, and I do what the good ol' doc tells me to do. So, it won't do any good scheming on how to get out of here. We know all the tricks."

I sigh and turn away from her, not wanting to make eye contact. I wish I could drop-kick her out the window. I giggle to myself with the thought, doubting her fat ass would make it. I put my head to my knees so she can't see my grin.

The light is streaming in through the window next to me. The sky is clear outside. Only a few splotches of clouds break a beautiful bright blue. I get up to look outside and take in what I'm missing. The window is open, but there is no breeze this morning. The heat from the sun makes me perspire more. Beads of sweat gather on my cheeks and run onto my lips.

Beyond the tree line, I can see water and more trees and houses. I smile at the familiarity of it all. I try to focus but can't tell for sure if it's South Beach. That is, until I see my Vug parked just outside the window.

I'm on the north side! I grab onto the bars, holding myself steady so I can look at my new car longer. It's waiting for me, just sitting there patiently. My ultimate escape.

Then, it hits me.

I'm never going to be able to drive it again—not as long as I'm locked up in this room and in this cage anyway.

I *must* get out. I have to get back to Todd and my life again.

I wonder how long Todd waited for me last night. I can't think of him standing there, watching for me. I look at South Beach to see if the tower is in view, scanning the coastline for familiarities. Just above the top of the trees, I can barely see it. Such a happy time seems so far away now. If only I could let him know that I'm right across from the tower.

I miss Rick, too. He's got to be searching for me by now, but he probably thinks I stayed at a friend's house at this point. Once he finds out that's not the case, I'm sure there will be hell to pay around this place.

I turn back toward Dolores. She's writing something in my chart.

Shit, she's probably writing incriminating evidence on this morning about me. A whole play-by-play on how I lost it.

"When do I see the doctor?" I ask, as I wring out my hospital gown through the bars.

Dolores looks up at me without answering at first, seeming surprised by my sudden pleasant interaction. Then, she looks down at the chart, continuing to write and talk at the same time.

"When he tells me. Why the rush? Got somewhere to go?"

"Yes, I do, as a matter of fact. I've got a beach waiting for me."

"Yeah, well, that beach might have to wait a bit. You rich girls always have to go to the beach. You won't be visiting any while you're here at the Manor. You can look and wish though."

I look back outside at my Vug, wishing—and planning my departure.

You have got to get out of here, Jeannie.

The door to the attic flies open and Drake enters, carrying a note. Dolores reads it and gives it back to Drake. She turns to me without emotion.

"Take her to see him right away. Bring it in."

"Oh, come on! She's still hurting from last night."

"That's her own fault. We'll follow protocol with this one."

I look over at them both, not wanting to know what they are planning.

"Come on, Dolores. It won't be very comfortable."

"Since when do I care? This is just a job, Drake, nothing else. Remember that. Just go get it."

Drake looks at Dolores for a long minute, before he sighs and walks toward the doorway, glancing back at me.

I look back at Dolores to watch her expression, but she has none. There are no hints on what Drake is about to do. I suddenly feel nervous again, and trapped even more. There is absolutely no escaping whatever is in store for me. I brace myself against the back of the cage and wait.

9

It feels like I've been waiting half a day for Drake's torture device, and he's still not back yet. I can't imagine what he and Dolores are referring to, but I know whatever it is, it isn't going to be pleasant. I close my eyes and try to calm myself down, dreading their arrival. I just need to concentrate on proving myself to the doctor. He's got to be reasonable on some level. He's a doctor, after all.

Then again, he *is* a friend of my dad's, so maybe that's wishful thinking.

I turn back toward the window to look at my Vug again and tears well up in my eyes. Watching the car that represents such freedom to me from my prison window is killing me. It's way worse torture than anything they could conjure up to do to me. The ironic part is that I don't think they even know about my car being parked out front or the fact that I'm looking at it on a daily basis. I think they really are oblivious. Here, they're coming up with all kinds of different ways to torture me, when I'm looking at the very vehicle that I drove to my prison, and the same vehicle that taunts me to escape. Not just to escape from this place, but to find Todd. I want to be with him so bad. He's got to be thinking I snubbed him for good. Ugh! And to find Rick who will probably disown our dad. He's always wanted to get back at him for me. Maybe if we both refuse to include Dad in our lives, he'll die a miserable man.

The door to the attic flies open, and Drake enters the room

with a thud. I slowly turn toward the doorway to see what evil contraption Drake has for me. I can hear the rolling noise before I focus in on it completely.

Shit, it's another cage.

It's not as big as the one that I'm in right now. It's more like the size of a dog pen on wheels. Cuffs and chains are hanging within it too, ones that I'll have to be strapped into with my sore wrists.

"Drake, please don't put me in there!" I beg, but he keeps coming at me without hesitation. I guess Dolores is right. He's a man with action and no foresight, one who will never really care. All she has to do is give him an order, and he follows.

I cry at the thought of being put in such a small cage and kick at Drake when he tries to drag me out of my sanctuary. It's the only place I feel safe now, because I'm locked away from them. I know screaming and crying won't work, but I can't help it. Drake looks like a drone, as he grabs me by the waist and forces me into the cube. He locks the side door and then stands up over the cage and opens the top door, grabbing for my wrists with swift arm lunges, as if afraid of being bitten by an animal.

I don't bite him, but I don't make it easy either. I try to hold my arms behind my back and away from him. He attempts to grab for them, but eventually gives up and digs his fingertips into my arms instead, forcing me to flinch enough for him to grab hold of my elbows and jerk me forward until his hand lands on my wrist. With little effort, he twists my arm into an uncomfortable position, and I have no choice but to let him cuff me. Nothing else could be more demoralizing. I fight, but lose the same battle with my left arm as well. Before I know it, I'm attached to the top of the cage with cuffs that are cutting into the sores from the night before. Pain chops through my arms, as if I'm caught in a rattrap. I start breathing in and out erratically until I pull myself up a little so the cuffs fall lower on my arm. Blood droplets form along the sores on my wrists. Drake seems to give me a couple of minutes to get myself together, or at least I hope that's the reason why he's hesitating. I look into his eyes and then back at the cage.

The cage is a typical dog kennel with steel crosshatched bars. I feel huge inside of it, sort of like Alice in Wonderland when she expands in the small room. Even the thin cushion beneath me might be meant for canines. I sniff for any sign of wet dog smell, but there isn't any. I cross my legs with my arms over my head, bending over somewhat since I can't sit up. At least I can position myself in such a way that I'm not touching the wounds with the cuffs. That's until Drake starts to move me. The movement shakes my hands and rubs on the sores again.

I whimper when he rotates the cage around to head out of the room and rolls me toward the doorway. I feel Dolores' eyes on my back and figure she's enjoying the whole scene.

"Bye, bye, dear Jeannie. You have a wonderful trip now, ya hear?" Dolores says. "Oh, wait a minute Drake. I almost forgot!"

Drake stops rolling the cage and jerks back toward Dolores. "No, she's fine. It can wait until afterwards," he assures, quickly closing the door behind him without waiting for an answer and continuing to move me toward the stairs. I brace myself for the flight down the stairs as he moves the front of the cage to the first step, but am pleasantly surprised that he makes an effort to softly move the cage down each step, catching the front of it before it flies forward. The back of the cage, however, slams on each step, sending shocking pain through my wrists with each jolt and causing me to bite my lip while trying to hold back the gasps.

At the bottom of the stairs, I can see a small landing followed by a second set of steps in the opposite direction. Oh God, not again! As luck would have it though, Drake stops pushing the cage at the bottom of the first flight and moves my cube against the wall, leaving me there as he walks around the cage.

"You ready for your adventure? Hold on tight, sweetheart!"

Okay, so I'll be going down the stairs, like it or not.

I brace myself for what I know is going to hurt, as I envision myself flying uncontrollably down the next set of stairs.

But there's no liftoff.

Instead Drake opens a latch along the wall and slides a pocket door open about the size of the cage. I only have a few seconds to examine the dark space within the wall, when he kicks the cage into it. I quickly brace my legs against each side of the bars, not knowing if I'm going to land on solid ground anytime soon. Luckily, there seems to be flooring within the wall, and the free fall never comes.

"See you on the other side of eternity!" Drake says, quickly sliding the door shut again, leaving me in complete darkness. I look around in all directions but can't see anything.

Panic sets in. "Drake! Let me out of here! Please! Please!" I scream, but I'm left in the wall. "Oh, God! What's going on?"

I try to get a grip on where I am. The noise in my head from my ear is making it hard to comprehend whether I'm hearing phantom noises or the real thing. I see flashes of light also, but I'm not sure which direction they're coming from.

"Help me, somebody!" I scream, but instead of an answer from someone else, my senses kick into overdrive, and I'm hearing louder noises from all directions. I feel wild with fear, pulling my hands through the cuffs as much as I can, and tugging at them with all of my weight. Am I being buried alive in a wall?

My heart palpitates loudly in my head. I pull more and more at the cuffs, not caring if I pull off my hands in the process. Then, suddenly, with a loud clank, I feel the cage move, causing my shoulders to hit the top of the cage. Once I gain my bearings, I squat and wait as the cage continues downward, looking around me for any signs of light.

Finally, the movement halts and there's silence again. I think I hear a noise from above and protect my head from anything that might be falling, but then I realize I can't figure out the direction of sound. I begin shaking uncontrollably within the unknown. I wish I were standing in front of my dad again, as he scolds me on something I didn't hear. That is better than this.

Okay, Jeannie, just calm down. Try to relax. This is just worse because of your hearing. Just relax.

As I squat in the dark, shaking uncontrollably in fear, a screeching noise begins enveloping the cage from which direction I can't tell. Finally, I see a light come through and a man's legs standing within it. He kneels down and peers in. It's Drake. I breathlessly curse him for scaring the shit out of me.

"Oh, you're alright—just giving you a little thrill ride. It was probably the best ride you've been on in a long time. It's a dumbwaiter, dummy! Just think of it as the Tower of Terror at Disney. Been on that ride? You know, the moving elevator?"

"You are a fucking asshole," I say, weeping.

"Oh now, let's not be too mean. You should be on your best behavior when you see the doc. I didn't let Dolores at you, did I? That ride would have really freaked you out if you were stoned."

I shudder at the thought of it but try to quickly pull myself together.

"Seriously, I wasn't being an asshole. It was either that or a really rough ride down two flights of stairs. I think you got the better end of the deal, sister."

"You should have warned me."

"What fun would that have been, huh?"

Tears well up in my eyes again.

"I'm not arguing with you anymore. Let's go see Doctor Feelgood."

I wipe my tears on my forearms, trying to hide my anguish, as we head down the hallway again.

Come on, pay attention to where you are. You'll need to know the layout of this place for when you get the hell out of here. Take mental notes!

Quickly, I focus in on the world around me. The hallway is much brighter than my hellhole. It is almost cheery. To my left all I see are blue-green walls and white doors jetting by. Most of the doors are closed but a few are open to what looks like empty patient rooms. To my right are endless windows. Are these the same windows I glanced up at when I was standing in the entryway during my arrival?

Before I can orient myself and put together a mental map, Drake slows down at the last door on the left. He shuffles me through the doorway until we enter a richly wooded library with floor-to-ceiling bookshelves that hold volume after volume of medical journals and reference materials. The room is warm, dressed in golds and browns that remind me of my father's office at home. In the center of the room, Doctor Wiggins is sitting in a black leather chair with his feet on an oversized desk. As I'm wheeled closer, day-old smoke smell stings my nostrils, reminding me of the first day I met Doctor Wiggins—the day of my imprisonment.

"You can let her out of that dog cage now. Why do you insist on bringing all of my patients to me in that contraption?" asks Doctor Wiggins, seeming generally concerned. "You can't handle a girl who's three quarters your size, Drake?"

"Well, I didn't want to bring her in this, but Dolores insisted. This one bites though, doc. You sure you want her out?" Drake asks, talking over my cage.

"Wait, maybe not if she bites."

"I am here, you know!" I proclaim. "I can hear you both. No need to talk over me as if I were an animal. I'm not going to bite you."

Doctor Wiggins bends down in front of my cage, smoking a cigarette and assessing my stature.

"Let her out and uncuff her."

Drake reluctantly frees me from the restraints and backs up. I crawl out on my knees and try with all the dignity that I can muster to stand up on my own accord without the assistance of anything nearby and without wobbling. My knees almost give out, but I manage to rise to my feet with minimal swaying. For this I'm grateful, since I can't be looking like I'm drunk off my ass right now. This guy's my ticket to freedom, so I must impress the bastard, despite his connection to my dad. I walk over to one of the burgundy leather chairs, as if I were walking on a tight rope, and sit in front of his desk.

So much for the good impression, damn it! Why won't my legs work? I pat my hair down and straighten out my hospital gown. I've got to admit, the leather on this chair feels like I'm sitting in butter.

"You can go now, Drake. I've got it from here. Come back in an hour," Doctor Wiggins directs as he continues to smoke his cigarette.

He doesn't say anything at first while looking at my chart and glancing up at me occasionally. Behind him are several official diplomas encased in gold-leafed accented frames, all perfectly aligned with shiny glass fronts to make him look legit. One of the diplomas is from London. I would have never guessed he spent any time in England, since this guy is far from a class act. They probably kicked him out. His desk is littered with cigarette ash and piles of papers.

After sizing me up for what seems like forever, he finally moves back in his chair and asks, "What's up with your arms and legs, Miss Kynde? They're bleeding."

"It was a rough ride."

I wonder if he knows about the old kitchen shaft ride.

"Uh huh—not self-inflicted?" he asks, his voice slowly becoming baritone.

I look down.

Guilty. Shit.

"Not totally. The cuffs irritated them."

The doc takes a deep breath and exhales strongly. "So, you didn't hang yourself from your limbs last night?"

"I did, but that was because I didn't want to lie on the same mattress as the dead girl."

"Did you tie your neck up, too?"

I'm surprised at the question at first, but then figure out where he's going.

"No, no, I'm not suicidal."

"Hmm—okay. How about the biting? Any additional attacks on Deadwater personnel?"

Did he not hear my comment on the dead girl?

"No, but I did that before because you were capturing me against my will."

"So, biting was okay in your mind?"

"In self-defense, sure. I was scared."

"That I believe," he remarks without moving his teeth.

He lights up another cigarette and inhales deeply, drawing bright red from the end of the tip.

"So, let's talk about your dad," he says. He takes a big drag off his cigarette again and exhales the smoke, which floats to the top of the room.

"What about him?"

"He tells me you're always angry with him. Is that true?"

"He is abusive."

"He hits you?"

"No—but—he makes fun of me a lot, especially my hearing issue."

"A little teasing is hardly abuse. You're kind of young for a hearing issue, aren't you?"

"I had an accident. It makes it hard to hear in crowds or buildings with tall ceilings."

"Well, it's not my job to worry about that, but we can have it evaluated if you want." Doctor Wiggins pauses to write more down in my chart. "You hate your dad?"

"Yes."

"You ever want to see him again?"

"No."

"Just because he picks on you?"

"He constantly picks on me."

"You ever thought of hurting him?"

"Sometimes," I answer.

He looks up at me. "So, you want to hurt him?"

"I want him to leave me alone."

"How do you want to hurt him?"

"It's just random thoughts—"

"What was the last one?"

"Um—I guess it was about running him over with my car mostly. No biggie. I would never actually do it. I just want the pain to stop."

"Uh huh. Didn't he just buy you a car?"

"Yeah, but he just bought it so I could unknowingly drive myself here to my prison."

"So, you've hurt yourself and thought of hurting him before, correct?" he continues.

"It's not like that. You're twisting things around."

"I just state the facts. Your wrists and ankles look sore, and the nurse's notes indicate finding you hung like a crucifix. You think this is normal behavior?"

"Of course not, because these are not normal circumstances.

It is desperate behavior because I was in a desperate circumstance," I answer directly at his confrontational question.

"How old are you? Eighteen?"

"Yeah."

"You seem pretty well-versed for an eighteen-year-old."

"Yeah, well, when you can't hear too well, you end up picking up hobbies that don't require hearing, like reading."

"So you're book read?"

"Very. Is that a problem?" I ask, anticipating his next attack.

"No, not a problem. How did you lose your hearing?"

"During gym, some kids decided to practice hitting baseballs just as I was walking toward the field. The ball hit me just right. All I remember is seeing a white blob, like the ball was huge. A few days later, I lost all hearing on my left side. No one's really sure why. I probably should have a hearing aid by now, but my dad won't take me to a specialist. Because—he's an ass."

"Everything's your dad's fault then? How old were you?"

"I was twelve, and half of me ended that day. The other half ended when my mom died. I was fourteen. So, I basically have nothing left in that house."

"Your mom was the parent you were closer to then?"

"My mom was an angel. She always supported me and loved me. My dad is all about appearances and pretending he's perfect since my mom died. I don't fit the mold."

"You don't think your dad misses your mom?"

I grow silent. I want to answer that sharply too, but can't fathom how to answer it. He never really told me how he felt. He never verbalized how his world ended, too. We're both in pain, only I don't have any children to hurt.

"I think he's still mourning her and taking it out on me—over and over again. I'm not sure why I get the brunt of it. His favorite is to call me handicapped and tell me he should put me somewhere so that they can throw away the key. Guess he got his wish."

"I know it seems harsh right now, but this is more like an intervention."

"There's no intervention needed. I have been functioning fine, despite his constant demeaning approach to parenting."

Shit, what happened to keeping it simple? Shut up, Jeannie!

"So, you're feeling trapped?"

"Yes. Wouldn't you if you were locked in a cage?"

"Cage? What cage?"

"The one I slept in last night."

"I'm not sure what you mean. Maybe I have your medication dose too high."

"I'm not dreaming this! Nurse Dolores and her doting Drake are keeping me in a cage in the attic."

"Uh huh. We have no human cages at the Manor."

I stand up in front of his desk, frustrated with his denial.

"Are you shitting me? So, I'm just imagining all the sweating and claustrophobic panic attacks I have from cage dwelling?"

"You've been having panic attacks?"

I bend over his desk to get his attention and say firmly, "Listen, I know you're in this with my dad. No getting around it. Tell my dad that if he leaves me in here, he'll have a dead daughter. Better to have me deaf than dead. Well, you'd think—but with him, maybe he'd rather I be dead." With that, I sit back down.

"Okay, Miss Kynde. I think this is enough for today. I didn't mean to upset you."

I look beyond his eyes to flush out the big lie.

I know he knows about the cages.

"Walk me upstairs yourself and see my room. Make a home visit."

"Uh, that's against hospital policy. I'll see you here in my office every day for a while until I feel like you're coping better with your new surroundings."

"No, I'm not staying here! I want to talk to my dad," I demand.

I never thought those words would cross my lips.

"No family correspondence for the first month, at least. We need to work with you, Miss Kynde, without outside influences. You'll feel better about all of this when you're farther into the treatment."

"A *month?* How long is this going to last?" I say with a gasp. "I don't need treatment!"

"Okay, enough for today. I'm going to have Drake take you back to your room now."

"You mean the pink cage in the attic?"

The doctor starts writing notes in my chart, ignoring my question. "I'll reduce your medication a little bit and you should feel better. Oh yeah, and I'll sign you up for some therapy."

"I don't want *any* drugs or therapy! What is it about that you don't understand?"

"Oh, I understand perfectly, Miss Kynde," Doctor Wiggins says. He slowly looks up at me with a slightly crooked grin and dark eyes. "We're going to take very good care of you."

There's an edge to his voice now. He's being sarcastic, actually. This is the clue I've been looking for. He's definitely enjoying his part of the scheme.

His grin grows wider as he describes the kind of therapy he's prescribing. Ones that will make someone like me calmer—heat, ice, and shock.

I don't disappoint him when I run for the door, giving him a reason to call Drake in to control the crazy girl.

I begin yelling, "No!" to him, screaming for my dad to come out and be a man, but he doesn't show. Doctor Wiggins doesn't even flinch at my tirade. He just looks at me and smiles.

"Good day, Miss Kynde. Enjoy your accommodations and beneficial therapies."

So much for persuading yourself out of here.

10

I stare at my car for hours, plotting ways to escape and drive away. I fully realize there's little chance I will succeed, but thinking about it is a kind of meditation. It also keeps the boredom at bay. My arms are fatigued from grasping the bars so tight for so long. My head grows heavy.

Dolores has stabbed me with my new dose of medication to calm me down which is enough to make me quit yelling at least, but the day's events have made me tired and even more worried. I know I really have no hope of leaving now. No one is coming to get me. Rick, Todd, and my friends don't even know I'm here. My friends may come around my dad's place to see where I am, but he'll tell them the same thing he's probably told Rick—that I've left home and didn't leave a note. There's no way they'll think to look at the place we all stared at just two days ago. I have to face it. I'm going to be here for quite a while.

Worse yet, I'm losing it. I'm constantly panicking, constantly shaking. Sometimes it's evident to Dolores and Drake, and sometimes I hide it well. I can feel the internal shaking, even when it's not outwardly visible. It is almost as if every blood vessel is twitching inside me, which I fight against instinctively. The fight makes me even more tired. This is worse than anything I experienced with my dad. During those attacks, my arms and legs would shake for a few hours and then my symptoms would go away. Now the attacks are relentless, causing me to wonder if I am actually having a nervous breakdown.

Who wouldn't?

Being stuck in an enclosed cage right in front of your new car would be too much for anybody. The thought of getting to it consumes me. Over and over I dwell on pulling myself behind the steering wheel and driving out of here like a maniac. Before I thought Dolores and Drake didn't realize what view I had. Now I wonder if they did this on purpose to taunt me.

Even worse, the backdrop beyond my car is my favorite place, South Beach and the tower. That time feels forever ago already. I miss my freedom rides, my brother, my friends, my beach, my mom's picture, and my Todd. I miss the salty smell of the Gulf that's now only faintly distinguishable through the breeze. At this point, I'd even welcome the annoying high-pitched, squeaking calls for food from overhead seagulls. Hell, I'd throw them bread if I could and watch everyone clear out before they got soiled on.

All this because I'm a family embarrassment and because Dad thinks I was involved in some horrific lie. Why didn't he just come out and ask me about whatever it was? I loved my mother and still do. We enjoyed each other's company. We were inseparable. He knows this.

Lunch arrives, but I'm not hungry. I'm too focused on getting out of the predicament that my dad created for me. I think back to the night he gave me the car.

I should have waited to take the keys until I could look him in the eye. Then I would have seen he was hiding something.

I should have left that night and never come back, like I planned.

I should have brought Rick with me to the hospital.

I should have told Todd where I was actually going.

I didn't. It was all too good to be true. Now victory is his. I'm going to become a victim of him and this place. God, Rick. Where are you?

I wonder what I'll be like a couple of months from now.

Probably wrinkled with straw hair and speaking in tongues like that crazy lady escapee at the intersection with the police dragging her away.

I grin. Well that's an interesting thought. At least the crazy lady escaped from here somehow. Maybe there's hope. I just need to keep it together and find an opportunity.

I never realized before that I could actually talk to myself without anyone else hearing. Maybe this will be my new form of escape for a while. That, or I truly am as crazy as everyone else in this place.

"Are you going to eat that, poor mistreated one?"

I don't turn around to look at Drake, but unfortunately, I can hear him. I'm not in the mood for him. I don't want him looking at me or touching me or harassing me.

Just leave me the fuck alone.

"I'm going to take that as a no and get the tray out of the cage now, so don't come flying at me with your teeth again, you hear?"

I close my eyes and sigh. This guy just needs to get over it.

"Tomorrow will be a better day. The treatment won't be that bad. Some patients don't come out of it for hours sometimes, but afterward they all say they feel more relaxed."

I'm shaking harder.

"What kind of treatment is it?" I ask, turning the right side of my head in his direction.

"Cold as ice, baby! The new and improved therapy for all that ails ya. You're cold anyways, so no biggie for you. Right?"

I exhale sharply in return. "You don't even know me, asshole. Don't be thinking you do. Is there any way I can get out of this?"

"Nope, you're in for it. You better heal those sores up overnight. They'll probably hurt the worst."

I shake my head in disbelief as he leaves the room. I look back briefly to see Dolores sitting in her chair, sweating profusely as usual. She constantly has sweat stains down her back and along her sideburns. As usual, she's eating her dinner at her desk, which always ends with a pretty disgusting show of licking underneath her long, fake fingernails after she's done. I'm not sure if the licking that accompanies it is just exaggerated for my benefit, but it usually makes me gag. I'm not quite sure why she chooses to eat in the attic, where the sweltering heat makes it close to impossible. She certainly could eat downstairs somewhere, not that I'm going to spend any real time caring or thinking about it. I do wonder, though, what she meant about the mean girls she dealt with in high school. I wonder what they did to her to make her like this. It had to be pretty bad for her to have so much pent up anger. I was never mean to anyone in high school or ever, really. If anything, I always felt bad for anyone getting picked on and would console them later. I knew what it was like from my home situation. I remember the time when a classmate was being ignored suddenly and blatantly by her best friends. They snickered behind her back on the lunch line and left her to sit by herself during lunch. She looked mortified, so I invited her over to sit with Todd, Derrick and me. Melissa never went back to her old friends after that. God, do I miss her too.

A breeze drifts through the window next to my cage again, cooling my skin as it passes. I can tell by the sun that it must be around seven in the evening or so. I'll see the painted sky again soon. This is one of the few moments I will enjoy at my new "apartment." I turn toward the other window on the opposite end of the attic to look outside as well, glancing down at the other cage and suddenly focus in.

Someone's in it!

I quickly look over to Dolores, but she's oblivious to my stare.

How did I miss someone coming in?

I try to remember if I looked in the cage when I came back from the doctor but can't recall for sure.

This person is thin like the one from the night before, only his or her head is larger with thinning hair and his or her body frame is larger. I move over to the front of my cage to see if I can get a closer look, but I can't see the face. I sit down in the corner to observe for any movement for a while, but there's only an occasional jerk.

"Quit staring," Dolores states sharply.

I turn to her with a frown, not sure what the hell she expects me to look at otherwise. It's this or Dolores. I choose this.

"Who is that?"

"His name is Christian Blaylock. Should be some interesting company for you when he comes to," she answers with a sarcastic edge, grinning down at her chocolate cake. "He's pretty close to your age, except he's been here longer."

I'm surprised. He looks more like eighty, or at least the top of his head does. "There's no way he is eighteen."

"He's not, but he's close enough."

"What have you people done to him?"

"Nothing more than what's done to the rest—and what'll be done to you, by the way—a little of this and that. He's just weak. Probably has no immunity."

He moves his leg out and stretches, turning toward me. With wide eyes, I wait to see his face, wondering if it looks any better than the twisted limbs Dolores calls young.

It is. In fact, he's quite handsome. Despite the distortion of his head, his face is symmetrical with dark eyes and strong jawline. He kind of reminds me of one of those alluring cologne models.

"What happened to his head?"

"He experienced a little allergic reaction to shock treatment. Everyone reacts differently. Poor guy. Looks like he was handsome at one time. Wonder if he'll do okay living like us ugly ones now. I feel bad for him," she replies sarcastically. "I can't wait to see what *your* reaction will be."

I close my eyes, trying not to let her get to me.

"He'll probably look better by tomorrow—well, at least until the next treatment anyways. I gave him some Benadryl. I'm out of here by the way. You're on your own tonight. There's no one available to cover for me and I've already been here too long."

She comes over and checks the lock.

"What do I do if I have to go to the bathroom?"

"Oh yeah," she says. Rummaging through her bag, she pulls out a long plastic tube and throws it into my cage. "There ya go. Just don't spill it."

She laughs at her own wit and throws one over to Christian as well.

"You'll be fine. Just hit any rats with the plastic tube," she says. Then she opens the door, flicks off the lights, and quickly locks the door behind her.

It's still light. I watch the painted sky as the sun goes down.

After about an hour, the parking lot lights brighten up the room and my eyes adjust. I quickly cover myself with a blanket in case she wasn't kidding about the rats.

Turning toward Christian, I wonder if he's okay and if he's ever been in this attic before. If he hasn't, he'll probably wake up scared by the cage and darkness. I know I did. Hopefully I can be more comfort to him than my dead predecessor was to me.

The wind picks up. It whistles through both window openings in a high enough pitch for me to hear. I can see Christian rustling around but can't hear well over the background noise. His corner of the room is the darkest, so I can't see much. I have the eeriest feeling that he's watching me, though. I flip over, facing my back toward him just in case, feeling nervous about this stranger and losing my nerve about being a comfort to him.

The wind continues to whistle loudly through the open windows, allowing rain to drip along the inside wall. I swear there are squeaking noises coming from his side. I try to bravely turn back to see, but I can't. My breathing becomes more labored, and my imagination starts to get the best of me. The good thing is that if I sleep on my right side, I can't hear anything through my left ear. It's like having an earplug that blocks out sound. Well at least most sounds. Tonight, though, I keep hearing an occasional squeaking noise that seems to be coming from his side, causing chills to run through me.

What the hell is he doing?

Finally the wind dies down a bit as well as the squeaking noises, making me feel more comfortable. It wasn't the wind that was bothering me, of course.

The rain is coming down hard and flashes of lightning are glowing in the distance. At times, the rain pelts against the roof and tops of the windows, back and forth, with the movement of the wind. I always feel comfort in Florida rainstorms, though. They relax me.

I'm almost asleep when something suddenly smashes into my cage, shifting me forward. I grab onto the bars to brace myself. I can't imagine what could have just moved my cage. My chest starts heaving in fear, and I draw in deep breaths, trying to calm myself.

It's still dark, with only the faint light of the parking lot entering the room, but I feel like someone is staring at the back of my head. I don't know if it will do me any good to look back, since I probably won't be able to see anything in the dark, but I quickly turn around to face it.

I don't see anything at first, but as the distant storm flickers light into the room, I suddenly see two eyes staring back at me within inches of my cage. I yelp, throwing myself backwards as far away as I can. Thoughts quickly flutter through my mind.

What the hell am I looking at? Could it be Christian? Is it a rat? What the fuck is it?

As I focus more, I can see double bars along my cage. It *is* Christian. He has moved his cage all the way over to mine. I sigh in relief a little until I realize that he hasn't said a word yet. I look closer toward his cage, but can't see him anymore.

Is he hiding from me?

I feel exposed, like somebody is peeping through my window.

"What the hell are you doing?" I ask out of reflex. "Are you still there?"

The cage squeaks.

"You scared the hell out of me! Don't fucking do that to me again," I say angrily, trying not to show the panic in my voice.

There's no response, but with each flash of lightning, I can see that he's shifting around in the sheets.

I wonder what his head looks like at this point and if it causes him pain or if his mouth is swollen shut. Will he be normal looking in the morning?

"Christian?" I whisper, looking back and forth into nothingness. "You okay?"

There is still no answer.

"Okay, I'm not sure what kind of game you're playing, but this is ridiculous. Go back over to the other side," I demand, still fearful of him, but taunting him to talk back.

He's moving in the sheets again, and I can feel weight shifting from the floorboard vibrations. He suddenly screeches out a high-pitched, "Help me!"

I jump.

"I can't take this misery anymore!"

He continues screaming in agony as he paces back and forth in his cage, banging against the sides.

"Christian? Is it your head?"

"Oh God! I hate this," he hisses. "Make it go away!"

"Christian, I wish I could do—"

"Please, please whoever you are, please make the throbbing stop," he interrupts.

"Try to relax, maybe meditate?"

"I'll do anything you want. Just name it."

"No, Christian. Help! Help! Somebody help us!" I scream, but no one enters the attic.

Christian continues screaming in agony for what feels like an hour. I finally press my hands to my ears, trying to block the sound, especially on my right side.

Then, he stops. I bring my arms down and all I hear now is his sobbing—deep sobbing. It's the kind that wrenches your whole body, and reminds me of the anguish I felt when I lost my mom. They are torturing him. I can see his hands grasping each side of his head through the faint streams of light now and then. I want to help, but I am too scared to move and not sure what to do.

After a while, his sobs turn into smaller bouts of whining, until he finally calms down. His chest moves erratically. I'm not sure if he's breathing correctly. I close my eyes, exhausted by the whole event and tired by my sympathy for him. I cry, too, but this time, it's for him, not me.

11

The hue of the morning sunrise is dramatic despite my being on the west side of Florida. Only thing I can tell is that the storms have recently pushed away, leaving an eerie glow behind. The wind is still and the room is stagnant already. I lift my head to try to hear any room noise, but there isn't any. I don't want to turn around.

If only Dolores would get here, or even Drake.

God, what the hell is wrong with me? Why would I wish for them?

I close my eyes, attempting to gain enough gumption to look toward Christian. He's probably staring at the back of my head. I can almost feel him.

I roll to my back as a compromise, listening, but only hearing the static in my head. Wrong ear. I sigh, as I roll over to my left side, facing him with my eyes closed, and bring my sheet over my mouth to hide any sign of gawking I might show when I see him, just in case.

First, I look down toward my legs, trying to tell from my peripheral vision if his cage is still next to mine.

It is.

Oh God, I don't know if I can look.

I slowly shift my eyes to the blue and pink bars, keeping my gaze downward, but trying to focus on his side. Two feet are sticking out of the sheets in his cage. My eyes follow him upward toward his torso, which is covered.

My breathing grows heavier as I look at his chest and arms. He's taller than I expected for some reason, and in shape.

Please make his head normal too!

I brace myself as I finally glance up, unable to fight against my curiosity of his condition. My gaze meets his, looking straight at me without any movement on his end. Startled, I jerk back a little but quickly regain my composure with my concern for him. He's staring, but not blinking, as if no one's there.

I stare at his face and chest to see any signs of breathing, but I can't tell. Lunging forward, I grab the bars and scream, "Help! Dolores! Somebody please hurry! I think Christian needs help!"

Small drips of drool start to dot his pillow.

"Dolores!" I continue bellowing.

Oh God, what the hell am I doing here? I don't know how much more death I can take!

Shivering, I grab his cage and jerk it to try to shake him awake, but there's no reaction. It's then that I notice his head. It's normal size with no sign of the events from the day before. I sit back down, wishing I could do something.

The door swings open and Drake enters the room with breakfast.

"What's up, sweetheart?" he asks, taking in the proximity of Christian's cage to mine. "You guys getting cozy or what?"

"That's hard to do with a corpse, don't you think? You are all nothing but a bunch of murderers here!"

Drake throws the trays onto the desk and runs toward Christian's cage.

"Shit. Dolores!" he calls out, his hands shaking while he tries to get the lock open. I can hear Dolores' footsteps, as she slowly makes her way up the stairs.

Finally, Drake is able to open the lock and starts inspecting Christian's condition. I grasp onto one of the pillows and hold it to my chest as I sit, watching in horror. His eyes are still open, now looking at the ceiling. Drake pulls Christian out of the cage and it's there that Dolores and Drake work on him, trying to save him. I can't see what they're doing but eventually they both are less tense, looking down at Christian. Drake looks over at Dolores who's emotionless as usual.

"He'll come out of it, Drake. They always do. Get his cage back where it belongs," she demands. She helps him get Christian back inside. The cage squeaks as Drake pushes it to the other window with Christian watching me the entire way. I didn't want to stare but his gaze is luring me to see if he will blink. Half way there, he not only blinks, but he also flashes me a wicked grin, making my hair stand on end.

He's awake.

I look up at Drake and over to Dolores, but neither of them notice. When I look back at Christian, his eyes are closed.

Did I imagine this? Was it the drugs I'm on?

"So, did you pee in the container or all over yourself?" asks Dolores with a wicked grin of her own.

"Neither."

"Good thing, cause I would have made you clean it up," she says as she turns to Drake. "Get her to the bathroom before she shits all over the place."

I roll my eyes and gather myself to go with Drake. My wrists and ankles are still sore from the day before, but I'm glad to get out of the cage for a while despite the shackles.

"I'm going to take you downstairs to the bathroom so you can see the light of day a little. Okay with you?"

I nod my head and stumble from the chains. They're heavy, and with the lack of eating over the past couple of days, I'm getting more fatigued. It takes a while, but we make it down the stairs and into a long series of hallways until we enter a round room with glass windows near the ceiling and a central nursing station. The vastness of the room feels good with its tall ceilings and open space. Several patient rooms are located along the periphery of this circular building. Most of them look dark, unlike the area I'm standing in.

"She doesn't belong in here, Drake," warns one of the nurses we pass. She's an elderly woman who's wearing an old white nurses' uniform—black and white cap included.

"Oh, come on, Barbara! The patients aren't even up yet! She

needs a good shower and bathroom break. You've got the best facilities."

I look again into the patient rooms to make sure no lights are on yet, feeling more uncomfortable about this idea.

"It's against the rules. Get her out of here."

"We'll only be a couple of minutes," says Drake. He pulls me toward a door next to the nurse's station and hurries me inside. The bathroom is as grand as the room outside with tall ceilings and an old-fashioned bathtub. The pink and blue tiles leave a lot to be desired, but I don't care much at this point.

"I'll stand guard outside, so hurry up. I want to get you out of here before Dolores starts searching for us and the patients on this floor are out of bed. You don't want to meet them."

He unshackles my wrists and ankles quickly and heads for the door. "There's no way out of here, so don't get any ideas," he says over his shoulder. "When you're done, call for me and stand in the middle of the room. There are fresh hospital gowns underneath the sink."

I nod and wait for him to close the door.

I quickly head over to the bathtub and turn on the faucet. I can hear Drake arguing with the nurse again about my presence here. Just the sound of the water is enticing. The tub fills with cool water, something I have been yearning for since I was kidnapped. I slowly submerge myself, taking in every wonderful moment of the comfortable temperature of the water. After rinsing the soap from my hair, I relax for a few minutes and float in the water. It feels good to have my guard down and to be alone and able to think.

Me time. What a concept.

I close my eyes and concentrate on everyone I miss and how I got myself into this situation. I wonder if my friends and family are searching for me and are concerned with my whereabouts—all except my dad, of course. He masterminded the whole plot, working with the doctors—and probably lawyers too—to commit me.

I was pretty gullible to believe he was doing something nice for me with the new car. I knew it didn't feel right. Why didn't I listen to my gut? That bastard let me drive myself here so he didn't have to face me as they hauled me away. Fucking coward.

What about my brother? I wonder if Rick knows where I am. I'm not sure how I'm surviving without him, actually. He's always been my support system, egging me to move on despite the constant struggle with my dad.

I have to get out of here, but how the hell am I going to do that? Drake said a few weeks, but the doctor mentioned no timeline for my release. They all just keep drugging me up and caging me. What kind of therapy is that? Does that shit ever heal *anyone*?

A shiver runs down my spine when I think about what is next for me—not in the long-term, but in the near future. What's involved with hydrotherapy? It must have something to do with water, but maybe I don't want to know. Of course, if it has anything to do with water like this, I'm all for it. I doubt it will be this nice.

I have to get to my car—my savior.

The only thing I can think to do at this point is cooperate. Maybe get out of my room more and check the place out, so I can look for escape routes. One way or another I'm getting out of here. It's just a matter of when.

There's a knock at the door.

"You ready?"

I leap out of the water and run to the cabinet for clothes. No way do I want to take the chance that he'll get a good look at me without them.

So much for peace.

"Hold on a second!"

After another minute, I'm standing in the middle of the bathroom floor, looking around at my former sanctuary with a smile. It was nice to have some alone time, even if it was only for a few minutes. Regenerated, I call for Drake to come in.

Drake enters the room, shackles in hand and binds my limbs without a word. I'm confused by his lack of interaction but allow him to attach them without a fuss. He methodically locks them into place and pulls my arm toward the door. This time, I notice that he doesn't attach the center chains from my wrists to my ankles and I'm freer to move.

"What's going on?" I ask.

"The patients are out."

"Oh no, not *patients*," I tease, sarcasm dripping from my words. After all I'm a patient too, and perfectly sane, and they keep me locked up in a cage.

"I'm not going to give you your medicine until we get upstairs, so you can concentrate."

"First of all, for the record, I'd prefer not having any meds ever. Second of all, how much concentration is needed to walk down a hall—"

He turns quickly to me. In his eyes I read no humor whatsoever. "This is the high-risk ward."

"What does that even mean?"

"It means it can be—dangerous."

"Why—Why would you bring me here?"

"You enjoyed it, didn't you, all alone in this big bathroom? I was trying to be nice, geez. Just shut up and follow my instructions. We have to get across the recreation room without causing much stir. Being you're a young girl, it might be difficult not to attract some male attention. They are not used to females. Let's hope they are tame today."

Drake grabs for the door, but I pull his arm back.

"Aren't they in shackles, too?"

"No, they don't have to wear them while they are in their own ward. There are guards everywhere to handle them, but patients can move fast. Guards don't intervene until a patient behaves badly. That can mean—after the patients are in the process of hurting someone. It's a bad system, I know, but I didn't design it. Besides, it wouldn't be fair for the guards to constantly be tackling patients before they do something wrong."

"Everything is *so* fair to patients here, after all," I mutter. "Just ask Christian, up in his cage. Hell, just ask me!"

"Will you just shut up? All we have to do is get across the room and through the double doors we came in."

Drake opens the door and peers out to see how they're behaving.

"Looks peaceful," he whispers and reaches for my arm. "Come on, you'll be fine."

I have no choice but to trust him. I'm sure he doesn't want to get hurt either. As we nonchalantly walk into the recreation room, I see several patients sitting around tables, reading books and walking around aimlessly. Some are talking to each other and some to themselves. I stay behind Drake as much as possible, but the chains are rattling loudly as I walk, attracting some of them to look our way. More and more hollow eyes are on me as we come closer. I try to walk more softly but it just makes the noise louder. At one point, Drake pauses to negotiate our way through several patients that are walking toward us. He glances over to the nurse's station and then over to the guards. I can feel the pulse in his wrist.

"Get back to your seats. Nothing concerns you here," Drake warns those approaching us.

"How is that, Mista? You seem to be lost. We can help ya—and—the girl," says one of the patients.

He walks closer to me, but Drake steps in the way.

"Nothing concerns me here, Mista," continues the patient, wringing his hands, as he smiles at me with his crooked teeth. Several other men are watching and waving me to come over to them. The guards close in and Drake continues pulling me through.

A sudden cry pierces the room. "Wait!"

We look over to see a man standing on top of one of the tables, completely naked except for a floppy hat and patterned socks. "Do you want to see President Kennedy?" he calls. "I can show him to you!"

His nudity doesn't faze Drake, who looks over and politely answers, "No thank you, Sir."

He hops off the table and rushes over with excitement, pressing the issue.

"No, Sir," Drake insists. "I have to get this patient to her room. Maybe another time."

"It'll only take a minute," he says, his hair standing outward.

"Yeah, I know, but I can't right now."

"Okay, after you're finished with her, then?"

"Sometime later, okay?"

The patient is elated, fluttering around the room.

I'm surprised at Drake's patience with him. He knows it's ridiculous, but doesn't badmouth him. As we round the other side of the room, another patient flies in front of us.

"Did you let her use our bathroom?"

"Yes," replies Drake.

"Are you serious? You contaminated that bathroom with a female?" the patient continues, grinding his molars back and forth. He's an elderly patient with long, gray hair tied into a ponytail. His slippers have holes and his big toes are sticking out with yellow toenails. "We don't allow any females in there."

Drake respectfully responds to the inquiry. "She's a patient too, and allowed to use all facilities. Kindly move on."

"No, you should have asked first!" the patient responds with one finger in Drake's face.

"I got permission from the nurse. It's okay. Don't worry. We're done now and are leaving."

"No! We're not letting you through here until you clean it! Right boys?" Several of the other male patients respond in agreement.

I try not to make eye contact with any of them in case that provokes them all the more.

"It's clean already. We—we already cleaned it. Just sit down and we'll be out of your way."

Several of the "inmates" are crowding us now, making Drake back up and pull me behind him. One starts chanting, "Leave her, leave her," and the others join in.

Panic jerks me backward. I can't help looking at their wild-eyed stares and desperate behavior. Several start clawing at me with rigid arms that do not work properly. The place is definitely out of control. I grasp onto Drake's waist braced for the pulling and dragging that is about to occur, as several of them are distracting him and others are moving toward me. Time slows. I watch mouths moving but can't understand everything that is said.

Suddenly, they're all flying across the room, slamming against the wall—victims of a power-wash fire hose with no mercy on where anyone lands. As the guards flush them out under full force, several are left bleeding and confused on the opposite side of the room. I stand stunned in front of the nurse's station, unable to believe the pure force of the guard's actions. To them, the patients are nothing but worthless scum.

The patients were scary, to be sure. The guards treating them as though they are not human is even scarier. It's disgusting, actually.

"Get out now!" Nurse Barbara demands. "I warned you about this, Drake. No more patients in this ward, understand? Especially females. Shit, now I've got a mess to clean up."

As we hurry to the double doors, I look back into the room against my better judgment. The most demanding patient is still watching me, as he sits within the pile of patients who are still gathering themselves. I can hear moaning as they move along the flooded floor, slipping on each other's garments. This doesn't seem to distract the patient. He is still staring at me, forcing me to catch his gaze. He no longer has his slippers on. Somehow I know this won't be the last time I see him.

"Come on. Don't look back. They're nuts and don't know the difference. It isn't their fault. Remember that."

I don't want to remember anything. I just want to be back in my cage.

Isn't it funny how things change?

12

I try not to dwell on the earlier events of the day. In the middle of my crib, I'm glad that I'm safe from the angry group of mind-dead patients. I wonder how much shock treatment they have endured. Did it cause their current states?

My hair is still damp, keeping me cooler than usual. It feels nice when the wind occasionally blows through the open window. Birds chatter and the occasional car goes by. It isn't a busy part of town—a perfect place to torture inmates—so there isn't much to entertain me outside. I press my face onto the cool bars and stare at my Vug, still waiting for me. I'm surprised no one has moved it. Hopefully, no one knows it's mine and won't notice it sitting there for—how long? Weeks? Months? Maybe Dad will slip up and tell Rick where I am. He'll come searching for me and once he sees my car, he won't give up until I'm free.

That's probably wishful thinking. One of these days, I'll look out the window, and it will be gone.

Just like everything else.

"Feeling refreshed?"

Not looking back, I answer, "Yes."

Drake tugs on the lock and slips lunch in. "Well, this ought to help even more. There's fresh fruit today. It seems healthier than the normal fare."

"Great." I keep staring at the car.

"Wow. Your hair is really long when it's wet, huh?"

Oh God, he's looking at me. I don't want him to.

I don't answer.

"Maybe I can find a brush somewhere—help you get the tangles out."

Wait, is he talking about me doing that or him? Why is he being so damn nice?

"I'll see what I can find, Jeannie."

Jeannie? Now he's using my nickname?

"Come to think of it, your cage is like Jeannie's lair in the show 'Jeannie in the Bottle'. Maybe I should get you some more pillows. Make you more comfortable. Perhaps you'll welcome some guests."

Is it my imagination, or is he saying that—*suggestively*? I cringe from the thought of him in here—from the thought of whatever he is suggesting—but don't look his way so he can't see the panic in my eyes.

Figuring I'd better squelch the thought of it, I answer, "I doubt I'll ever do any entertaining in this hellhole."

Drake sighs, then leans close and whispers into my good ear, "We'll see how you feel in a couple of months when you're aching for your boyfriend. I might be able to help you. In the meantime, I'll get you some more pillows."

I jerk my head in his direction with serious eyes, but his are soft, almost begging.

How did he know I have a boyfriend? He just guessed?

I study his face, as I think of the right way to handle this. I don't want to piss him off, since he's so much nicer than Dolores. He's usually the only one trying to make this place more pleasant—using the dumb-waiter instead of pulling me down the stairs, risking safety to let me use the nice bathroom—but I don't want to encourage him either.

This is the first time I've really taken any time to look at him. He's actually not a bad looking man. He's perhaps in his mid-twenties, average build with blonde hair and blue eyes. He kind of reminds me of Kevin Costner. Will he be my Robin Hood, and rescue me?

Doubt it.

Maybe it isn't a bad idea to have an ally though, as long as I'm careful about it. I'll have to be smarter than him, outwit him, which will be hard with all the numbing effects of the medication in my veins. Before I can answer, Dolores slams the door open.

"Get the fuck away from that cage, you idiot! Don't you pull this shit again. I need you to keep your mind on your work."

Drake looks a bit embarrassed. He backs away without saying anything and locks me in. "Just getting her lunch."

"Yeah, right, and looking like you wanted something in return. This is not a brothel, you hear?"

"Yes, ma'am."

Christian stirs in the other cage. I almost forgot he was there. We all look in his direction to see if he'll stay conscious and say something, but he just stares out the window.

Dolores' eyes narrow as she watches him, calculatingly. Drake sees it too. He starts trying to sidetrack her with duty assignment reviews, but she's focused, almost animal-like—predator on prey. I grow concerned for Christian but am not sure if I should be, with his evil grin and pretend unconsciousness from earlier. Then he sees it too, backing up in his cage, hissing at her to stay the hell away.

Is this what I look like too, when Dolores is on the attack with me?

Dolores approaches his cage, keeping her eye on him. Drake calls to her, but she ignores his plea. She pushes Christian's cage away from the window, making enough space for her to walk through, circling him around and around. He follows her with his head, keeping her in view. Waiting for her attack.

"What do you say to me in the morning, Christian?" asks Dolores. She pauses for his answer. He just growls—not just any growl, but a deep, low tone from the gut. It echoes off the rafters though, scaring me. "Oh, come now, Christian, tell me what you want—or you know how much worse it'll be."

"I want you to leave me the hell alone."

"Nope, that's not it," she says gleefully, dancing her fat ass around his cage now. "Today is going to be fun!"

Christian looks panicked. His eyes are wild with worry. He

sighs, stands up, faces me, and mumbles, "I want shock therapy."

Did he really just say that?

Dolores stops dancing and turns toward him. "What was that? I couldn't hear you."

He announces it louder, looking at me with pure fear now. I'm breathing harder in disgust at Dolores.

No, not again!

"And?" she prods.

Nostrils flaring, Christian answers, "I want you to be the one," his voice quivering on the last word.

"Beg me then. I'm not easy."

I close my eyes and cry into my pillow.

"Please, Dolores, please give me shock therapy," he says quietly through gritted teeth.

"Louder."

He repeats.

"Louder!" she pushes.

Christian screams it and burst into tears.

"Okay, okay—since you insist!"

Christian looks at me desperately, like I might be able to stop the agony of the next several hours.

Dolores walks back to her desk and scribbles some notes with Drake reminding her that Christian can't take anymore, but she just keeps writing.

"Not only will you get him set up, but you'll get her set up too," she says.

Christian looks over at me with pity in his eyes and leans back against the bars.

"You mean I'm getting shock therapy too?" I ask, searching both of their faces.

"No, no, Miss Jean," Dolores responds while she writes. "Yours is hydrotherapy—for now, anyway."

"Why do I need that? I'm not doing anything uncontrollable!"

"Doctor's orders. Don't give me any lip or I'll set you up for shock therapy right next to Christian."

"What is hydrotherapy?"

"You'll see soon enough. Just shut up with the questions,

would you?"

Drake glances back at me and then frowns at Dolores. He appears to be uncomfortable with the whole situation, but he waits for her to complete her writing assignment. This is not good. I know I can't fight my way out of their clutches.

Am I really stuck with this?

Yes, I am. Before I know it, I'm drugged, thrown into the rolling cage, and dragged down the stairs to the first floor. I can hardly focus but see several patients and attendants walking around, watching me as I pass. The patients are wearing regular, everyday clothes and the attendants are wearing scrubs.

Why the hell am I stuck in a hospital gown?

As we make our way down the hall, I try to prepare myself mentally and physically for what's about to happen. It's only water, right? They wouldn't drown me—at least not on purpose.

Oh God! Mom! What if I drown like you?

I can't let that happen.

"Drake, get me out of here, I mean it! Get me out of this place! I don't belong here. You guys are trying to kill me. Help me—somebody!" I scream, and continue to rat Drake out to anyone who passes by. I'm mostly met with hollow glances or dilated glares. Abruptly, Drake stops the cage. The glimmer of hope I feel that I've gotten through to him is short-lived. He plunges another needle into my thigh. Within seconds, I can't feel my tongue, but I'm still panicking.

He pushes the cage through a set of double doors. Inside is a row of tiled rooms. Each room contains an elevated bathtub, sink, and side table. Above each bathtub, several metal pipes run up the walls with knobs and digital displays. Straps are stretched along the sides of the tub, attached to hooks on the outside.

Am I going to be strapped into this contraption?

"Okay, Drake, we've got it from here," says one of the nurses, as she guides him out.

The other nurse comes around and unlatches the cage from the side. "Alright, sweetie, bath time."

No way am I going to make this easy for them. They'll have to drag me out.

Easy enough. They take the top of the cage off, and pluck me from it like I'm a newborn, kicking and screaming inside but totally helpless due to the meds.

Shit.

They hold me in front of the bathtub, since I can't stand for myself, and completely strip me. With whatever control I have left, I don't make this easy for them, knocking the nurses back on their heels a few times. Not that I thought it would work, but I can't just make it seem like I'm okay with the whole thing. This leads to them trying to reason with me.

"Now, come on, Jean. You're going to really like this, so quit fighting."

"The more you resist, the harder it will be."

"Think of it as your own personal spa treatment."

"Yo—no—goin—ta—win—"

The drugs are making me dizzy. I try to focus on each of their faces, looking at any distinct feature I can, so I'll remember them when the county sheriff finally finds me and I put an end to them and this place—a place that commits crimes against innocent people.

One of the nurses starts the bath water and adjusts the knobs while the other moves me closer, holding my arms to my sides. I try resisting but I'm too exhausted, too drugged up, and too overpowered.

"Come on, Jean. You'll feel better very soon," the nurse whose name starts with the letter B explains. If only I could make out more of her name. As I try to read the nametag, it changes to several possibilities, likely thanks to the meds—Belinda, Bernadette, Beatrice, Beverly—

Shit, I don't know what the fuck it says. I'm just going to call her Beast. The other one I'll call—Boobie.

Boobie and the Beast are dragging my ass into some cool water to get me under control, I tell myself for entertainment, so they can get it on with each other when no one is looking. The thought of it makes me laugh hysterically, until they quickly flip me around and dump me back first into the water.

It's frigid.

My fingertips sting.

Within seconds, I feel paralyzed, barely able to move my limbs.

Surprisingly, they don't attach me to the straps. I flail around initially, then float a bit as I freeze. I can think of nothing else but how to keep my body from quivering, to try to somehow warm myself from within. Minutes later, I'm shaking uncontrollably. They stick my head through a hole in the tub drapery, which they attach along the sides. I'm entombed, and all becomes quiet, except for the occasional check on my pulse, which Boobie reads to the Beast. This situation should freak me out, but I'm too numb to worry about it. As I look upward, I see a sign titled "Patient's Rights." I can't focus enough to read the text underneath. It probably just says, "None," anyway.

Scattered thoughts of my mom come in and out of my mind in rhythm to the short pulses of water at various temperatures that are shooting in from the sides. Ever since she died, I haven't been able to submerge my head in any water—tubs, pools, spas, and lakes. It doesn't matter what. I can't brave it. It feels almost as if, when I try, I'll feel like I do now—that I can't breath. I'll even wake up from my dreams, gasping for air, panicked that I'm drowning like her. I can't imagine the pain of drowning in water. What a terrible way to die.

My worst nightmares are of her being cold and alone. What irony that I am just that right now.

Wait, where am I? Oh yeah, psych ward. Why can't I concentrate? I'm just so tired, I can't fight it anymore. I have to let go. I hope they keep my head above the water—

Mom, please don't let me drown.

13

Streams of sweat connect the dots and move along my face as they drip, soaking the area below my cheek and chin. It reminds me of the game Plinko on The Price is Right, as each droplet moves in random patterns toward the money prize. I used to watch that show every morning with Mom while I was on summer break. We couldn't believe how idiotic some players were when it came to the Clock Game. They never got the idea of bracketing their guesses, and the ones that started out doing so only ended up panicking near the end and got completely scatterbrained.

Was it the ticking? Or Bob's constant badgering about the time? Peer pressure? Fear of failure? Neither Mom nor I knew, but I'm sure that most walked away kicking themselves for the wasted opportunity to change their lives in some way.

Now I'm kicking myself for not driving straight up U.S. Highway 19 toward the state border when I had the chance. I had a plan, and I got off the plan before I even started. I've screwed up on so many levels, but this one has me spinning with regret.

Where am I?

The onslaught of various ways I doomed myself keeps me away from reality. This lack of focus is probably drug-induced, I figure, but it's difficult to keep my concentration on any other thought for long.

I force my eyes open and only see the blankness of nothingness. All around me is white—no color, not even a hint.

Is this death?

The thought makes my heart race. I struggle to move, only making me lunge forward and hit the tip of my nose on a fabric in front of me—white fabric. It covers the tub.

God, I am an idiot. Stupid as always.

As my senses come to, I feel the water pressing against my limbs that are now shackled to the sides of the porcelain. I pull on them vigorously, trying to shake them loose from their stronghold to no avail. My neck feels fatigued from being in such an awkward position. My head fell forward while I slept, so I throw my head back and look up to see nothing but more white—white curtains, white ceiling, fluorescent white lights. Everything is hospital-sterile white.

God, what I wouldn't give for just a little color right now. I'll take anything, even my pink cage. Why did I think that about being in a cage? Shit, I don't want that either. No human should be locked in a damn cage. Has their therapy actually made me nuts?

I fling my head forward again and feel my swollen tongue move between my teeth and stick out a little. I press my fingertips together. They are wrinkly, as if they belong to a ninety-year-old. Luckily, the water is warmer than I remembered from earlier. I'm not sure why my face is sweating, and I'm not sure why they have left me here by myself, but I don't like it. I don't like any of it.

God, please let Drake come in here and rescue me.

Before I can even feel the shock of my thinking of Drake as the hero here, it is already too late. The double Bs are back.

"Why is she sweaty? Did you add warm water instead of cold the last time?"

"No, it was at the same temp as always."

One of the nurses pulls my head back and opens one of my eyes.

"Shit, she's dilated and has a protruding tongue. Get her out of there!"

I feel a hard squeeze on my arm, as I'm unlocked from the tub and flung onto the floor.

"Fucking accelerated hypertension, I bet. Go get a beta blocker from the cabinet."

"Shouldn't we get Doctor Wiggins?"

"No time! Her blood pressure is dangerously elevated."

"Oh, God! I can't lose my license. I've got the kids to think about—"

"Stop thinking about your license and hurry up!"

The squeezing on my left arm continues two more times. I'm sure she's pumping the life out of me because now my hand is going numb. My head and neck feel warmer than the rest of my body, and I begin to feel drowsy again.

"Stay with me, Jean."

Footsteps rush toward me, and I'm forced to sit up.

"Force it down her throat if you have to" says one of them, before I black out.

* * * *

I'm not sure what time it is, but I feel relieved when I see that bars surround me again. I look out the window. By the angle of the sun, I can tell it's close to evening, probably around five o'clock in the afternoon. Feeling tired still, I don't move much. Sometimes it's better not to engage. I try to figure out how many days I have been imprisoned, but I'm losing count.

Has it been three days?

I'm not sure, but as I slowly regain my memory, I realize whatever happened at the end of my hydrotherapy, the nurses were pretty damn sure I was close to death.

I immediately start re-focusing on how to escape this place. My next task will be to get Drake to take me on a grand tour. I need to start getting to know the place, doors to the outside, open windows, attendant schedules. It'll take time, but it'll be worth it. He's my best bet. He's the only one who has given half a shit about me and other patients like the dead girl and Christian.

My muscles ache from staying in the same spot, so I switch sides, keeping my eyes shut at first. I can smell dinner. My best guess is roast beef, mashed potatoes and carrots, but I don't dare go for it until I figure out everyone's position in the room.

I slowly open my eyes. Dolores and Drake are sitting at the

desk. Dolores is fanning herself as usual. They aren't engaging in much, just reading paperwork. Soon they'll both leave for the night. I quickly glance over at Christian and end up staring at his enlarged head again.

They are slowly killing him. I wish there was something I could do to help him.

I contemplate attacking my dinner for a few minutes and finally dive in before it becomes cold. Within seconds, Drake makes his way over. It isn't until then that I notice the extra pillows—nice ones with embroidery. They are the kind I'd have on my bed at home or my living room sofa when I move into my own place. The pillows are homey, comfortable. I like the new addition to my apartment.

"I was wondering if you were going to ever eat again," Drake says as he nudges the cage with his knee. He has hands behind his back as if he were a schoolboy.

I look up at him, but only manage a slight smile while I chew.

"Sorry you had to go through that hell today. If I could have stopped it, I would have. I mean, I tried, actually. I just don't have any power, and I'm kind of in—well—a bad situation here. I mean, I need my job. I can ask or suggest things, but I can't piss off people around here. Are you okay?"

I nod, but don't speak.

Dolores cuts in. "Oh, she better eat up, Drake. She'll need her strength so the doctor can evaluate her again tomorrow and see what treatment he's planning for her next."

Drake scowls at Dolores, his eyes meeting hers as if he were challenging her to a bull fight.

She brushes off his agitation and continues with her badgering. "Yeah, well, let's see. You have a full suite of opportunities here at the day spa. Hmmm—let me think. Well, there's the gentle massage of shock therapy, the cooling wraps of hydrotherapy, or the high of insulin therapy. Any requests?"

I spit my food at her legs. "Yes, how about you fucking keel over and die?"

Drake gulps, like he can't believe I dared.

Dolores looks down at her food-spattered shoes.

"You fucking bitch—that's it! I will not allow you to disrespect me. We're not in high school!" she bellows, almost losing her balance on a glob of mashed potatoes. "I'm going to drug you up harder than you've ever experienced. Now goddammit, where's my medicine tray, Drake?"

Drake catches my eye. "I haven't seen it. Can't we just go cool down and think this over before you do something that could end up with you losing your job?"

"Oh, Drake. I didn't realize how much you really cared. I always thought you were just using me to get close to all the young girls in this place. Now I find out that you just really wanted to get down *my* pants instead of theirs. How flattering!"

Drake stops with a grimace that makes his forehead wrinkle. "That's disgusting, Dolores."

Christian stirs in his cage and turns over to watch the show.

"What? Don't you find me attractive?"

"I meant the young girl comment, but no, I don't find you attractive with your big-ass ego thinking you own the fucking place. You think you know me, but you don't."

"I'm going to get your girlfriend over there high for you then since you like her so much better. This way you can do what you want, and no one will know the difference, except maybe big head over there."

"Come on, Dolores. Calm down. This isn't the first time a patient has spit food at your feet."

"Move out of my way."

Suddenly, Dolores spies the medical tray beneath my cage. Drake grabs for the syringe, but Dolores pushes him aside with pit bull eyes on me.

Out of reflex, I brace myself against the back of the cage, knowing that she'll win.

She does.

Within seconds, I can barely keep my eyes focused on anything except the pointed petals lining the outside of my pillow.

Maybe this isn't so bad. It's now my only real escape.

* * * *

I'm not sure what time it is, but the room is pitch black, so it must be night. The drugs tend to only last four hours, with haze for two hours more, so I'm probably in the clear until sunrise. I look up at the sky and feel relieved that the stars are sparkling back at me tonight.

I can barely make out the silhouette of Christian's cage on the other side of the room. All is quiet. I wonder if he's dead. I wouldn't blame him if he gave up on life with the constant electric torture he endures. It's surprising that he's not screaming again tonight.

Standing in front of the window, I long for my car. It's shining back at me under the parking lot lights that are angled far enough so I can see her.

Her? Why am I thinking that?

For some reason, I feel the urge to name her—my real friend. Someone I can confide in—trust. After all, she's there for me every day, giving me hope. It would have to be a good name though, not some lame one. She *is* a Vug—that's not who she is though. She needs a name that signifies a free spirit.

Shit, what the hell was the name of that movie I saw last week with the two ladies who picked up Brad Pitt in their Thunderbird on their way to Mexico? God, if I could only concentrate. Oh yeah: Thelma & Louise. Okay, so which name? Well, which one was cooler? I'm thinking it was Thelma. Besides she gets Brad Pitt, so if he thinks she's cool, then so do I. I agree. Who the hell am I talking to? Fuck. You've got to get yourself together and stop having conversations with yourself. It can't be healthy.

Out the window, Thelma seems to be telling me to just relax, her smooth yellow lines shimmering in the light. I can't wait until I can be Louise and laugh back at this place, as we drive away to freedom. I lean my head against the bars, staring at Thelma for what must be an hour. Then my thoughts are fully bent on how I'm going to escape this prison cell. When I was young, I tried to be Houdini and remove chains from my hands and legs while my brother cheered me on. I wasn't good at it, but managed to get loose a few times out of pure luck. If only I had kept practicing.

"Hey."

Startled, I jerk my head around to see Drake unlocking the cage door. Panic sears through my limbs. Moving backwards, I wonder if I could possibly knock him out with one of the pillows if he tries to molest me.

"Hey, it's okay. Just stopped by to say hello before I leave for the night—I've been working long shifts lately. Besides, I wanted to know how you like the new pillows. Comfy?"

I can hear Christian starting to move around in his cage.

Drake crawls onto the bed with me, propping himself up with several of his presents. He draws in a deep breath as if he were making himself comfortable at home for the night—as if we were married and I just made him a big meal.

I'm not sure what to do, but it does feel kind of good to have company.

"Arrrgghhh!" The sound comes from Christian. "This fucking head of mine! Make it stop!"

Christian has impeccable timing. He continues with his moaning, screaming, and begging so loud that I cringe. Drake does not. His attention never wavers from me.

"Can't you help him?" I ask.

"He'll get over it in a few minutes. Just sit back and relax. Let's talk," Drake says.

"But he sounds so awful. He's got to be dying."

"He's not. He'll be fine. Like I said, let's get to know each other."

I do as he says, gathering the pillows around me.

Christian screams loudly for a few minutes more, followed by achy moans.

"I hate this place," says Drake.

"Me too."

"We're both stuck here in our own ways. You're trapped because of your dad. I'm trapped because I need income to live. I hate seeing you in here. All I can do is try to keep you comfortable."

I study his face for a bit to see if he's sincere. His eyes are soft, velvety.

I can't respond.

He shakes my leg. "Hey, I'm the enemy. I know that. You don't have to talk to me. See you tomorrow."

Puzzled at his behavior, I watch him lock up my cage and leave as if he were going to work for the day. He looks back at me and waves as he heads out the door. I'm pleased that he didn't try coming on to me. He was respectful—kind even. This is hardly like the Drake I met in the beginning. Of course, I did bite him, so maybe I deserved it. Maybe I shouldn't be so hard on him. At this point, he's the only person who genuinely cares. Is it real, though?

How far am I willing to go to secure his protection? Is kissing him too far? What about making him think I love him? Will he want sex? How far will he push it? Besides, can he actually protect me, or is he as powerless as I am?

I look around my space filled with pillows, rearranging them so the place looks tidy. Why? I don't know, but it feels good to do it.

It's funny how a place can be a home no matter what the nightmare.

14

I must have slept the entire day, because it's light out and the dinner tray is next to me. I listen for Drake or Dolores, but hear no one. All I hear is the occasional car going by and birds chirping as usual and only hear this because I'm sleeping on my left side. If I were on my right, I'd only hear the hissing from my inner ear. It is louder today than normal. Most of the time it sounds like I'm in an airplane with wind gushing by, but today there are several high-pitched noises adding to the ruckus going on in my head.

Maybe they should try shock therapy. It might be a way to get rid of this constant noise in my head. What? Did I just think that? Why the hell would I want to end up like Christian? *Get it together, Jeannie.*

I shudder at the thought.

I'm still not sure what to make of Drake, with his thoughtfulness these days. I kind of like it. At the same time, it doesn't feel right. I don't, however, want to push away the one person who cares about me in this place. It's not like my daddy is going to drive up in his Maserati anytime soon to save me. It isn't like Todd will save me either, and it doesn't seem like Rick will either. I guess he can't find me.

What is worse? Being alone or spending some time with someone who's actually making an effort to get to know me? Besides, I kind of like him. *God, what are you thinking? Are you completely out of your mind?*

Well, if nothing else, maybe I can at least get him to take me on a grand tour of the place, so I can plan my escape out of this hellhole. Maybe I can talk him into another downstairs bathroom visit with the crazies. It will be worth the risk. This time, I'll study everything going by even closer than the last time—every nook and cranny.

What would he want in return? The thought of this scares me. This courting effort on his part has to come with a price. Will I sleep with him? Would I mind? Would it be dirty? Is it selling myself out if I actually sort of like him too? I don't know. I just wish I had a clear head.

It dawns on me that I hadn't checked on Christian yet. It's getting dark outside again. I feel stressed with the thought of his squeaky cage making its way over to my side. Who is this guy anyway? Why the silence?

I glance over toward him and see that he's sitting, staring at me. When my eyes meet his, he doesn't flinch. He just keeps on staring with dark, empty eyes. My breathing grows faster, and his gaze paralyzes me. I'm afraid to turn my back on him. It's as if he positioned himself to just look at me with his legs crossed Indian style, facing me.

"Hey, you okay?" I ask.

He makes no attempt to answer me, but shifts his weight back and forth to readjust his position, or perhaps reaffirm that he's not going to stop staring at me. His head is now normal size and all he has on is his pajama bottoms. As he continues to stare, he brings his arm up to scratch his neck. His arms flex with his movements, but his stare doesn't waver.

"Christian, are you okay?" I ask again, hoping he's just in a trance from his therapy today.

He grins. Is he just happy about how much he's disturbing me? His piercing eyes continue staring, as the room gets darker. Eventually his black eyes are lost in the shadows of the room. I strain to find them again, not wanting to take my eyes off him—I don't know what he'll do—but they're lost.

Then it is pitch black.

The hair stands up on the back of my neck. I look around

frantically, not wanting nightfall to overtake the room so soon. I clench my pillows and listen for him, trying to hear past my head noise. I can't pick up on any movement.

"Ah! I hate this!" Christian screams suddenly and makes horrible screeching sounds.

I jump.

"This place," he hisses, "is killing me. I hate these fuckers! Ah!"

Loud, hollow, banging sounds follow. They sound like a head on metal joining in on his screams. I have never heard the pain of pure agony before until now. I've felt it though, I remind myself, thinking of the night my mom died.

He continues for what feels like hours.

I finally grab two pillows and cover my ears to drown out some of the madness. I wish I could help him, but even if we were both uncaged, I would be afraid that he'd hurt me. He is so out of control during his treatment recovery, yet so vulnerable too.

Then, as quickly as it started, it ends. There's silence again.

Trembling, I approach the other side of my cage to hear his breathing, but all I hear is my own. I glance back and forth around me to see if he's possibly out of his cage, but it's so black, he could come at me from anywhere and I wouldn't know it until it was too late. Again, I move to the back of my cage.

I wait for what I know is coming. The sound of rusted cage wheels will grind against their supports as Christian rolls over eventually. The screeching noise will echo through the room and into the darkest fears of my soul. The fear is deep, cold, and lonely—a fear of the element of surprise. I really don't know if his intentions are good or bad. All I know is that he wouldn't stop staring. This means I'm the center of his focus, so I keep my good ear to his direction.

Seconds later, the initial squeak throws me up against the bars. I whimper as the noise grows louder and louder, moving—or so I think—in rhythm with my beating heart, until finally stopping to silence.

"Give me one of your pillows!" he shouts, sounding as if he's directly in front of my face. "If you don't, I'll come in there like

Drake, only I'll stay for the night."

I immediately grab one of the pillows and hold it against the cage bars so he can reach it.

"You are most kind. Jeannie, isn't it? That's your name?"

I can feel his breath on my legs as he waits for my answer.

"What, you only speak to Drake the Fake? You know he's just using you, right? I mean, what would he have to lose with convincing you to be his friend? He'd be gaining a playmate and losing nothing. Are you a virgin?"

Stunned by his boldness, I finally answer. "You have no idea what you're talking about. Drake hasn't tried anything on me."

"Oh, but he will! You wait. Then you have a choice to make. Will you let him in, shall we say?"

His insensitivity is insulting. I wait several minutes but before I can answer, I hear him snoring.

Christian is asleep.

* * * *

The next day, I awake high up in my cage, nestled into a makeshift hammock I strung together from sheets to get away from Christian's grasp. The sun is beaming in on me. My forehead sweat is beading already. The days are getting hotter and hotter, earlier and earlier. How am I going to bear this room through June, or worse, the whole summer?

I turn over and see Christian's cage still situated right next to mine. He's lying on the pillow I gave him with his face toward me. His expression is peaceful. It's the first time I've seen him like this. He even has a hint of a smile. It's hard to believe how handsome he is when his head is normal size. His jaw is strong and broad. His hair is shiny brown, except for the spots where they attached the electrodes. His skin is smooth with hints of stubble here and there along the chin, showing his youth. I watch him sleep for a few minutes, trying to study him while I have the chance. His pajama pants are sitting low along his belly, showing the top elastic of his white underwear. If he hadn't been ruined by this place, he could probably pass for a model.

The door flies open. In comes Dolores with her piles of files and snacks for the day. She pauses in front of Christian's cage briefly and continues toward her desk, strewing her files around to grab the bottom one.

"Christian, oh, Christian, what do I have for you today?"

So much for his peace.

His eyes flutter at the sound of her voice and slowly open with what looks like dread. He peers around the room until his brown eyes rest on mine. Then, he jerks back to look behind him, anticipating the inevitable stabbing for the day.

Dolores is holding the needle in her hand, tapping the tip of the syringe like a professional, getting it ready for the deep injection into the first thing she can grab on Christian's body. Unfortunately, I know I'm next.

"Hey, baby, how's it going today? You're looking really good again. Have you decided on how you want to handle my proposition yesterday?" asks Dolores with a sick smile. I'm surprised how brazen she is about her unprofessional behavior.

"No, I won't do that. I don't need to think about it at all."

"Oh, really? You're not longing for anything these days, even a cuddle?"

"I'm not desperate enough to want an old, fat broad like you."

Dolores looks disappointed for just a second and then immediately turns and stabs him behind his knee. Christian yelps, swatting at her hand.

"We'll talk again when you're feeling better, sweetheart."

I close my eyes and try not to imagine what she has in mind and roll over toward the window. I don't want to look at her. The only view I want is the glimmer on the waterway that stretches along the coast. This morning, there are two pelicans flying along the shore with their beaks raised even and proud as their wings pump them toward their destinations. How I wish I could climb onto the back of one and fly away.

"Hey, remember me?" Drake says.

I turn over and am startled that he's already inside my cage with the door shut.

"Where is Christian?" I ask, wondering when it will feel

normal to miss major sounds going on around me.

"Dolores is—uh—taking him out for a while. We have an hour or two until they come back. I see you've made yourself comfortable with the pillows. I've got another present for you. Want to see?"

"I guess."

"Okay, let me get you down from there first."

He draws his hands around me, gathering me into his arms and gently withdrawing me from my haven. He keeps me close, drawing his lips near mine.

"You were so beautiful up there, I had to be close to you."

Drake's chest is strong as he draws me up against him, laying his head on my neck and gently kissing me beneath my ear, brushing his hand against my breast.

I push away from him, unhappy with his advance. "Get off of me."

"Oops, sorry about that," Drake whispers. He pulls me in closer and then lets me go. He arranges the pillows for his own comfort and sits down for a chat, prodding me to sit with him. "I really mean it. I'm sorry about that, and it'll never happen again. I totally respect where you're coming from. If you're not ready for me, then so be it. At least we can be friends in the meantime."

I study him as I sit on the pillows opposite of him, squeezing one up to my chest so he can't stare at my breasts. He's quiet, stretching his neck back and forth. He relaxes and closes his eyes. I'm not sure why, but he seems more handsome today with a bit of a red tint on his nose and arms from the sun. A black undershirt shows around his neck beneath his scrubs with white letters that read "Deadwater Manor" stitched on the right side of his chest. The shirt is slightly snug, accenting his physique beneath. I feel like I have just woken up with my husband, as he rests.

"Hey you," Drake says, still keeping his eyes closed, "are you ready for your present?" This is eerily familiar to last week's encounter with Todd, making me reminisce about the fortune cookie.

"I guess," is all I can manage, quivering at the thought of Todd's touch. God, do I miss him.

"Well, I brought you some more decorations for your apartment," he says with a smile, reaching his arms through the bars and pulling a package behind his back.

Snapping out of my Todd thoughts, I grow interested in what Drake has behind his back. He smiles at me and brings one arm slowly forward with a bouquet of colorful silk flowers toward me.

"Oh, how beautiful! They're perfect for brightening my day," I say excitedly and look them over. "How nice of you!"

"They're just a little something for the place."

I tuck the stems behind the mattress in one corner to hold the flowers upright and swoon over them more, rearranging them so they are perfect.

"From now on, Jeannie, I will protect you from everything bad here—as much as I can, anyway, even if I have to work extra hours. I don't want anything bad to happen to you. I won't be able to stop the treatments—those are doctor's orders and beyond me—but I will be able to make you feel better afterwards. I promise I will be here for you."

Flushed, I smile shyly and sit back down on the mattress. This time, I'm within arm's reach.

"So, have you worked here long?"

"Too long. I really want to move on from this place. Maybe find a job in a regular hospital."

"I'm sure you can if you try. I wanted to go to college. Guess that's out of the question right now. Can you get me out of here?"

He reaches for my hand. "I'm sorry this is happening to you. If I could do something, I would. All we can do is make the best of this." I start to feel an ache for him, his touch—just like I had for Todd.

Drake draws me in, closing his eyes while inhaling the smell of my hair. Then he kisses me on the cheek, wiping my other cheek with the back of his hand.

"You are a beautiful woman, Jeannie," he whispers. Then he lets me go and backs out of the cage. The aching turns into a burning desire for him to be close again.

What the hell is the matter with you! Stop it! You can't feel this way about him. He's one of them!

I can't help it, though. All I want is for him to come back home.

15

I must have spent five hours looking out the window today, glancing back and forth between my getaway car and my tower at South Park. Memories of my birthday party, driving in my car the first time with Rick, and being close to Todd monopolize my thoughts. Sometimes glimpses of my dad trespass into scenes where I was the happiest, causing me to become rigid and tense with these fleeting moments. I try hard not to think of all the sleepless nights I cried over my dad's insults, the only thing he was good at nurturing.

He's the reason I'm in this horrible hospital, locked away in the attic with bars for my walls. Worst of all, he would see nothing wrong with this picture.

I snuggle into my pillow more, hanging one foot off the hammock and push off the bars to rock back and forth. This is the only comfort I've felt since I arrived.

"I'm not sure that hammock is within code, especially with a suicidal maniac such as you."

I don't even need to turn around to know that Dolores is standing there with her hands on her hips, glaring at the back of my head. I know there's no use trying to shield myself from the next dose. Sure enough, a surge of pain gouges through my butt, causing me to wince out of reflex. This is something she loves, I can safely assume.

Throwing my weight backward, I swat at her with my arm,

which causes my hammock to turn upside down and drop me onto the mattress. Dolores bends over in laugher.

"Serves you right, you good-for-nothing piece of shit. Stay down from there, or I'll use your ass as a pin cushion even more."

Within minutes, drowsiness accompanies the weird sensation in my limbs and lack of concentration that occurs every day after each shot. It comes in constant waves of every six to eight hours, leaving me only a couple of hours of function. The rest of the time, I'm in and out of the fog. I try to concentrate to see if I feel good, like a high from marijuana or my favorite mojito, but the feeling of pure loneliness is all that I can muster. It's a deep, depressing place where images of scattered memories flash in floating patches back and forth in front of me sometimes. It is almost as if they are real, as if I can touch them and be a part of their fluttering world as they slide on by my peripheral vision.

When my mom comes to see me, I talk to her.

* * * *

Mumbled voices talk over me, as I gain consciousness from the day's drugging. My head hurts. I don't want to open my eyes, but I am curious over the sound of these voices. They are muffled, but different somehow.

Who are they? Where the hell am I?

I jerk myself awake and slowly focus on my surroundings. The talking stops as soon as I open my eyes, and then resumes. My cheek is lying in a pool of wetness from the drool still flowing down the side of my chin.

Man, Dolores got me good this time.

"Are you awake, my dear?"

I focus on the voice, trying to answer, but can't respond.

"Do you know where you are?"

I struggle to open my eyes again.

"Get her out of there and into the chair."

I feel strong arms around me. I'm lifted and gently placed upright. My head hangs down. I flip my head back, trying to gain my composure.

Ah yes, it is the good ol' doc. *Shit, how are you going to convince him of your sanity when you look like this?*

"So, Jeannie, how is your treatment coming along?"

I try to form words, but I only end up breathing heavier and the effort to move my lips causes extreme fatigue.

"You don't feel like talking today?"

With every ounce of energy I can force into my neck, I nod.

"Oh, so, you do want to talk?"

I nod again.

"Well, then, catch me up on what's been happening over the past week?"

Week? Wait, I just saw him two days ago.

Panic sets in. I try to remember. Finally, my senses come back enough to speak.

"What do you mean, a week?" I mumble.

"Well according to my records, the last time I saw you, it was a week ago. I prescribed hydrotherapy for you to see if this would help with your suicidal tendencies."

My eyes race back and forth as I search for any minute detail of the past five days.

Nothing.

"Have I been getting hydrotherapy every day?"

"Every other day." His eyes study me as I try to process this. "You don't remember?"

I look down at my folded hands, ashamed. My head is cocked to the right a bit as I try to hear him.

"Your depression is worse."

"I'm not depressed. I'm not anything. You are causing me to be like this—and Dolores' constant injections."

"Of course you would think that. Jeannie, you need to start taking responsibility for your own actions. I know a lot of your withdrawn behavior has to do with your difficulty relating to your dad since your mom died. You need to start focusing on yourself now."

Dad? Dad who?

"Try to forget that for now, and just relax as we bring you back to a better place. Eventually, we can mainstream you again, one step at a time. It'll be a while, though, considering your state at this point."

I look at him sharply, barely able to focus in on his hard lines and elongated ears that show his age.

"Why are you doing this to me?" I ask through sobs accompanied with uncontrollable gulps of air between each one. I cry for myself. I cry for my life, my bedroom, my Todd, my mom.

"There now, sweetheart. Listen, I will reduce your medication and skip the hydrotherapy today, so you can get yourself together. How are your room accommodations? Will your roommate let you sleep?"

I stand up and pound my fists on his desk. "I am not in a room, you bastard. I am in a cage in the attic—the hot attic, where I can barely breathe. In the hot attic where you cage your victims away from the rest of the world! My roommate, since you asked, is suffering greatly from Dolores' torture."

He backs up in his chair, somewhat alarmed at my aggressiveness, and reaches for the phone.

I quickly sit down. The last thing I want is for him to change his mind about the reduced meds and therapy.

"I'm sorry about that. Look, I just want you to understand the seriousness of my living conditions. I have no room. I have a cage. Come see for yourself. Please, come see."

"Listen, Jeannie," he says, setting the phone back in its cradle, "I'm trying to help. Treating your doctor that way is not going to make your stay shorter, that's for sure. You need to control these angry, out-of-control attacks on me and my personnel. I will not stand for it. Do you understand?"

"Look at that cage behind me," I demand, realizing too late that I'm losing control again—just proving his point. "That's the smaller of the two. Why do they bring me in that if you have no cages in this place? Please, just come look!"

"We're out of time, Jeannie. We can continue this next week."

"Next week? No—please! I want you to check on me sooner. Either they're not giving me my medication correctly or they're overdosing me. I should not be forgetting the past five days, for God's sake!"

"Again, Jeannie, you don't make the rules around here, I do. The sooner you understand that, the easier you'll have it. I'll see you in a week. Try mingling with the other patients here and stop shutting yourself out. Socialization would do you good."

I sigh and again start to plead with him, but he ignores me and rings for an attendant. It's not Drake. Why no Drake?

Before the attendant can put his paws on me, I climb into the cage on my own, sit cross-legged, and stare at the doctor, taunting him to look at me.

He doesn't.

16

I fall into my pillows when we reach the attic, crying in frustration. I'm losing it again. All eyes are probably on me, but I don't care. Every inch of me hurts, especially my head. In fact, it more than hurts. Parts of my scalp are tender, and I can't find a comfortable spot without feeling stabbing pain, which seems to be spreading to my jaw and even my hand. There's a bandage on the top of my hand covering a bruise with accompanying puncture wounds. I check the rest of my body and I also have pain around my head area, including a sore in my mouth, as if I have bitten my cheek.

Bewildered, I glance into the room to see if anyone is watching me. The only face I see is Christian's, and he's staring at me with sad eyes. I can't understand why. He looks perfectly normal; no head trauma today. In fact, he looks better than I've ever seen him.

So why the sad eyes?

"Is something wrong, Christian?"

"You don't know?"

"No, I haven't been here. At least, I don't think I have. I mean, I went to the doctor today."

Suddenly, an incredible pain shoots through my head as if someone is piercing a knife through my temples. I grab my head. Then I notice my toes twitch.

What the hell is wrong with me?

Christian now has his hands on his head as well, almost

mimicking me—only his head is normal. It's as if he's cringing.

My toes twitch again.

I grab them with my fingers, trying to stop the involuntary movement. A circular white pad lands on the top of my foot. It reminds me of the ones Christian sometimes has on after his electric shock therapy.

Through the confusion, I grab the silver dollar-sized pad and peer out at Christian again.

Why can't I remember?

I clench my temples again in response to more pain. There's gel on each of them and more pads on my forehead. I hold the pads in front of me, trembling.

Oh, my God. No!

At that moment, Drake enters the attic holding a large department store bag. Dolores follows him in and both of them head for the desk without paying much attention to me. Drake drops the bag near his legs and continues his relaxed conversation with Dolores.

I whimper, still holding the pads out in front of me. Tears stream down my cheeks.

Drake does a double take during the conversation and moves the bag out of his way, once he notices my distress.

"Jeannie, you alright? What are those?" he asks gently, pointing to my hands. He walks closer, peering in between the bars. His eyes grow wide.

"Dolores, you didn't! She does not have that down as a treatment option," he shouts, racing toward her. She turns her back toward him. "You fucking monster! I should strap your fat ass in that chair and watch you fry! In fact, maybe I will!"

Dolores is indifferent and licks her index finger as she pushes pages in a book she pretends to read, only glancing up at him once over her reading glasses. I think I even see her smile. It almost seems like she has a vendetta against him. But why would she? Is she jealous? Is there some story between her and Drake?

Drake punches the book. It flies through the air and lands on Christian's cage. Then he picks up the shopping bag and heads my way. "I'm not going to let you do this to her again. That's final. Just wait until Doctor Wiggins hears about this."

"He's already seen her," she replies with a grin on her way out.

Drake hesitates for a second and then continues toward me without responding. I'm not sure I really want him to come in. At this point, I'm not sure about anything.

As Drake starts reaching for the lock, Christian screams so loud that it sends Drake reeling backwards until he catches himself on the bars. I look over at Christian. He's standing with his arms stretched outwards, trying to reach the bars of my cage.

"You get the fuck away from her you disgusting ass-wipe of a man! I can't fucking believe that you're taking advantage of her like that."

Drake turns away from him.

Christian bends down and picks up one of the pillows that Drake gave me and caresses it in his arms. "She gave me one, you know," he says as he pulls it close to his head, smiling at Drake.

Drake looks back at me to confirm Christian's statement, only to confirm it himself with the matching embroidery. He sighs for a moment and then his attention is fierce toward Christian. In seconds, Drake grasps onto Christian's cage and kicks it toward the other side of the room, sending Christian backwards and forwards, slamming his head on the bars until the momentum stops. I move forward to see if he's okay. Drake walks over too, but only to grab the pillow. Christian whimpers in pain, but I'm too weak to protest.

Drake heads back toward me. "Now, where were we?" he asks, looking at me with nothing but adoration.

Unlocking the cage, Drake crawls in, dragging the bag and pillow across the mattress.

I'm sitting in the same position, still holding the pads.

"Here, let me have those," Drake requests. He picks them out of my hands and throws them on the floor, gently touching my face and inspecting the areas around my temples and forehead. "Do you have any side effects?"

"Side effects of what exactly?" Then I decide to just answer— Drake's the one person trying to help me after all. So I nod and point to my toes which are still twitching at random increments.

They don't hurt, but it's disturbing to have no control over them. "My head is killing me."

"I'm sorry, Jeannie. I can't even give you ibuprofen, since I'm not the nurse. The pain will go away in a couple of hours though and so will the tremors. I promise. Just hold it together in the meantime, okay?"

My lip quivers. I lie down on my side with my back facing everyone.

Drake moves the hair from my face and says, "I have a present for you."

I close my eyes.

He wrestles with the bag a bit and I eventually feel the warmth of a blanket over my legs.

"I know it gets hot up here, but I thought you might like a comforter to match your pillows and give you more of a cushion to sleep on during the night. In winter, it'll come in handy when it gets cold up here. It's pretty drafty."

I draw in a deep breath and turn over toward him. "It'll be a cold day in hell before I end up in this hellhole for the winter. One way or another, I'm checking out of here."

"Don't talk like that Jeannie," Drake answers. "Or, if you do, be careful not to say it in front of Dolores. If she were here, you'd be back in shock therapy for sure."

I roll back over and contemplate his words. I'll never survive until winter. At the very least, I probably won't remember who I am.

I've got to get out of here.

* * * *

I awake to Drake's arm around my waist, which is limp. He's sleeping. From the position of the sun, I surmise it's about four o'clock in the afternoon. My headache is gone, and my toes finally feel like they don't have minds of their own. I'm returning to normal, except for my memory. God knows what has happened to me today—or over the past five days.

Then there's Drake. What am I going to do about this

situation? Sleeping with me? This can't be ethical. Dolores must be off duty. I look down at his forearm. It's muscular like a baseball player's. His hands are tan and smooth except for a couple of calluses on his palm. I want to entwine my fingers through his, but think better of it. Having another human's comforting touch is a nice change.

This is dangerous ground. You must keep your head together and be smart.

Drake stirs and squeezes me tighter, drawing me close. He takes a deep breath in and lets it out slowly. On some level, I guess we are a couple. We're not dating, and I'm not his girlfriend, but what are we? I don't know what to think of it all, but what I do know is that I have to accept Drake's offer of shelter and protection. I need him and am feeling more and more safe in his arms—in our bed, on our comforter.

Maybe, in time, he'll just sleep in the apartment for the night instead of going home. That would be the ultimate protection. Maybe I'll just let him kiss me. Maybe that would be okay given the situation. After all, he will be helping me, and he's already given me all these nice things. Maybe I need to make him want to stay.

I examine his face to determine if he's awake. His eyes open and he meets my gaze.

"Welcome back, Jeannie. You slept for quite a while. Feeling better?"

I nod but am uncomfortable with the way he's looking at me. He's so close, I'm afraid he'll try to kiss me.

Didn't you just tell yourself you would let him? What's the problem? Let him!

He draws me even closer and presses his lips against the nape of my neck, slowly, methodically, keeping his eyes locked onto mine. His tongue outlines part of my clavicle, sending waves of delight to my center being.

See, you're attracted to him. He's handsome, strong—and has keys to every door. Use him to get out of here. In the meantime, enjoy him.

"Hey, you mother fucker! Get away from her! You don't

belong in there!"

Shit, Christian, what are you doing?

Drake becomes agitated right away, jerking his head around toward Christian and climbs out of my cage. He then makes his way over to Christian's cage and opens the door. Christian doesn't budge.

I cringe.

"Say it to me now, you crazy bastard! Who are you to judge me when you're screwing Dolores?"

Christian stays still and replies, "You're just jealous, because she doesn't let you do it anymore."

"Oh, you think so, eh? Well, if you're such a better man, get out here and prove it. Kick my ass."

Oh my God. Drake will kill him.

"No!" I yell out of reflex. "Drake, please come back here and hold me. I can't take this today. Please?"

Drake immediately turns around, forgetting to lock Christian's cage. He joins me again, returning to his sensual licking of my shoulder and rubbing my waist and back with his hand. He cups his hands around my face and begins kissing my temples and forehead as if trying to heal them.

"You left the door open, you shithead!" laughs Christian, standing outside of his cage, leaning on its door.

Drake jumps up immediately and ejects himself from my cage, but Christian is faster and disappears out through the doorway of the attic. Drake follows. I listen for screaming from Christian or maybe thuds from fighting, but I hear nothing. I can't be sure if this is due to my deafness or if they're already down the stairs. That's when I notice, in his rush to chase Christian, he forgot to lock my door too.

A jolt of excitement jets through me, as I contemplate the possibility of freedom—getting to my car and driving myself out of here the same way I drove myself in. I quietly make my way over to the cage door and push it open, but hesitate.

Should I do this yet? What if I get caught? Maybe I should plan this better.

If I do nothing, I'll gain Drake's trust. How do I get out of sleeping with him when he gets back, though? I'm not sure I want him that way.

Before I can decide, Drake comes back in with Christian and throws him into his cage, head first. Christian is knocked out cold.

I look up at Drake, praying that he'll just see that I stayed put and not remember that he had shut the cage door.

"You okay?" I ask.

Drake melts and walks toward me. He stops abruptly when he sees the cage door open. "Wow, Jeannie. You could have escaped but you didn't. Thanks for not forcing me to have to hunt you down tonight."

"Well, I didn't want to leave you just yet," I reply, flirting, trying to strengthen his trust. With that, he crawls into our apartment and shuts the door.

17

I have just found out it's Monday again, and I'm feeling a new day on my skin with the warmth of the sun that's shining into my cage. Will it be a good day? God only knows. My forehead is already melting, and it's first thing in the morning. I'm concerned with how hot the room will be by midday.

The place is silent too. I wonder about what's waiting for me when I turn around. Anxiety is setting in along with the dread.

I need to start planning. Can I? Will I be able to concentrate through the endless hollow mind that I seem to be constantly fighting against? I'm getting tired—absolutely fatigued. Besides, why should I go through the struggle? It's not like my dad is going to come in and save me, and no one appears to be wanting me "healed" and out of here anytime soon.

Where's Drake? Where's Dolores or Christian? I'm surprised I'm not getting stabbed yet.

How should I do it? Do I figure out a way to escape my cell in the middle of the night? Should I climb out the window? Maybe I could knock out Dolores and Drake and make a run for it? Is slashing my wrists an option?

No, it is not.

Take a tumble down the stairs?

Yeah, right. With my luck, I'd break something and end up recovering in here. I need to come up with something that won't end up crippling me.

Under better circumstances, it would eventually dawn on me, but with my mind lately, it's unlikely. My pillows tell me the best way is to use Drake. I need to get him to want to save me.

Could I talk him into running away together?

"There's the slut. Have a good time with Drake last night? I couldn't believe what I saw when I came in here at shift change—you two sleeping together, pawing each other. Well, I can tell you one thing, the guy is good in bed. You'll learn all kinds of things. At least, that's what I hear from all the young female patients he seduces."

When the hell did she sneak in?

"He'll find another young girl to sleep with soon, mark my word. He's conquered you, so he'll move on. Maybe next time he'll pick a girl who has actually grown a set of tits, or at least is more experienced. I'm sure your bed post is shiny and new—or was before last night."

I ignore her and try to concentrate on how I'm going to take the syringe she's bouncing around in her fingers and jam it down her throat. Maybe I'll hit her voice box while I'm at it. Then I'll heave her lard ass into one of these cages, shove it through the back window, run it through the back parking lot and push her right into the harbor. Nothing would give me more pleasure than hearing her beg for mercy while I watch her drown. The big cage would teeter back and forth as she fights to free herself. Her eyes would grow desperate as the water reaches her neck, bobbing up and down to try to catch a breath. She'd gulp in water. She'd suffer. Nothing would give more pleasure to watch.

It should have been her and not my mom.

As she leans back to get a good stride before she strikes me like a viper, Drake grabs the syringe from her hand and dangles it over her short stature, taunting her. She grows angrier with every leap, swinging at his torso to try to make him drop it. He's too quick.

"Forget it, Dolores. Doc says no drugs today. I talked to him about your drugging rituals, and I think your license may be in jeopardy."

"What?" she responds with her final swipe at the syringe. "If I go down, you go down, Drake. Is she really worth it?"

"I don't have a license, idiot! All I'd lose is my crap job. You think I care?" Drake replies.

Wow, he's a pretty good liar.

He puts the cap on and hides the syringe in his pant's pocket. "By the way, I'm taking Jeannie out today. She'll get a shower, real clothes, and time in the pink room. She'll be fucking coherent for all of it."

"You wouldn't!"

"Oh, yes, I would. Today is a day without chains, cages, or any restraining devices for Jeannie."

"You can't do that. It's against policy."

"Yeah? Well, how about this? I'm going to take her outside, too." He draws his hand up to his mouth in an exaggerated way, as if he were Scarlet O'Hara herself.

I don't know whether to be excited or not at this point, since I'm not sure if he's just making her crazy or if he really means it. The thought of going outside, however, is more than I can bear.

"Are you serious?" I ask.

Drake turns around, winks at me, and grabs one of the leather restraints from my cage.

"Okay, Dolores. Now it's your turn."

Time slows down. To my shock, Drake forces the restraint onto her wrist and drags her to my cage, attaching her to the outside of it.

I back up so she can't reach me.

"Drake, get me out of this!" she cries, pulling on the strap, but only making it tighten.

Then he grabs another strap and restrains her free hand to another bar.

"See how you like it, bitch. You're lucky Jeannie's in there. Otherwise you'd experience caged life for yourself."

She continues to yell at Drake. He ignores her, unlocks my door and nods for me to exit. I'm a bit timid, but follow his lead.

"We'll be back and maybe I'll let you free then. Hope your tree trunks don't give out with the hours of standing you're in for. Go ahead and struggle—please do. Keep struggling until you wear your ass out and become immobile from the exhaustion. Maybe next time you'll stop and think before you kick me out of our little home. We are a couple and you can't do a thing about it!"

Drake reaches for my hand and closes the attic door behind us. I can't help but worry about Christian and the wrath she might take on him if she frees herself before we get back. His expression is begging me not to leave.

I'm walking for the first time in weeks. I feel wobbly, but the adrenaline from a drug-free mind and unstrapped extremities has me skipping down the stairs. How I've missed being able to take a normal-sized stride and be without the extra weight from the chains. I'm light—almost floating—as I dance back and forth with the air. Never before have I felt so elated.

Drake's watching me with a smile

"Thank you," I say, barely audible.

"You're welcome. I like it when you dance."

We make our way to the hallway that connects to the main rooms on the bottom floor.

"Where are we headed?"

"Well, I thought I'd take you back to the nice bathroom again."

I start to feel concerned, but before I can respond he says, "The patients are back in their rooms this time of day. Don't worry."

Relieved, I continue skipping and jumping my way down the hall until we reach the bathroom. He was right, the place is dead quiet. I rush in and turn on the faucet, getting my bath ready as if I live here. Drake comes in with two towels for me and closes the door behind him. His eyes are on me.

I'm quiet at this point. I prepare everything around the bathtub. Drake doesn't move or say anything. I turn off the faucet. While a few drops continue to fall, I ask Drake if he intends on staying to watch.

"You're my wife, aren't you?"

"Well, not officially. We haven't talked about anything like that. I think I'd prefer to bathe in private for now, okay?"

He throws the towels at me, surprising me by the outburst.

"You don't want me to look, then cover yourself up, but I'm not budging."

"Come on, Drake. You can't be serious."

"Look, you've given me nothing in return for everything I've given you. Even if Dolores wouldn't have come in, you probably would have stopped me or fallen asleep. How can I take you seriously as my wife if you're not willing to share your bed in a way that is satisfying to me? You need to learn that I do expect some affection in return."

Oh shit, what do I do about this?

I figure as soon as I'm naked, he's going to come join me. If I protest, he'll have another outburst about what I *owe* him—or he'll just take it. I hope I'm wrong. I carefully undress behind the white towel cloaks and ease myself into the water, trying not to get them wet. Then, I drape them across the bathtub to try to shield most of my body parts.

Drake is still staring.

I figure I'd better make this quick, so I submerge my hair, move the water through it and bring it to a lather. Being clean feels so refreshing. Drake watches my every move and never wavers. I feel funny washing myself in front of him, but I don't get this opportunity often so I continue until I'm finished and then relax in the water, feeling soft and cool. One of the towels falls in the water, bringing me back to reality. Drake is standing right over me with a replacement. I grab the other towel to cover myself.

"You should not be this close, Drake!"

"Here's a fresh towel. Get out of the tub. I want to take you somewhere else, and we need to get going before the crazies are back."

He holds another towel so he can't see my body as I exit the tub. Then he wraps the towel around me, pulling it taut.

I back up a bit from him, and he waits.

"Put your clothes on," he commands

I know I can't do this without dropping the towel.

Turning my back to him, I dry off and begin trying to put on the hospital gown Drake brought me.

I can hear Drake moving closer—slowly. I turn around to look

133

at him with "no" in my eyes.

He doesn't stop or slow his approach whatsoever. Instead, he puts his hand on my shoulder and strokes it with gentle caresses. I sigh in worry. I'm not ready for this.

I thought I might want to sometime, but that was before he added all this entitlement talk. Why would he think I'd want him after this? I'll play nice, but somehow I'll have to distract him.

Then he turns me around and grabs the towel away from my hands, holding it out so he can't see me.

Thank God.

I dress quickly before he changes his mind and walk to the large mirrors over the ceramic sinks and begin fingering my hair to get the tangles out. Without a brush, it's pretty much an impossible feat.

Drake carefully pulls my hair to my back and begins brushing it. I'm surprised when I feel the bristles on my back. He starts methodically with the bottom of my hair and slowly works his way up, getting the tangles out along the way. Eventually, he's brushing it in long strokes over and over. His entire focus is on my hair. I surmise this has been a fantasy of his. As he detangles a few groupings at a time, he lets them drop forward over my chest and continues until he's able to smoothly get the brush along my scalp and through to the ends. I can feel coolness on my back as he finishes. Finally, he turns me around and pushes my hair back behind my shoulders and my ears. He then looks down toward my chest.

I look down too and see that the wetness from my hair reveals most all of my breasts through my top. I shove him backwards as I lunge for the door, running as fast as I can. He rears up quicker than me and blocks the door before I can open it.

"No leaving unless I'm with you, understand?"

His eyes are dark and serious. I know it won't be long before he has his way with me. He's a man, strong and healthy, with a need that is growing more and more every day, and I know it.

"Drake, I know, but you're scaring me."

"Really? Well, I don't know why, since you share your bed with me, remember? I even hold you when you're hurting whether physically or mentally. All that comes with a price. You know that, right? If you don't want it, then I can take that protection away. I don't want to spend that kind of time with you if I'm making you feel uncomfortable. I just thought you liked it."

"I do," I quickly respond. "I just don't want to rush into anything. This is the first time my head has been clear in a while."

"That's shit, and you know it," he replies and pushes himself up against me. Holding my wet hair in his hand behind my back, he pulls my head backward as he engulfs my mouth with his tongue and gyrates against me. His free hand comes up to my breast and outlines my nipple. I'm totally at his mercy.

I'm too scared of him and his conditions to remotely get into it. Realizing this, he backs away.

"Okay, fine. Maybe I do need to give you more time. I'm not going to just be used, though. Keep that in mind."

It is a stunning victory.

He pulls me away from the door by my arms and opens it to see if there are any patients. There aren't, so we head back down the hall toward the attic.

Does this mean I didn't "earn" a trip outside?

I stay close behind him but peer into every patient room to see if there is any possibility of a future escape. My hope diminishes with each footstep, though. Room after room reveals barred windows and bare beds without even a sheet.

Then he swiftly pulls me through a set of double doors, which leads us into an empty grand hall with floor to ceiling windows and intricate, white metal latticework, like you'd see in old mansions. There are fireplaces on each side of the room that have been painted white and the rest of the room is painted in bright pink. The enormous windows allow streams of sunlight to enter the entire room and it feels cheery and bright, like no other room I've seen in the place. I immediately feel welcome in this beautiful space. He lets go of my arms, so I can wander around aimlessly, taking in the grand ceilings and wooden floors.

"Come here, Jeannie, I want to show you something."

I meet Drake at the opposite corner of the room. He's standing next to a telescope on a tripod.

"Some of the patients like to come in here and look at the stars. Maybe we could do that sometime."

"Can I look through it now?"

"Of course, but first give me a small kiss," he says before his voice lowers and he looks at me with warning in his eyes, "and this time, kiss me back."

He grabs me by the waist and brings me in closer, wiping my hair from my cheek, and begins softly nestling his lips against mine, waiting for me to part them and let him in. I do.

"Okay, go ahead," Drake says as he steps out of the way of the telescope. I'm a bit frazzled by his kiss, but move forward toward the telescope and peer through, eager to see anything that could assist in my escape. First I see the rooftops of the buildings. As I focus in, I can see beyond the hospital grounds and out into the swamplands and river waterway. It's amazing how close the boats look as they race by. I can even see South Beach and the tower, making me more eager to get back to my favorite place on earth.

How great it is to see this place from a fine room!

I focus the telescope even more on the beach to see if I know anyone and even further on the tower, but see no trace of my friends.

Or did I?

I move the telescope quickly back toward the tower and focus more on the figure on the top of it.

Could it be Todd?

In my excitement, I almost pull the telescope off its brackets.

"You okay?" asks Drake.

"Ah, yeah, just amazed by how well you can see everything."

It *is* Todd.

My heart skips.

He's just as I remember him with his board shorts and shiny hair flapping in the wind. His hand is resting under his chin, as he looks out toward me. I wonder if he's thinking of me, missing me. He looks right at me, and I jerk back quickly in surprise. After a second, I return to his gaze—return home, my place, my tower. If only he could really see me.

Don't look away, Todd. Stay with me!

If only he could hear my thoughts.

I look back at Drake who's been distracted by another attendant and is chatting about something I'm sure I couldn't care less about.

How can I get Todd's attention? I look around the room to see if there's a flashlight or something else I could use to bounce light back his way, but I don't see one thing remotely metallic or electronic.

Quickly, I peer through the telescope again, hoping that he's still with me, but he's not. He's not with me at all. He's not thinking of me, missing me, or trying to find me. Melissa has made sure of that.

I see their embrace. His lips are on hers. No, Todd!

I finally look away, unable to take anymore. When I return to the telescope once more, I cry as I watch him pull Melissa down behind the guard rails, out of sight, protected from any onlooker's view—my view, my tower, my Todd. Damn him! I've been gone a week—maybe two! That bastard!

I jerk my head from the eyepiece and feel myself lunging downward—not physically, but mentally. Todd was my last hope. I thought he'd figure it out eventually and find me here. Now, I have no one.

Feeling numb, I look toward the beach without the help of the telescope, and wonder if he's smiling at her the same way he use to smile at me. Are the birds singing for them too?

"You okay?" Drake is close behind me, rubbing my shoulders. "You look upset. What did you see?"

"That bastard."

18

I never did go outside. After telescoping, Drake escorted me back to my cage, because I wouldn't confide in him. He even looked through the telescope himself, but saw nothing. It was probably because Melissa was getting her brains fucked out behind the wooden guardrails. I can't believe they're together now. I guess I meant absolutely nothing to him.

I hope a seagull shits on his head.

The only high point was returning to see Dolores hunched over and still attached to my cage. Drake released her and all she did was snarl at him as she headed toward her desk, rubbing at the redness on her wrists. No threats, no screaming. Then Drake threatened to strap her again if she did any more treatments on me. She seemed to resign to him—whatever he had on her was that bad—so he helped me into my cage and left.

Here I sit, depressed again and doped up, of course. I can't even cry. Dolores made sure to stab me as soon as Drake was gone. She must have used a lower dose this time though, because I'm actually coherent.

That figures. I think I'd rather be oblivious to my situation right now.

The memory of Todd and Melissa enters my mind, but I quickly divert myself.

I wonder how my car is doing.

I pull myself up so I can see. Leaves have started to

accumulate along the edge of the back window, and there's a thin coating of dust, making the windows look foggy. Thelma needs a bath, but to me, she's still a vision of beauty. She's waiting patiently for me. I know she is. She's like a best friend, my support system. She's always there to reassure me. She's my beacon of hope.

Wow. Hope. I've got to keep hope.

I have to keep the faith despite Todd and Melissa. Besides, I've been the one thinking about Drake in a romantic way sometimes. What better am I? I suck too. Besides, I didn't show up to meet Todd. Maybe he thinks I changed my mind. I don't know.

What I do know is that I will not die in this place. I will not allow myself to succumb to the depression. I will control what does or does not happen to me from now on as much as I can. I will not be victim. I will fight. I will do what I need to survive. I'm only eighteen. I still have a lot of life to live.

I can't believe my energy level despite the drugs. Maybe I can fight through the fog more too.

"Are you in la-la land, or do you want dinner?" asks Drake from directly behind me, causing me to stumble backwards and fall onto the mattress.

"Christ, Drake, can you please let me know when you're near my cage? If you announce yourself, this is the ear I can hear out of, for the record," I say, pointing to my good ear.

"Well, fine then. I'll take this picnic dinner out to the back myself. Thought you wanted to get outside, but guess not. I'm getting pretty sick of putting up with your shit, you know it?"

Did he say "outside"?

Drake opens the cage door and throws a grocery bag toward me with something soft in it.

"Yeah, it's another present. Too bad you don't appreciate me. That'll be the last one you get." He slams the cage door. He has the picnic basket in one hand and the key in the other. "Are you going to be nice, or should I lock this?"

He's playing me, isn't he? He knows I want out of here, so he's using it to entice me to become dependent on him. He wants me to trust him so he can get down my friggin' pants. Why, though? He

SANDIE WILL

could probably get any girl he wanted outside of this Godforsaken place. Why would he want one of the supposed loony ones?

"Well?" he demands.

I reach over to the bag and pull out its contents. Curtains. Long, flowing white ones with a row of holes at the top similar to a shower curtain. They could be easily hung up with string along the top of my cage to provide privacy from Dolores and Christian. In the bottom of the bag is a spool of string.

"I'll help you get those up, if you want—but only if you want."

Christian stirs in the next cage over. His head is swollen again.

I'm not sure about this. It'll be great to get some privacy, but I'm sure he's got another motive in mind.

"Don't worry, Dolores isn't here tonight, and Christian is out of it. We can have dinner and then come back and hang the curtains. They'll look great in our home, don't you think?"

"Yes," I reply, still looking down at the curtains. I agree not because I want this, but because I want to go outside.

"Great! Let's get going before it gets dark, then," Drake insists. He reaches into the cage for my hand. I pat down my hair and then take his hand.

"Our first real date," Drake says with a smile and lifts me out of the cage. His arms are solid, as they carry me to the doorway. "No chains tonight, Jeannie."

Probably so he can have easy access. Right now, I don't think I care. They've taken my freedom, drugged me, tortured me, and locked me in a cage. It was only a matter of time before someone realized they hadn't included sexual assault to the list yet. Somehow I'll fight him off. I'm going outside!

Drake carries me down the stairs and through the hallways. We pass the pink ballroom before heading down another set of stairs and out through a pair of double doors. The sun is bright and hot, but not as hot as the attic. I can tell that my weight is getting tough for Drake to carry. He breathes heavier, but keeps going. We pass the circular crazy wing and along the grass. It feels like we are on the west side of the building. Then we pass by a basketball court enclosed in a screen room. No one's playing, but I can see patients dressed in orange pajamas inside the next room

140

that looks like a cafeteria. These patients are not shackled or restrained. They aren't even attended.

What's to keep them from slicing a hole in the screen and running away? Why couldn't they have brought me there?

Drake's breathing becomes labored. He walks down toward the water, an inlet with meandering sawgrass as far as I can see. His gait slows just before the waterfront, and he turns toward a cluster of oak trees to the left. Finally, he puts me down.

"Don't move, Jeannie. I need to get the blanket out for our picnic."

He's thought this out.

The blanket flows out like a wave, the wind from it bustling through my hair, as it escapes from beneath. I can tell I'm in his peripheral vision the entire time.

Then he lifts me toward himself, hovering over me like a man with a woman who knows she wants to run away. He holds my wrist tight and I hear a click. It sounds like it came from behind me—I can never be sure with my damn hearing. I jerk back to see. There's nothing but trees and weeds. Then Drake backs off and rolls onto his back, satisfied with himself. I try to move away from him, but I can't. I'm handcuffed to him.

I'm fucked. I mean screwed. No, I mean fucked. Shit, what am I saying? I need to get out of here!

Drake's demeanor has changed from begging to dictator. Instead of asking me if I'd like to have dinner now, he empties the picnic basket contents and tells me I will eat. He doesn't just tell me I will eat, but what I will eat, in what order, and how I will eat.

"You see this nice, big, yellow banana? I'm going to undress it for you, and I want you to let me slide it into your mouth and then I want you to eat it slowly," Drake says suggestively.

I want to puke.

"If you don't, I'll make sure you never see this beautiful view again," Drake promises, "or your car for that matter."

Oh, my God! He knows about my car!

The grin on Drake's face is like that of a serial killer just before the capture.

I eat the banana to Drake's satisfaction.

I kiss him to his satisfaction—on the lips, nothing more.

"You have very soft lips," Drake hisses in my bad ear. At least, I assume that's what he's saying based on the sounds I'm getting from my other ear. No way am I asking him to repeat it though.

He pulls back to look directly at me. "You know, Jeannie, I find your living quarters very sexy. You're my Jeannie in the cage. I feel like I'm visiting a nightclub when I come home to you. One of these days, you're going to have to dance for me in it."

His penis is hard against my thigh.

Maybe I should just let him. It would be easier. What does it matter, since Todd's no longer there for me? He's going to do it anyway. Fighting will just make it worse, and he'll punish me for fighting him. Now, I know I have no one. Just Drake, who thinks he's my husband.

I try to relax, but I can't. Deep down I know this is wrong. I can't just let him have his way.

Drake kisses my bad ear, murmuring some incoherent phrase.

He's got to have the key to the handcuffs somewhere. I slide my free hand down to his pocket and braise it with the back of my hand. No luck.

Suddenly, out of nowhere, it starts to rain. Within seconds it's pouring.

God, I love Florida.

Drake jumps up as if he's being doused with acid and runs toward the manor, barely paying attention to my hand, which is still attached to his, or the fact that I'm literally being dragged across the wet grass. My foot slips while I try to keep up with his pace.

"Drake, hold on a sec!"

"Hurry up! We can't both show up drenched or they'll know I was outside with you."

"You're pulling my hand off!"

"Well, keep up or I *will* pull it off. I'm about to get shit-canned!"

He drags me around the buildings until we finally make it to the threshold of the double doors.

"Okay, I've got to get dry clothes on," Drake says as he tries to catch his breath. "I'm going to take off the handcuffs. If you bolt, I will find you and stick you back up in that cage and leave you at Dolores' mercy. Got it?"

"Yeah," I mutter, rubbing my wrist.

I wonder if that would actually be any worse.

"I want you to stay here for two seconds. Can I trust you?"

"Of course."

"Okay. You better be here when I get back," Drake warns when he's halfway down the hallway.

Can I help it if he's an idiot? As soon as he's out of sight, I push on the double doors, but they're locked. I scramble around the hallway trying to find a goddamn unlocked door, but they're all bolted tight.

"Jeannie?"

Fuck.

"Yeah, I'm here. Just snooping around."

Drake comes around the corner fast and grabs my elbow. "Okay, I need to get you back upstairs quickly."

I'm sure my disappointment is evident, because Drake took a second look at me while dragging me down the hallway.

"Why do I need to keep telling you not to worry? I'm going to protect you. Remember too that Dolores gets off early today. That means no shots and no hassle. Just you, me, and—privacy." Drake winks at me as we enter the attic.

Thank God, Christian is here. Maybe this will be my saving grace.

Drake follows me into the cage and immediately removes the curtains from the cardboard they're pinned to. He grabs the string out of the bag and ties each panel securely along the top of the cage. The breeze is flowing in at a steady stream from the window behind me and forces the curtains up against the bars. As the wind changes, the panels free themselves from the bars. I envy them.

I can no longer see Christian, the desk, or any part of the attic. All I can see is the ceiling, the window and the wall behind me. It reminds me of being in the hospital room the day my mom died. I didn't know what to do back then, and I don't know what to do now.

Should I just give in? Will I have a choice? If I don't, am I doomed to this cage with no one to watch out for me? Will he let Dolores fill my days with drugs, hydrotherapy, and shock therapy? I don't think I can take anymore. I'm tired and weak. I'm sick of this place. I'm sick of fighting. Todd is fucking Melissa, so why shouldn't I fuck Drake? What does sex really mean, anyway? Certainly the act of sexual intercourse doesn't mean anything to men. Maybe I should feel the same. Just fuck him and enjoy knowing it will allow me some freedoms, and make sure it means nothing else.

Jeannie, stop. Don't do this.

Drake sits across from me, legs crossed. I see his penis bulge in his pants. He begins the mating ritual with long, gentle strokes along my calves, and I begin the process of leaving my body.

19

It doesn't take long for him to slide me on top of his lap, both of us with legs crossed. He's gyrating toward me and pulling my chest toward him. My breasts are directly in line with his mouth. I'm losing myself to him. I'm losing the battle. I like this.

No! You can't like this. Stop before it's too late! Why are you being so stupid?

He circles my nipples with his fingers, as he reaches his tongue into my mouth, and explores every inch of it, pressing his penis against me in rhythm with everything else. I'm panting, wanting more. I want him to touch me. I want him to tease me. I just want someone to love me and hold me. I've been so scared.

He starts licking my earlobe, nibbling. He lets go of breath into my good ear.

"Dance for me, Jeannie," he expels between tugs on my earlobe. "Give me a lap dance. Give yourself to me."

Everything stops and he leans back against the cage, smiling.

"Do it!" he demands. "Use the cage bars."

I lean back away from him, stunned by the tone of his sudden demand. None of this feels sexy anymore.

"Come on, Jeannie. It's my fantasy. Turn me on. Seduce me."

It's at this point that I notice the figure on the other side of the curtain.

"You bastard! Get the hell away from her!"

Drake begins to turn around, but we're suddenly jerked

backward as the cage topples over onto its side. Drake's head hits the cage hard, knocking him out. Through the top of the cage, I see Christian is free from his cage and looking down at me.

"Are you crazy?" I yell at Christian once I gather myself. "You could have really hurt me, you idiot!"

"Better to be hurt a little by the sudden jolt of the cage, than raped by this asshole!" Christian yells back. "Don't you see what he's doing? He's a slime ball who has locked you in a cage to force you to fuck him. News flash: that is not love. He's in cahoots with the rest of the staff around here! I need to tell you something—"

He suddenly stops and drops to the floor in agony. "Headache," he mumbles.

With the comforter wrapped around me, I move to the corner of the lopsided cage.

God, please get me out of this insane asylum! I'm the only normal one in the place and soon I'm going to turn loony like the rest of them.

Wait a minute. How did Christian get out of his cage? Why didn't he just run while he had the chance? I mean, who cares if a girl he doesn't even know is being seduced by someone. He stayed the last time he was out of his cage too. Why?

I put my nightgown back on, scoot up and move over to the top of the cage to see how he might have freed himself. His cage door is open, but I don't see a key.

"Oh God, please make this stop! Please, I'll do anything," Christian whines.

I look over to the desk, but there's no key.

Christian must have it on him. Shit.

I need to get it from him before Drake wakes up, but how? I can't even try to move the cage now. Maybe if he moves closer, I can try his pockets? How can I shake him out of this episode he's experiencing long enough to free me?

After a long minute, Christian is still wiggling but it's starting to subside. The veins on the top of his head have become less pronounced too. He should be out of it soon. He always sleeps afterward.

If only he'd come closer. I need to at least try to get the key.

I sit and wait, praying that Drake doesn't wake up in the meantime. Two pins fall out of Christian's pocket.

Oh, my God! He used pins from the curtains. Are you fucking kidding me? I quickly rummage around the inside of my cage through the curtains, sheets and pillows until I finally see a pin next to Drake's leg. I grab the pin and find another. The only problem now is that I have absolutely no clue how to pick a lock with pins.

I must figure this out. There's a first time for everything!

I crawl over Drake and grab the lock. Working from behind it, I quickly jab the pins in and out of it. This does no good.

Come on Jeannie, you've got this!

I use one of the pins to feel around the mechanism inside of the lock, frantically. Suddenly, by a stroke of luck, I hear a click. The lock is hanging open.

I look back at Drake. He's still sleeping. Christian's out too. Relief starts to creep in, but I catch it before it spreads. This isn't over.

I remove the lock and open the cage door, not yet ready to believe this is happening.

I'm free!

My eyes fill up with tears as I crawl out of the cage and onto the floor. I stand up on my feet. Oh, thank God, I'm halfway steady!

With a half-crooked stance, I run to Christian and beg him to wake up, but he only moans and rolls over.

I try to drag him but it's no use. I'll just have to come back and get him after I get my car. I fling open the attic door, but then remember I have no keys.

Oh, my God, no!

I halt in the hallway at the top of the stairs.

Where are the keys? Someone will catch me if I don't have my car. I'm just going to have to figure that out later.

Before I get my foot down onto the first step, I'm grabbed by my waist and pulled back into the room.

"No!" I scream. "Let me go!"

"We have some unfinished business, little lady," Drake says, all tenderness gone from his voice. "You're going to like it, or at least you better pretend to."

Every ounce of struggling I'm doing has no bearing on the absolute physical dominance he has over me.

"Christian, help me!" I scream, but he's still passed out.

In an instant, I'm back in the cage with both hands strapped to the top of it. The cage is now standing upright. I'm on my toes. Drake rips off my hospital gown. A belt buckle touches the back of my thigh as Drake drops his pants onto the mattress. He's going to take me from behind, and it's not going to be pleasant.

Before he has a chance, though, a knock at the attic door interrupts his advance. He quickly pulls on his pants and frees me.

"Put your hospital gown back on. Not a word about this to anyone."

He leaves the cage and locks it. Then he quickly drags Christian to his cage, locks it, and heads for the door. I can manage to get only one arm through the sleeve of the nightgown, because my hands are trembling so badly.

Drake looks back at me, anxiously waiting to open the attic door. I can tell he wants me to act like nothing happened. Instead, I start to sob uncontrollably.

He opens the door and stands in the way so the attendant can't see in. All I can hear are mumbles and they depart.

"Jeannie, what happened?" asks Christian from his cage. "Are you okay?"

I push the curtains to the side and bunch up the comforter around me as I sit, needing some kind of comfort. Tears continue to stream down my face.

"You—you were right, Christian," I finally manage to say. "He tried to rape me. Thank God, he was interrupted."

"That no good, fucking bastard. I wish I had been awake to help you. I'm so sorry, Jeannie."

I lie down, still holding onto the comforter. "Please help me get out of here before it's too late."

20

"You doing better now?" Christian asks.

I open my eyes and pull back the curtains. It must be early morning. The sunlight has started its ascent across the floorboards, and Dolores isn't here yet. He's watching me from inside his cage.

"Yeah, I think I'm over the initial shock. I'm just so grateful nothing happened."

"Well, he still put his hands on you and has been seducing you. This is not acceptable. He is misusing his power."

Christian rubs the sides of his face, which is normal size now. He looks frustrated. "Okay, I need to tell you something, and I need you to believe me. Just listen."

I nod.

"Were you in the attic when the other girl was here?"

"You mean the one that died? How did you know about that?"

"Yeah, that was my client's daughter."

"What?"

"Her name was Brianna Danner."

"You know this, how? What do you mean *client*?"

"Her family hired me to find her. Unfortunately, I was too late. My name is Detective Christian Blaylock." He extends his hand.

I'm not buying it, and I'm not touching him.

"Uh huh. So, Detective Blaylock, if you're an investigator, then how the hell did you end up in this attic? I would think someone with your background could manage to somehow get away."

He doesn't look fazed by my insult.

"I committed myself to investigate this place and to find Brianna. At first, the staff was accommodating and told me to rest. I searched for Brianna whenever I could, but never found her. Then I started to notice personnel heading up a set of stairs with food trays. Rumors were spreading that there was a girl in the attic who had died. I didn't know whether to believe them, but I hung out near the bottom of the stairs, pretending I was confused. That's when I saw her emaciated body being carried out. Something about me attracted the attention of Drake. He quickly handed her to someone else and jabbed a needle in my arm. I hurled that fucker around like a rag doll and advised him he was under arrest, but soon I had no control over my body. I slumped to the ground, unable to fight the effects of the drug anymore. Next thing I knew, I was in this cage writhing in pain."

"Well, why didn't you tell me before all those creepy nights when you slithered over to my side of the room?"

"It was my way of calling out for help. Have you seen the size of my head after the treatments? The after affect is so painful, I can barely think straight, much less confide in someone whom I don't even know. As time has gone on, though, I see that you're trustworthy. When you're not drugged up, you're also level-headed and innocent." His cheeks flush when he says the last part of the sentence.

"Why would they put you in here? Aren't they afraid your cop buddies will come find you?"

"It doesn't look like it. I was working on my own, though. It's a side business. No one has a clue where I am."

If this is true, we're in the same boat. If it isn't, then I'm just part of this guy's fantasyland.

How can I tell? Christ, for all I know, I could be whacked out on medication myself, and he's part of my fantasyland. Shit. How do I know what's real anymore?

"You don't believe me?"

I keep my eyes on the mattress, not wanting to meet his.

Christian moves over to the lock and frees himself from the cage with one of the pins.

Wow, he's good. Where did he get the extra pin? I hope he's not going to leave me.

He walks over to Dolores' desk. Oh, thank God.

Hastily, he looks through files until he finds the one he wants.

He scans the interior and hands it to me through the cage.

The name on the file is his.

"Why aren't you leaving? You're free!"

"Look at my bio."

I open the file. Christian is twenty-four years old with brunette hair and brown eyes. He weighs one hundred and eighty-five pounds at six feet, two inches. He is listed as having no allergies, and checking himself in for depression.

His next of kin is blank. His employer is blank, but occupation is listed as "detective." A copy of his business card is attached. Dolores' signature is at the bottom of the page.

"Jeannie, I'm telling you the truth. I'm going to leave and you're coming with me, but we have to be careful about this. We can't just walk out of here. You need to be careful with Drake, too. Don't let him con you into doing things you don't want to do."

Oh yeah, *that*. Suddenly, I want to cry, but I refuse. "I can't believe that despite just being assaulted, I'm actually feeling stronger right now."

"That's a good thing, Jeannie. That makes for less trauma. Be mad about it. That guy is a piece of work. You have to try to keep him away from you or he will get his way sooner or later. You can do it. Use your instincts." Christian exchanges his chart for another. "Here, read this one too."

The chart is labeled, "Brianna Danner."

Brianna was nineteen with brunette hair and hazel eyes. She lived in Palm Harbor, Florida. Her parents, Drew and Alice, live at different addresses. It looks like she lived with her mother. Brianna was a student at Saint Petersburg College and was studying business. The hospital admission form has her father's signature on it.

Where was her mother?

"What does this mean?"

"Keep reading."

She had an allergy to Penicillin, and listed under her medical condition is, "manic depression." The doctor's scrawl suggests shock therapy for six weeks, followed by—

I look up and meet Christian's gaze.

Oh, my God.

"They wanted to sterilize her?"

"They didn't just want to—they did. They sterilized her because her father was embarrassed about her depression. Some rich families can't have a black mark on their heredity. She died from complications, but no one will admit to that. Take another look at the chart, if you don't believe me. Her death certificate is in there."

The reason for death is listed as heart failure, cause unknown.

I slam the chart shut and throw it onto the floor. This is just too much.

"How did you know all of this if you've been locked up in a cage?"

"Let's just say that some of the screams were real and some of them were exaggerated. After I found the pins from your curtains, I've been a busy boy."

I sit back and look at my cage. She was the previous tenant, and until now, I had forgotten about that. I forgot she died in the same cage, forgot how she was mishandled afterward, too. I still can't figure out why they forced me into the cage that night either. What could have been the purpose for that? Did they want to break me? Well, it worked.

"I promise you, there is nothing wrong with me. I have a hearing issue, that's it. I don't know which direction sound is coming from. I have to ask people to repeat themselves when they're on my left side, and I even have to stare at people's faces while they talk so I can read their lips if I'm in loud areas."

"Don't tell me. Let me guess. Your rich dad is embarrassed by you too."

"I'm nothing but a handicapped idiot to him. Before that, everything was fine. We were all fine. Until—" I cut myself off from thinking about Mom again. I'm getting sidetracked.

"Until what?"

Dolores slams the attic door open and steps heavily onto the floorboards with a newspaper stuck beneath her armpit. As soon as she sees us, she stops and about drops her coffee.

Christian makes a run for his cage and slams the door shut.

"Shit, now look what you made me do! I spilled the coffee all down the newspaper I was going to read. You guys are both dead. Just wait until I get my hands on you."

My heart races as Christian frantically locks his cage. Hopefully, she forgot her key or Drake never gave her one.

Wait, why is he acting scared? He could probably take her down easily. Then we could get out of here.

I pull the curtain back down and wait behind it for the attack.

Well, that was stupid—now I can't see anything. She can roll this stupid cage in any position she wants. It's just a matter of time before I'm stabbed with a needle that holds the venom that will leave me paralyzed.

I stand up and wait. Maybe she'll catch me in the thigh. It hurts less there. I turn my back toward the curtains and look outside. My car still patiently waits for me. I can see the yellow hue reflecting off the doors and onto the white car next to it. It's funny how some days it looks cheerier than others. Today, she is less energetic, duller, more worn. She needs a fresh wax job. She needs me.

I hear Christian wince.

Then the viper flies through the curtain and stabs me in the back of the knee.

"Next time one of you leaves your cage unsupervised, you will get ten injections each. Do you hear me?" Dolores screams from behind the curtain. Her shadow looks round, like a big blueberry. No neck, just a stick protruding from the top. I don't know how she gets around really. It's too bad I don't have something to pop her with. I'd watch her fly around the room as the air leaves her body and she shrivels into nothing but a piece of waste. That's all she is anyway, something to throw into the garbage and forget about.

* * * *

I wake up to Drake and immediately jerk backward on my elbows to get away.

"Jeannie, it's okay. I'm really sorry. I didn't do anything though."

I can't even respond because I'm so dazed right now. My head hurts. My eyes hurt. I feel funny.

Drake's holding a grocery bag filled with all the things bad husbands bring to their wives after they've abused them. He has brightly colored flowers, a box of candy, a card addressed to "the love of my life," and a wrapped present. He hands me the card and waits for me to read it.

"Despite what happened, I'm a good husband. I'm your husband. I will wait until you're ready, I promise to never push you again."

When I look up, tears are streaming down Drake's cheeks. He hands me the present. It's glittery and wrapped with precision. My fingers aren't coordinated enough to open it though, so he opens the present for me.

I remove the paper that's hiding its contents.

It's my car keys.

21

Over the past few years, I've lost hope for life. Not in every way, but in many ways. I lost my mom. I lost my hearing. I lost my life, or life as I knew it anyway. When I think about it, I lost my dad too. My family basically fell apart on the night my mom died. It's engraved on her tombstone, and it's engraved in my mind.

Now, I really have hope at last. Does this present mean that Drake will help me get out of this hellhole? I don't know. If he doesn't, I'll find my own way. I can feel hope creeping in again. It's actually more dangerous than anything I've experienced here so far, because with hope, I'm opening myself up to more disappointment. I just can't let that happen.

I grab the car keys and feel the coolness of the metal against my palm, and in seconds, I feel a sense of peace. It's almost as if they're calming me already.

Drake is still waiting for a response, but his weeping has continued. Christian is also watching me from his cage. His eyes are wide. Dolores is reading her newspaper and paying no attention to this significant moment. She's such a dumbass.

"What's going on, Drake? Can I leave?" I whisper, trying to hide my excitement.

Drake leans forward and says, "No."

"Then, I'm confused. Why give me my car keys?"

"I just figure you'd like to have them. That they would mean something to you, like a souvenir of times past."

What the fuck is he talking about? I need to bust out of this place!

I try to remain cool and put the keys back in the box. I'll hide them for later along with the pins to pick the lock again. Drake doesn't look fazed by my question at all. I think he really believes I'll never get the hell out of here.

"I wish I could give you more than this," he says. "It's the only thing I could think of to make up for my bad behavior."

"This means more to me than you know. It is the best present ever. I feel like I have a little part of home. What time is it?"

Drake smiles and pulls the curtain back so I can see into the attic. "Dinner time." He places my tray inside the cage and wipes the sweat from my brow.

"How many days have I been here?"

"Sweetie, you've been here for a month now."

God, don't call me that.

Wait, what? How did a month go by?

I gather myself. "Oh, really? Wow, where has the time gone? I'm out of it most of the time. What's the date?"

"Glad you asked. Tomorrow is the fourth of July, and we're going to celebrate! They always let the patients go outside to see the fireworks over the river around nine. I'll make sure you get out there."

I catch Christian's eye beyond Drake's shoulder. Christian glances at Dolores who is still reading the *Tampa Bay Times*. He grins.

Drake gently pulls my chin so my eyes meet his again. "You okay?"

"Yeah, I was just wondering if Dolores would really let me go, or if I'm getting my hopes up for nothing. That seems to be the case most of the time around here."

"I will make sure you get to go." He gets up to leave. "I'll be back after my shift is over."

Dolores pulls the newspaper down and watches Drake leave. As soon as the door shuts, she proceeds to fold the paper neatly and methodically, placing it carefully onto the desk. She's silent, but I can see from her body language that she's calculating something—or she's about to destroy me, Christian, or both of us.

My nerves rear up again and my breathing becomes shallow. This is not good. If only I could scream for Drake to come back. What happened to him protecting me from her medication tirades?

"Well, ladies and gentleman. It's my duty to tell you that I, as nursing supervisor, am making a very important change that will be effective immediately." Dolores walks slowly toward Christian's cage, her heels echoing throughout the attic on the way over.

She shifts her weight to one side and kicks Christian's cage. "Are you listening, my dear Christian?"

This can't be good, since she just found him outside of his cage.

Christian doesn't answer. This pisses her off, and she moans in frustration. I glare at him, but he doesn't look my way.

He needs to at least pretend to cooperate.

She quickly glances my way and starts walking over.

Oh, shit. Here it comes.

"Well, since you two seem to be inseparable, I've decided that you two should now share a cage. Then you can grope each other all you want. I will only have to keep track of one cage lock; that will be the main reason I give if anyone questions it, of course." Dolores puts her hands on her hips as she waits for our response.

Christian is now looking at me. He has a stunned expression. I probably do as well. We're both quiet as this new change registers.

"Well?" asks Dolores, annoyed.

We just watch each other.

"Okay, so whose cage shall be kept?"

Wow. This couldn't get any better! I hope she picks my cage, since I have the extra pins and curtains. We'll be able to hide away to plan. I better ask for the opposite from this sadistic bitch.

"Please, move me out of this death cage and into his. Sleeping in a hammock made out of sheets hasn't been fun."

"Okay, fine. Christian, you will move to the slut's cage, and that's final. I kind of like porn and it looks like she's ready for men with all her pretty pillows and curtains. I'm sure you'll be very comfortable in there, Christian," Dolores sneers, "except when

Drake visits. It is going to get a little tight in there with all three of you."

Oh, so this isn't about us at all. It's to get back at Drake.

Dolores slithers over and drags her fingernails across the outside of my cage. "You're use to sweaty bodies, right Jeannie? That doesn't bother you. You're already use to men pressing up against you, aren't you?"

"Shut up, you fat bitch! What the fuck is your problem anyway? Don't talk to Jeannie like that. You fucking make me sick!" Christian says, both hands clenched onto the bars. He catches my eye, letting me know he's distracting her.

Dolores' eyes are wild. I press myself up against the back of the cage, since I'm not sure what her next move will be. Suddenly, she storms over to Christian's cage and jerks it away from the wall, sending Christian hurling forward. Then, she pushes the cage hard in my direction, her heels slipping as the cage fights against the momentum. Finally, she gets it going and Christian rears back up and continues his ranting. She doesn't pay any attention, though. She slams the two cages together, door-to-door. Christian's opens toward him but mine stays shut. Dolores quickly grabs her keys from her pocket and reaches in my cage to unlock it.

"Get in!" demands Dolores.

Christian sits down inside his cage and pretends to resist. "Go fuck yourself."

Fuming, Dolores goes back to her desk and pulls open one of the drawers.

She then grabs something from the desk drawer and holds it behind her back as she heads toward the bars he's leaning against.

"One more chance, Christian," she warns.

Christian ignores her, laughing again.

An evil smirk is on Dolores' face while she brings her arm from around her back and immediately starts to press on something.

It takes me a second, but I suddenly realize it's a lighter and before I can say anything to Christian, his shirt is on fire at the hem. He doesn't realize it yet.

"Christian," I scream, "your shirt!"

Dolores steps back as the flame starts to lick up the back of his shirt. Christian jumps up and runs toward me. He tries to quickly pull his shirt off, swatting at the back of it. He pulls it over his head and flings it outside my cage, which extinguishes the flames. His chest is heaving as he looks at me in desperation.

Then the cage door slams shut. Dolores now has us trapped in the same cage.

"You crazy bitch, you come near me again and I will kill you, I swear," Christian yells.

Dolores turns around without a word, flings the cage toward the window, and slams the attic door so hard the sound hurts my bad ear, making me wince. I quickly move over to examine Christian's back.

"Is it bad?" he asks.

"No, no, it's not bad. Just hold still." I pick some lint from around the raw skin that extends along his lower back. It's inflamed. Once his adrenaline calms down, he's going to be in pain. "I can't believe this. You knew it was a good idea to be in my cage since I have the pins and curtains, didn't you?"

"Yes, but we can't have her thinking we're plotting. Besides, who the hell would have thought she'd set me on fire?"

22

I knew it. He's calm now and the pain has kicked in. At first, he tried to kid around about it, saying how Dolores didn't even know how to set a shirt on fire correctly—how if she really wanted to hurt him, she should have went for his shirtsleeve or hair. Now he's quiet, like he needs to concentrate on blocking out the stabbing pain. It's getting worse as time goes on. The heat in the attic is excruciating, too. Without water, I have no way of soothing the blisters beginning to cover his lower back. When he passes out from the pain, I believe it's a blessing.

* * * *

I'm not sure what time it is, but it's late. It may be around ten o'clock at night. I've let Christian take up most of the bed and am back in my hammock, clutching my car keys. The breeze is flowing in and the sky is clear with stars that look like sugar crystals. The parking lot lights are on and the palm trees are swaying in rhythm with the wind. At least it has cooled down the attic, even if only a little. My car is still in the same parking spot, collecting dust, but still the perfect escape vehicle. Now that I have the keys, I'm one step closer to climbing in that baby and getting the hell out of here. The thought of it makes me think about my mom, though I'm not sure why. The peace in the room right now is relaxing. All I can think about is getting in my car and leaving. Over and over, the scenarios are repeating in my mind. I'm here, then I'm gone. When I am, I'll never stop driving.

Suddenly, there's a loud crash. Something falls against the cage, slamming it against the wall.

Oh, my God! The attic door is open. It has to be Drake!

I scan the darkness for him, but it's so pitch black I can't see a thing. My hammock is still swinging from the jolt. Christian stirs.

"What the hell is going on? Aren't I enough for you?"

It *is* Drake.

"It's not what you think!"

The cage lunges across the attic toward the opposite window and slows before it hits anything.

"Dolores locked us in here and took the other cage out of the room," I explain, not to make him feel better, but to keep myself safe. I realize suddenly that I want to keep Christian safe too. "Look around the room! Do you see the blue cage anywhere?"

He doesn't answer.

"Then she set Christian on fire and now he's passed out from the pain. Please don't blame him, and don't attack him. This is all Dolores' doing."

I'm not sure which direction he'll come from due to the silence, but I'm sure he's not listening to me. He probably doesn't want to. Jealousy has taken over any kind of rational thinking.

Suddenly the lock on the cage door starts rattling. He's trying his key. If he gets in here, Christian—passed out and badly injured—is a dead man.

"Drake! Did you hear me? She is forcing us to share a cage. This is not our doing!"

"I knew this would happen. You'd cheat on me. You'd bring someone else in to sleep on our comforter and our pillows! So, I figured I'd check on you to see since I picked up a late shift tonight. I was right, of course."

He continues working on the lock but for some reason can't get it open.

"Christian is hurt. Look at him!"

"What the hell do I care? He's nothing but a fatheaded loser."

"I'm telling you the truth!"

"What the hell is wrong with this goddamn lock?" Drake gives up and rounds the corner of the cage, luckily toward me instead of Christian. "Prove to me what you said is true."

Prove it? How am I going to do that?

"Like I said, after you left, Dolores went ballistic. She knew it would hurt you by putting us together in here. That's why Christian is burned. He didn't want to come into my cage."

"No, I mean kiss me."

God, no! I'm going to have to, though, to protect Christian.

I hesitate for a minute, but then lean closer to the bars to find his lips, and as soon as I find them, he kisses me deeply, breathlessly. His tongue tastes like beer and his breath reeks. It's all I can do to continue. He gently caresses my face and kisses my forehead. His demeanor has changed.

"She took the other cage out of here?" Drake asks.

"Yes."

"Well, shit. She did a good number on me now, didn't she? I can't even get you two out of there."

"Christian needs a doctor. Can you help him?"

"Fuck that. Why should I care?"

"Because you're human and he was set on fire!" I snap, before softening my attitude. "At least bring some water."

He's silent for a moment, but resigns. "Fine, let me go see what I can find—including the other cage."

Drake slams the attic door shut behind him, which makes me jump. Christian stirs at last, but the movement makes him yelp in pain. He breathes in and out heavily for a few minutes until he slips back into sleep.

At least, I hope he's just sleeping.

I wish I could climb down to help him, but I'm not sure there's anything I can do. I'd just land on the mattress, which would cause it to move and probably hurt him. I'm better off waiting for Drake.

Minutes later, the attic door slams open again. The room is still dark, so I can't see. A shadow nears the cage, but the person doesn't say a word.

Now, what?

"Drake, is that you?" I ask.

No answer. The shadow doesn't move.

"Drake?" I ask again.

"No, Miss Kynde. It is Doctor Wiggins. I hear we have a hurt patient."

"Oh, thank God! Now you can see what it's really like in here. I told you we live in cages. Christian is hurt—Christian Blaylock. Dolores set him on fire to force him into my cage. Please help him," I beg, "please."

Doctor Wiggins doesn't answer, but unlocks the cage door and pulls out his flashlight, aiming it directly at Christian's back. He already knew all this.

I can't see if his face looks concerned, but the doctor exhales Drake's name and backs out of the cage.

"Drake, get this patient downstairs. He's got second to third degree burns and needs treatment immediately. I may have to send him to the hospital, but we'll see how he looks in the light. Speaking of which, what the hell is going on with the lights up here? The air conditioning is broken too? Get them both fixed, immediately."

Before Drake can answer, I interject.

"This is how it is all the time. Please get me out of here."

"Sedate her. I'm tired of listening to her ranting. You need to get these patients under better control or they'll end up controlling you. I think we've had this discussion before about Miss Kynde."

"Yes, sir," Drake replies without emotion.

"But, doctor. Please don't leave me here! I can't take another day of this," I beg. I cling to the metal bars until I hear his answer.

"Drake, do as I say."

I can't believe what I'm hearing. I reach out for my hammock and pull myself in. The reality hits me hard. Another panic attack is setting in and Drake is ready with his needle. He's not even supposed to be giving me shots. He's not even supposed to be here this time of night. I wish he would miss and just stab me in the heart. It would be quick and painless as my heart drained all signs of life right out of me. My blood would spill out onto my clothes, the mattress, and the floor, leaving a sign of me for eternity. Might as well be this way, because without Christian, I don't have a prayer.

The pain surges through my arm and within minutes, I'm opening and closing my mouth. No sound escapes. Drake comes in the cage to comfort me, telling me that he'll take care of everything—at least I think that's what he's saying. My thoughts are a jumbled mess. I shake my head to make pieces of my brain fall out—the ones that help me to care, to be cognizant. Unfortunately, it's not working. In fact, it's kind of ridiculous—like a young girl being penned up like an animal for months now in the blistering heat. I feel Drake's hand on my leg. It's warm but I can't see it in the darkness.

Here we go again. I draw my hands to my forehead, trying to stop my scattered thoughts so I can fight him, but I can't. He crawls closer. Good thing is, I'm throwing up now. Vomit runs down my shirt, onto the mattress, and onto the floor.

I've never been so glad to be sick.

23

I hate the smell of puke. Even the word "vomit" sounds hideous. Here I am, lying in it, alone. Drake was repulsed by the smell, so he left right away. Dolores isn't in yet.

Shit. The one time I do need them.

I hear a moan from the other side of the room. It's Christian in the other cage. Thank God he's okay.

I try to push my cage toward him, but my arms aren't strong enough.

"Christian, can you hear me?"

"Yeah," he replies.

A surge of relief rushes through me.

"I'm so glad you're okay!"

"Well, I'm not exactly okay, but I'm somewhat better than I was. They ended up being second degree burns, so Doctor Hell kept me here, and locked me back in this fucking cage."

"I'm so sorry. I puked everywhere so the smell is rank too."

"That's the least of my problems. Don't worry about it."

He's lying still during the entire conversation, so I know he must be in agony. At least he's back. For that, I'm grateful.

I begin removing the bedding when I'm reminded of my car keys. Where are they? I pull each elastic end over the top of the mattress but don't find them.

Oh no. Drake must have taken them back!

I sit and drop my head between my knees in despair.

I give up.

Then I hear keys drop onto the floorboards.

I peek down between the cage and the mattress. Sure enough, my keys are shining back at me in the morning sun.

"Christian! I still have my car keys!" I exclaim.

"Great. Too bad I can't move or I'd join you in your great escape."

"I'm not leaving without you."

"Oh yes, you are!" Christian replies, his voice rising. "I can take care of myself. You take those keys, jab them into Dolores' eye, and bust the hell out of this place first chance you get. Do you hear me?"

"I'm deaf in one ear, remember? That means I can't hear what you're saying."

"Jeannie!"

I don't answer.

"Jeannie!" Christian says, clearly exasperated.

I still don't answer.

I can't leave him. He's been with me almost the entire time. He's a victim too. I'll get us both out.

Dolores busts in the room like a Trojan horse, needles in both hands and a twinkle in her eye—the eye I will gouge out the next chance I get.

"Lucky day for you, Jeannie. Both of these needles are for your dearest, Christian!" I gasp as she sticks both needles into his sores at the same time and he screams in agony.

"Instead, Jeannie, you get another spa treatment special from the good ol' doc. He wants to make sure you're calmer today. I guess you upset him last night. That was probably not a good idea."

No. He can't do this to me! I'm so close to escape; I need to keep a clear mind.

I cry into my hands and my keys drop to the mattress with a clank.

Dolores jerks her head toward me. "What was that?"

My heart pounds as I search for some stellar response.

She squints while looking at me. "Well?"

"It was just my foot. It hit the bars."

"It sounded like metal."

I don't dare move to pick them up so I leave them beside me.

"Yeah. The last time I checked, bars are made out of metal, you idiot!"

She lunges toward me and I roll onto my keys and cover my head.

"That's more like it, you wuss. You should fall into the fetal position every time I enter the room. Fear me, bitch!"

I pretend to cry.

I hear her back up and sit down behind her desk. Her chair creaks from the weight and I sigh in relief. Now, what do I do with these keys? I need to get them hidden again before Drake gets here to take me to my bubble bath.

I pull myself up slightly to sneak a peek at Dolores. She's leaning back in her chair with her eyes shut. It is the same routine every morning now. I grab my keys and push them into the mattress to prevent their chatter.

"Holy Hannah! Is that puke I smell? Which one of you idiots puked in your bed last night?"

"Me."

"Shit. Now I have to clean up after you again? Are you shittin' me?"

"I peed too."

With that, she's more enraged and slams her feet onto the ground. "I can't believe this."

"I need a shower," I reply from my fetal position, still with my hands clasped around my exit keys.

All I need to do is get her closer. Maybe I can get her inside the cage or at least with the cage door open. Drake stayed late last night, so I doubt he's here yet. If she screams, no one will think twice—there has been plenty of screaming from this room and no one ever came to check on Christian or me.

"All over those pretty pillows too? You poor thing. You want me to clean those for you? Want me to wash all that sperm off from Drake too? That's probably why you peed yourself."

I give her a scowl. "No, I don't waste any of that, like you! He's always telling me how bad you are in bed."

"Jeannie, shut up," Christian warns. Good, he's lucid. Those needles must have contained antibiotics, not the normal drugs.

"Why, because I'm a better cock-sucker than Dolores?" I reply with a smirk.

Good. Now she's coming for me.

I scoot back against the bars as far as I can so I have plenty of room to get momentum behind me. As predicted, she grabs her keys and unlocks the cage door, her hands shaking in anticipation of her revenge. I stand up with one of the keys stuck out between two fingers, waiting for the right moment. Dolores tries to grab my legs but I avoid her, making her fall onto the mattress.

I quickly crawl up into my hammock. Before I know it, I'm falling down toward Dolores with outstretched arms, causing her to look up at me. The shock makes her eyes open nice and wide, and I jab my key into her right eye with one swift motion so she doesn't know what hit her. Blood gushes down her cheek as she scrambles out of the cage screaming. I squeeze by her, avoiding her hands, which are grasping for me. With one good kick—a kick that has been building up for months now—I shove Dolores into the cage and slam the door shut. Blood is now streaming down her breasts, staining the front of her crisp, white uniform.

"Jeannie!" she gurgles. "Wait until I get my hands on you!"

I grab the keys out of my cage door and run over to Christian's. He's already pulling himself up and climbing out of the cage by the time I get the door open.

"Let's go," he says with half a smile. "It's time to get the hell out of here."

I smile back and help him to the door and into the hallway. I search quickly to find the key to the attic door—every minute of delay we can buy is important.

Then I close the door behind us. I've closed the door on a chapter and I'm ready to turn the page.

Without a word, we scramble down the stairs. I pull Christian into the wall. I remember hating my first ride inside the wall, but now I feel elated to even know it's here. Christian looks at me with cautious eyes.

I lower the platform, pulling one side of the rope. We slowly inch down to the first level.

"Faster," Christian urges in a whisper, careful to speak into my good ear. "Faster!"

"I can't," I reply. "I don't want us to drop to our deaths."

Every inch is agonizing.

"They are going to find us."

When we're halfway there, the ropes squeeze tighter, causing the pulley to strain loudly and screech like a locomotive putting on the brakes.

Christian catches my hands to make me stop and listen. I look up. The door is still shut.

"We're going to attract attention with all this noise," Christian whispers.

"It'll only be a few minutes longer," I assure him and start pulling on the rope again.

"No," Christian insists. "Let's think of something else."

"Like what? We don't have time."

"Here, let me try." I let go and Christian grabs for the rope, wincing in pain as the motion pulls against his raw skin. The sound is quieter, but Christian can't continue.

He drops backwards, causing the platform to sway, ready to tip us out. My car keys fall over the edge.

Shit! Now I'm going to have to find them. I need to get a plan together—and quickly! If only I could concentrate. I'm not sure where they ended up in this dungeon of a place.

I steady myself with the ropes, but Christian is flying back and forth toward each side of the platform, barely hanging on.

I try to grab his arm. Before I can reach him, he falls off the side and I hear a thud. The platform is still swinging violently, but I continue pulling it downward, faster now. I have to get to Christian.

The sound from the platform was horrendous, but I finally reach the bottom floor and leave just enough space to jump off and find him.

He's not moving.

I whisper to him, but he doesn't respond.

At least he landed on his stomach. I frantically feel for a pulse and find one on his wrist. I don't dare move him.

As I crawl over to the half door that opens to the hospital hallway, I can see shadows passing by the light that's coming through the bottom of the door. None stop. I sit by the door to gather myself for a few minutes, watching the motion on the other side of the door through the cracks. There's not much to see, really. Not yet, at least.

"Jeannie?"

"Oh, God!" I scoot over to Christian and stroke his hair. I still can't really see him.

Eventually, he answers again. "I think I'm okay."

"Are you sure? You probably shouldn't move until—"

"Until what?" he asks, a hint of sarcasm in his voice. "Until you get a doctor?"

"You could have broken your back."

"I'm good. Really," Christian answers as he pushes himself up to a squat. "My back is still on fire, but I have a feeling I'll be worse off if Doctor Hell gets his hands on me. Let's move."

Christian crawls to the door and opens it slightly. He peers at the legs of each passerby. His breathing is labored, but overall he seems strong.

"I've been down this hallway before. It leads to the violent crazy ward and a bathroom. Drake brought me there a couple of times. That ward is not somewhere I'd like to go back to, but I guess we have no choice."

"Was there an exit?"

"I don't remember there being one. Maybe the bathroom window, but I doubt it. Not sure what would be in store for us if we go to the left."

Christian is holding his head in his hands.

"You okay?"

He better not be having one of his episodes. Right now, he needs to be okay.

"Yeah, just trying to concentrate. I don't know what to do."

"Maybe we shouldn't do anything. Maybe just stay here for a bit. We might have a little time before—"

A piercing siren goes off and scurrying feet begin heading to the left, away from the violent ward. Luckily, we're sheltered somewhat from the volume and my ear isn't in agony.

Christian leans over. "Guess they noticed we're gone."

24

We sit in silence, watching the activity through the cracks around the door for what feels like an hour, paralyzed without a plan. We're going to have to wait until my medication wears off before we have any prayer of escape. Christian is sleeping with his head against the door, still sore from the burn and fall. I can slowly feel panic rising in me the longer we sit, but I know trying to leave is useless at this point with Christian basically out of it.

"Hey," I whisper and nudge Christian's shoulder. "You alive or what?"

He lets out a short grunt.

"We have to get out of here soon. I'm telling you, Drake will find us here."

"You go ahead. I've got zero energy. Get out of here while you can."

I sigh.

"Jeannie, don't worry about me. Just go now and find help. You can come back for me later."

"I can't leave you, Christian."

"Why the hell not? You have to. I'm counting on you to get me some help. It isn't going to do any good if we're both caught. Can't you see I'm in misery here? You need to go get an ambulance or the police. Just go."

"No."

Christian drops his head.

"If I leave, I'm never coming back. We leave together."

"Goddamnit, woman! You are crazy if you don't take advantage of this situation before it's too late."

"I don't think you're hearing me. I'm not leaving without you. That's final, Detective. You would do the same for me. You have done the same for me—you had the pins from the curtains and saved me from Drake instead of just hitting the road."

One of the shadows stops at the door and begins jiggling the handle. We both wait in silence, alarmed. The sound of something pushing against the door begins with a few crackles coming from the wood. It sounds like it could splinter any minute.

I look to my right for another escape, but instead of seeing another door, or tunnel or some other route, I only see eyes.

I cover my mouth to catch my gasp, as I leap backwards toward Christian, causing him to hit his back on the wall.

Christian winces, trying not to scream out, protecting his back with his hand.

"I'm so sorry. Are you okay?" I whisper, but before he can answer, I turn my head back to the eyes, which are still staring at me. "Do you see them?"

"See what?"

"Look over there on the other side, past the platform."

I feel Christian's whiskers on my head as he turns to look. His arm is on my shoulder, tugging me over so he can get a clearer view.

"I don't see anything."

Suddenly, there's more pounding on the door, startling us both.

I still see the eyes in the same spot.

"You don't see the eyes?"

"Where?"

"Over there? To your right."

Christian's breathing is labored from the pain, and he can't seem to get past it to concentrate on anything else.

I guess this is up to me, then. It's weird that the eyes haven't really moved. I mean, this person knows I'm looking at him or her, but he or she doesn't budge.

I move forward but am stopped by Christian's arm around my waist.

"No way are you going over there."

"I have to or that person may come after us. If he or she doesn't, those people outside the door will make it in. We can't just sit here."

"Yes, you can. I just need a few minutes to regroup, and I'll take care of it."

"You're in no condition to do that. Besides, what if it's Drake?" I whisper back even quieter.

"It's not. He'd already be over here. Maybe someone else is hiding here, too."

More door pounding ensues.

"We are so screwed," I resign. "Either they're getting in or the eyes are coming for us."

We move away from the door together against the wall. Christian is careful not to touch his back. I watch the eyes in case there's any movement from that direction, but they stay put. The door pounding is intermittent but hard. I burrow my head into Christian's chest like a child. He wraps his arms around me instinctively. After a few seconds, I feel safe despite the chaos and the mounting danger that surrounds us. I feel safe despite the pain and emotional anguish I've endured here, despite my agony over seeing my new car waiting for me on a daily basis, despite my rage over Todd and my dad.

You even feel safe despite the fact that you left your mother alone to die in that car!

Wait. What did I just think? I left her? Did I?

I pull away from Christian and sit forward to try to remember. What was I doing before that phone call from the hospital about Mom? It's something I've been trying to remember for years. Why did my dad hate me so much over it? Why have I hated myself?

I remember being with her. We were laughing. She was driving. I remember the interior of the car. It was maroon with cloth seats. It was evening but still light out. We had dance music on, and she was swaying back and forth in rhythm. I loved those times when it was just the two of us, when we would just be silly and Mom acted half her age. We were coming back from Orlando where we spent the day shopping at the outlet malls. My new leather purse was by my side. Mom pulled the car over on the shoulder of a deserted street. It's foggy but I can remember our conversation on that day.

"Come on, Jeannie. You drive now," she urged.

I couldn't wait to learn to drive. When I was younger, I would sit behind the wheel for hours and pretend I was driving. The thought of the freedom was tremendous.

"Won't I get in trouble? I'm only fourteen."

"There's no one around to know and nothing to hit. You'll be fine," she reassured.

I slid into the driver's seat, and she helped me adjust the mirrors and the steering wheel. She even turned down the radio so I could concentrate.

"Now, just put your foot on the brake and move this into drive," she said. "Don't take your foot off the brake until I tell you to."

I followed her instructions, nervous, but excited.

"Okay, now move the steering wheel to the left and slowly let go of the brake until the car starts moving. Then straighten out on the road and push gently on the accelerator."

Again, I followed her instructions perfectly. Suddenly, I was driving! I was a natural—so she said—meant to drive.

I looked over to watch her excitement while I was driving. Her smile quickly turned to concern though as she glanced forward then back at me. It was only a split second in time, no more than that. I glanced over the steering wheel too and the road which was straight less than a second ago was now gone, and I stormed forward going full speed into a pond.

It was a deep pond. We sunk even faster—in a fraction of a second. Cold water quickly filled the car. Mom was frantically tugging at my seatbelt, but it wouldn't release.

Before I knew it, we were both under water, holding our breath. Her white blouse was floating around her like she was an angel. Her eyes were wide, scared more that death was coming for her daughter than with fear for her own life.

Before she gave up, she unlocked my seatbelt with the last ounce of energy she had in her. I floated upward to the air pocket near the ceiling of the car and took in my first breath.

It was the first breath of life without my mom.

I took two deep breaths and quickly swam down to release her seatbelt, but couldn't find it in the brown, murky water. I tried over and over to save her—even tugging at her, trying to get her loose, but I couldn't. She died and I couldn't even see her. It was cold. She had no one holding her. It was my fault.

I wanted to die too. I even stuck my head back in the water trying to drown myself, but my mind wouldn't allow it. All I could do was swim out of the car and to the shoreline where I sat, dazed.

I couldn't believe this reality, so I created a new one. At that moment, I believed I was nowhere near this scene. I had no idea whose car that was in the middle of the pond. I didn't go to the mall that day. Mom was working. I never drove.

And I walked home alone that night.

25

"Oh, my God!" I choke, and throw my head into my hands, sobbing.

"Hey, you okay?"

"No!" I cry, but I'm not answering his question. I'm yelling at myself to not allow this memory back in. I want to forget again.

Christian covers my mouth so I don't draw attention from the people outside. I let him, though it is the last thing on my mind right now.

No wonder my dad hates me.

More memories flood back including how the police figured out I was driving and left the scene of the accident. It was not just any accident. It was the accident that killed my mom. They took pity on me because I was a minor. They kept asking me about the details, but I just denied it. As far as I knew, I was nowhere near that scene.

Further door pounding jerks me back into reality.

"Why am I remembering this now?"

"Remembering what?"

"My mom's death; the worst day of my life."

"I thought that was the day you came here."

Not anymore.

Suddenly, the door breaks inward. Patients start flooding into the wall through the broken door and crouch in front of us, some with folded arms.

I don't care. I deserve whatever comes. They can beat me. They can kill me.

Whatever.

"Jeannie, back up," Christian begs and pulls my arms and legs toward him.

"Let them do whatever they want to me, Christian. I'll save you," I say with a soothing smile. "I want to save you."

"Very nice, but shut up. You deserve to get out of here, too."

"I deserve nothing!" I yell harshly at Christian.

"What the hell is wrong with you?"

I don't answer but look back up at the crazies. They're still just crouching there like they're waiting for an answer to a question.

"Get the hell out of here, you fucking crazy idiots!" I scream as loud as I can.

Christian looks at me in shock and tries to put his hand over my mouth, but I swat at him and wiggle out of his control. Squatting, I stare back at them and move forward, challenging them.

They don't show a hint of fear or budge for that matter.

The eyes are also moving now, getting closer.

"It's the girl!" one of the patients exclaims. It's the same patient that was obsessed with me from the crazy ward. They lunge at me, but before I can spout anything further, Christian pulls me out into the hallway and we're running toward the crazy ward. The double doors that are normally shut are wide open and a scattering of patients are roaming around here and there, not paying attention to us. Something's happened—something other than what I have done to Dolores—and it is chaotic. We pass the bathroom and into the main gathering area of the circular wing. Last time I was here, I was hiding behind my attendant. This time, I'm in front.

I don't care if someone hurts me.

Christian is running as fast as he can, but wincing also from his burn. He hobbles into the room and collapses onto one of the benches. No one is manning the nursing station.

"Come on, Christian!" I demand. "I remember the way out now."

Patients are now erratically heading toward us from behind. They don't seem to have any idea of where they are going, until they see me.

"The girl is back!" one of them yells. "She's contaminating us!"

They lurch forward in unison, eyes fixated on me. One of them is peeing himself. Another is licking his teeth back and forth as he concentrates on moving.

I grab Christian's arm to pull him up, but we're stuck. Patients are now entering the other set of double doors too, stopping our advance.

"Holy shit! What the hell do we do now?"

Christian doesn't answer. He's barely able to stand.

The patient who was urinating himself is standing in front of me now. A puddle has formed on the floor next to him. Out of desperation, I stamp on the urine, causing a splash onto the legs of several patients including mine. Then, I jump on it again, splashing more. The patients are repulsed, moaning.

Then, one of the patients tries jumping on it too. This causes a frenzy of jumping patients, who are now giddy and laughing like hyenas. This turns into frustration over sharing the puddles and soon there is pushing, causing several to fall into each other and onto the wet floor. This distraction was all we needed.

We pass through the double doors on the other side of the wing and make our way to the doors that I know will take us outside. These are the ones I entered when I was with Drake. We clamber to them and push on the door bar, but it doesn't budge.

"Going somewhere?"

It's Drake.

Thinking quickly, I say, "Drake! You're here for the late shift again?"

"Yeah, the shifts have been crazy lately."

"I'm—I'm glad you're here," I lie. "Please, for the love of God, help me get out of here. The crazies are loose."

He smirks and punches Christian in the back.

"He's hurt!"

"Really? How the hell did he get all the way down here then?"

His eyes are red and irritated and the veins in his neck are twitching.

I'm scrambling for what to say next to try to resolve this situation but all I can think to do is try to convince him.

"He was helping me get away. If you're angry with anyone, it should be me. What do you think is best at this point? Us running away together?"

"Oh, like you care about that! You weren't thinking of me when you were pushing on those doors just now, were you?" Drake screams in my face.

My breathing grows heavier, but I stand my ground. I glance over to Christian and he's not moving. Beyond Christian, I can see patients starting to return back to their rooms, as well as the nurses. All is starting to return to normal. I can't fight it.

My eyes fill with tears as I turn back toward the doors and stare out of the windows.

We were so close.

"I'm sorry. We're going to have to go back now. I saw what you did to Dolores. There'll be consequences for that, you know. You're lucky you didn't blind her. It's just a puncture wound."

I sigh, knowing it is hopeless, and let Drake handcuff my wrist to his. He calls to one of the other attendants to take Christian to the medical ward. Then he drags me into the bathroom on the opposite side of the crazy ward.

Drake unlocks the handcuffs. "You stink. Get cleaned up. You've got fifteen minutes before I'm back."

As he leaves, he turns back to me. "Oh, yeah. You are nothing but a patient to me now. There will be no more special treatment. No more, ever."

He slams the door on his way out. I head to the bathtub. The water fills it quickly, and I wash my legs and let the water drain. Then I fill up the tub and am submerged in a few minutes. The coolness of the water feels soothing against my skin, as my arms float along the top of the water. I splash it, watching its ripples and currents from my hand movement.

The composition of water is amazing if you take time to think about it. It can support the weight of an arm, yet it's broken with the easiest of force. It's all about bonds if I remember correctly from my chemistry class—broken bonds. Force breaks bonds. Energy breaks bonds, like the energy of a car speeding into a pond. My weight wasn't enough to push against the bonds to get to my mother. The water pushed back at me. It didn't allow me to get to her. Why couldn't I break those bonds when I can easily break them with my hand now?

Tears drop into the water.

I watch them break more bonds so easily.

I can almost see her in the water—her reflection from that night. Her white blouse is flowing. Her hair is surrounding her. I splash at her reflection and break the bond between us, just as it was that night. I don't deserve to have even the memory of her.

Dad was right. No wonder he wants me in here.

The door opens and Drake enters. "Crying over me?"

I breathe out. "Yes."

"Okay, come on then," he says, forgivingly.

* * * *

My cell is all decked out now. The pillows are clean. The comforter and sheets smell like fresh air. The curtains float on the gentle breeze from the window.

I guess they had to clean up all the blood from Dolores' injury.

The room is still, other than the breeze. Dolores and Christian are gone. Drake left as soon as he locked me in. The attic temperature is even bearable this evening. This is now my home.

I'm caged, just as I should be. My dad would be glad.

No, you're not going to think about Mom! Keep thinking of other things.

I pick at my nail beds, trying to remove the dirt from beneath them.

I hope Christian is okay. Hopefully he's getting the treatment he needs. Between the fall inside the wall and the punch from Drake, he can't be well. His cage is back on the other side of the room. I hope he's in it by morning. At least I'll know he's safe. I wonder what our punishment will be. Hopefully, it won't be more shock therapy.

Don't stop thinking.

I wonder what day it is. I remember Drake mentioned going to see Fourth of July fireworks, but that was some time ago. That had to have come and gone. I can't remember seeing fireworks, but I don't remember why not. Was I too drugged?

Evening falls. The room grows darker, and I run out of things to distract myself. No one has come yet, as I sit and wait. The more I wait, the more I think about Mom—the darkness of that night, the black water, the numbness in my arms and legs from the cold. Despite it, I dove down numerous times to release her. I'm not sure why I could see them, but her eyes were open—dull. I hate that I wasted so much time trying to save her. I should have swam out of the car right away and gotten help. The most abhorrent, unforgivable act though, was my inaction after it was clear I couldn't save her. I walked home and told no one. I denied it. I walked in the house and had conversations about my day with my dad and my brother, revealing not a hint of trouble or Mom. She was, at that point, belted into a drowned car.

"How could I have done this?" I cry aloud. I can't hold back the tears now, and I mourn for her with deep sobs that have never surfaced before—ones from the gut that make me heave uncontrollably. "Why didn't I go get help? Why? How could I have just forgotten it? Even when I went to see her at the hospital, my mind didn't allow me to remember, yet I've been obsessed for years on what I was doing the exact moment of her death. It's always followed me."

Now I know why.

The denial was fierce and unbreakable. My mind blocked out everything during the two hours it took me to walk home. Even when the cops rapped on our front door two nights after her death, it didn't faze me. They questioned me for hours because she wasn't in the driver's seat and they found a second purse in the car. It still had the new tags on it from the mall. Others told them they saw us together there. I denied all, even passing a lie detector test. I truly believed I had no idea who the driver was or how Mom ended up in the pond. It seemed like they didn't believe me but they never pursued it more. They had to have known.

Even as I stared at her in the casket with her discolored hands positioned awkwardly as if still clenched to the seatbelt, I didn't remember why she was lying there. All I could think about was how different she appeared, making me question if it was really her. Her hair was combed from a side part instead of in the middle, and her lips and cheeks looked bloated, distorting her face. The face I stared at since I was a baby—the one I saw die—was not the one I saw in the casket.

"I'm so sorry, Mom!" I sob. "If you can hear me, I'm so very sorry!"

I stand up in my cage and stare at the night. The palm trees sway under the parking lot lights. The clouds move in the moonlight. The whisper of an easterly wind wraps around my mind, releasing the years of memories into the attic. They're there in front of me, memories pass by minute after minute, floating in the air and then vanishing. Somewhere within this depression, a hint of recovery is occurring, and a longing to know more.

Some questions are light.

How could I have forgotten this and why is it coming back now? What actually triggered my memories? What kind of a person denies it for years?

Some are dark.

What kind of a person leaves her mom under water? There must be something wrong with me. They should just lock me up and throw away the key, just as Dad said.

"Maybe they should sterilize me like they did to Brianna while they're at it," I suggest out loud to the vision of my dad.

My hands are suddenly clammy and my mouth goes dry the more I think about this suggestion. I instinctively look over to the patient charts that are scattered on Dolores' desk.

They wouldn't!

26

If there was one thing my mom taught me, it was to seize the moment. Unfortunately, I haven't been doing a very good job at it. This is no exception. Here I sit, frozen in fear, but wanting to go over and find my chart. It may be my only opportunity to find out what's in store for me since I'm alone right now. The nagging concern over getting caught has won out for the past hour. I'm already screwed with the punishment that's on my way for busting out Dolores' eye, so do I want to exacerbate the situation?

Come on, you coward!

I muster the courage enough to peruse underneath the mattress until my fingers land on the balls of three pins just waiting for me to pick the lock. If Drake comes, I'll hear him before he reaches the door, if I keep my right side turned toward it.

The lock separates easily, and I gently run on the balls of my feet over to the desk. It's so nice to be coherent. I shuffle through the chart names quickly until I find mine. Scrawled on the outside tab is written, "Jean Kynde: Admitted 6/3/16."

I sit in the chair to read every last word in my chart. Well first off, I see from the newspaper lying on the desk that today is the second of September. I've been in here for about three months now. Luckily, the fog from the medication only allows me to remember a few weeks of the ordeal.

There are several pictures of me stapled to the left side of the chart. There's an attractive picture of me drugged up with eyes half open on the day of admission. There's another one of me drooling, strapped on a table. There's even one of me sleeping with my mouth open during hydrotherapy. Similar descriptions are written about me as there were for Christian in his chart.

I already know my hair is brown and I'm allergic to penicillin. I clench my jaw when I see my father's name listed as next to kin, but quickly skip down to the diagnosis.

"Post Traumatic Stress Disorder," I read aloud, "and Paranoia."

Are they on crack? This is ridiculous. Any excuse to lock me up in here, right Dad?

The doctor recommends a treatment of hydrotherapy, some medication I can't read, and shock therapy as needed. He's scrawled here that my prognosis is "good."

That's encouraging. I'm going to recover from something I don't have? A more accurate diagnosis would be "panic attacks caused by emotional abuse."

I keep reading.

"Future Treatment: sterilization, as approved by parent."

I slam the chart shut.

He can't do that! I am an adult! There must be a mistake. I open the chart again and peruse the rest of the papers. Sure enough, there's a signed release; however, it's my signature. How can that be? Thinking back, I remember the pile of papers I signed the first day. This one must have been in there too. I'm sure my dad was in on it, and I'm sure he wanted to take away any chance of my conceiving.

If I don't get out of here, there will be no babies in my future.

I lean back in the chair and throw the chart onto the desk. How can this be happening? It's not bad enough I have to deal with being treated for diagnoses that are totally bogus, but now I have to figure out a way to prevent myself from being sterilized against my will! I'm going to end up another corpse that's just shuffled around at the whim of some insane nurse.

I pull out Christian's chart to see if I can find any more information on him.

The diagnosis for him is schizophrenia. This can't be true either. They're just trying to cover up the deceptive business they've got going on here. I'm sure my dad is paying them a pretty penny to keep me locked up.

The doctor recommends a treatment of shock therapy and another medication of some sort. His prognosis: "Permanent Institutionalization."

My God. If I don't get him out of here, he's never going to leave! This place is covering up Brianna's death!

My heart's racing but I'm holding back a panic attack that's beginning its ugly course. I've got to keep going before someone comes in. I pull out my chart again to see if I can find some kind of incriminating evidence. Perhaps some telephone conversation Doctor Wiggins had with my dad planning this whole thing, or some other clue in this medical mumbo jumbo.

I don't find any correspondence from my dad, but I do find something else very interesting. At the bottom of the chart, buried behind endless accounts of my craziness, is a copy of a receipt dated June 3, 2016; the day I was kidnapped. It's a Deadwater Manor receipt for $5,689, made out to my dad for one month of services rendered to me in June. On the bottom of the page is also a copy of a check. It has his name and address on the top left and it's signed by him. His involvement is now confirmed.

27

I throw the chart onto the floor and walk over to the window that overlooks my old neighborhood. It feels like forever since I was riding my bike along the long, winding road to my favorite beach and Todd. I can see the blinking red lights on the smoke stack from the power plant tonight, signaling an alert that something is wrong.

I slowly put the chart back on the desk. One of the pictures falls on the floor and I quickly pick it up and look at my modeling debut in hydrotherapy. I'd be the perfect sponsor, looking all relaxed and passed out. I chuckle at the thought, but at the same time, I find it sickening. I clip the picture back in place and suddenly notice a hand on one of the wall levers—a male hand. I examine it closer: the fingers, the watch, the excessive hair on the forearm. I know this hand. I've known it for years, especially when it would hold my hand when I was younger and steady me the first time I rode my bike. This is the hand that used to comfort me every time I was upset over someone at elementary school making fun of me. My dad was there for me then. I guess he's been here for me now, only in a more demented and inexcusable way.

He participated in my hydrotherapy? He's been here?

I look back at the cage and the room. This whole thing is staged. Who puts patients in attics much less cages anymore? This is 2016, for Christ's sake. I thought I read somewhere that cages were outlawed a long time ago.

Then it hits me. Oh my God, this is to get back at me for Mom! Dad knew about my involvement in Mom's drowning, and now I'm facing the consequences.

I've got to get to my car—now!

I shake the ornamental bars that cover the lower half of the window to see if they're loose, but they're tight. I run to the other window and do the same, but they too won't budge. I try the door, but it's locked.

What about any attic doors along the eaves? I quickly examine each side, but there are no other escapes.

Okay, what do I do now? I've got to get out of here before they come back. I can't let them sterilize me!

Desperately, I search the room for any other options, but there aren't any. My only option is to protect myself, which will be hard to do again once I'm drugged.

What other choice do I have?

I look out at the sky for answers, or maybe a memory that will help me figure this out. I wait.

The window—

I examine the back window that overlooks the crazy patient wing. This type of window is familiar, like my bedroom window. I yank on the top windowpane, and it moves down slightly. I pull down harder on the upper pane. It's tight but it's moving.

Oh God, please! I get it down all the way and pull myself up onto the windowsill. I hope I can fit through here!

The night air is stale with the pungent odor of decaying plants from the swamp out back. I can hear the millions of crickets that have talked to me night after night. On this night, I'll finally be able to meet them. A hoot owl is calling me, welcoming me.

Wiggling through the opening, I grab the bars below me. When I pull out my legs and swing them down, I rip my hospital gown along the hip. My feet land on the roof below. I duck past the windows along the side of the building and look for options to get to the ground. A few feet away are the scrolled lattice bars that surround the pink room—the telescope room. I cringe at the thought of the moment when I saw Todd with Melissa, but keep going. I scurry over, trying not to fall off the roof, and grab onto the closest scroll I can find. Peering into the pink room, I see that it's empty. The lights are bright and the chandeliers sparkle as they move ever so slightly. Quietly, I use the ornate bars to climb down to the ground. My feet touch the grass and it grabs hold of me, steadying me.

I look around as I hunch down and move slowly around the building and away from the crazy wing.

God, I hope no one sees me!

I round the corner to a smoking area outside of a wooden service door and head toward the front of the building.

I'm heading to my car now. I'm finally getting to my car!

Once I reach the front side of the building, I peek around the corner to see if anyone is out front. I don't see anyone, so I hesitantly make my way around the hedges, keeping low. My car is only across the entry road now. I look up to see if I can find my attic window, but I'm not sure which one it is. Besides, they must not know I'm gone since all is quiet. I hear no screaming alarms.

A mosquito bites me on my thigh, but I just let it. That pain is nothing compared to Dolores' needle.

Okay, just get moving. What would be the worst thing to happen? You get caught and are in the same position as before? It won't be any worse than what you've endured so far. If I make it out of here, though, I'll be free of all the spa treatments and drug therapy. I'll be free of Drake and the "apartment." I will at last be free of the life that was determined for me.

I'm giddy with excitement by the time I reach the Vug. I slide my hand along the smooth yellow surface and head toward the driver's side.

The car door is locked. I have no keys.

Oh my God, what was I thinking? The keys! They're in the wall. I forgot to search for them!

I start to cry in frustration, ducking to get out of the line of sight from my window.

Okay, don't freak out. Just think, Jean, think! Where is that wall space from here? It's just outside of the crazy wing in the hallway. I'd have to go back past the pink room to the double doors near the crazy wing. Then, I'd have to get through the crazy wing and through the double doors on the other side, near the bathroom. Who knows if I could even get into the door that leads to the dumbwaiter.

I bite the nail on my pinky, contemplating.

What if I just leave without worrying about the car?

They'll bring dogs. I've heard them before.

What about Christian? I'd rather leave with him than have to come back.

So now what? I have to go back.

Do I want to go back to the room or try to get to the dumbwaiter? I'd set off the alarms trying to get in the back door. I guess my only choice is to go back to the room.

I rush back to the side of the building and up the ornate bars to the roof. It looks dark inside the attic. A cool breeze kicks up behind me, making me reach for the window.

Inside, all is where I left it. The attic is dark and quiet. The curtains float on the breeze. The smell of cooling boards and old metal bars lingers in the air. I'm sitting and waiting in my cage with the door locked, angry with myself for coming back.

So much for carpe diem.

Sorry, Mom.

28

I'm awakened by the sound of a cage door and immediately open my eyes, feeling hopeful that maybe they're coming to let me out to go home, but it's not my cage door. It's Christian's. Two attendants I'm not familiar with are settling him in with pillows to hold onto, so he can lay on his side and off his back.

A breakfast tray sits outside my cage. Drake is watching the attendants. He must be back on the day shift. I can't keep my eyes off Christian. He really is handsome—dark hair, strong chin, symmetrical features that are set perfectly. I'm so glad he hasn't had shock therapy today. I wonder how Dolores is making out. She must be in agony this morning.

Good.

Christian looks over at me and grins like he's glad to see me. He's more relaxed and in less pain. Once the attendants leave, Drake pulls my cage door open and slides the breakfast tray in without a glance or a word. He's probably still mad I tried to leave with Christian yesterday. Little does he know I tried to leave alone too, and I will continue to try to leave until they kill me.

"Thanks for breakfast."

He doesn't look back. He simply locks me in and heads out the attic door. My urine bucket is full. I wish he had cleaned it out. At least he didn't give me a shot.

That makes two days now of coherency.

"Hey, Christian. How's it going? It looks like your back is

191

feeling better, despite Drake's tirade yesterday."

"Yeah. Not sure what they did, but I'm feeling much better. Some kind of salve they're putting on every four hours. I don't remember much after Drake found us. Did he bother you afterwards?"

"No, he didn't stick around here. In fact, no one did. You won't believe what I found."

Christian repositions himself. "What?"

"I'm in line for a future sterilization."

Christian's face grows concerned. "What? No fucking way! What the hell is up with this place? No way is that happening to you. I won't let it," he insists.

"I need to get out of here before they do. In fact, I think I have a way if we can find the car keys."

"The car keys? You just had them, didn't you?"

"They're gone. I lost them down the damn dumbwaiter shaft yesterday. We've got to get them back."

"Why didn't you tell me yesterday?"

"I don't know. You were out of it, and it wasn't like you had a flashlight handy," I reply, irritated with his question. "The point is, I know where they are and we've got to get back there."

"Okay, they've got to be on the floor then. Can you get Drake to take you back to the bathroom again? Maybe you can sneak out and look around in the shaft."

"Probably not without acting like a slut, I can't." I cringe. "He's so mad at me, I'll really need to go over the top to get him thinking with his dick like usual, instead of his brain."

An awkward silence ensues. Christian stares at the floor. I wish I knew what he was thinking about. Finally, he looks up at me.

"No. Let's think of something else. We need to get out of here before he has another chance at you. What did you mean before about knowing a way to get out of here?"

"Well, last night I broke out through the window over there and made it to my car, but I didn't have my keys, so I came back and—"

Christian interrupts. "You did what? Why in the hell didn't

you make a run for it?"

"I've heard dogs before. Getting away on foot is not an option. They'll find me. No way am I swimming out back with the gators in the middle of the night. Besides, I didn't want to have to come back here to get you."

"Me? Jeannie, if you get out, don't you ever come back for me ever again. You just run and don't look back. Do you hear me?"

"You're not my dad, so quit acting like you are. You're not the only reason. I'm not leaving without my car."

"You can't be serious." Arteries are starting to bulge along his neck.

"Calm down. It's not good for you to stress out right now. Just relax. They don't know I have the upper hand. Now I just need a plan. Are you with me?"

Christian sighs but says, "Yes."

"Alright then. I'm glad we understand each other."

It's nice to have someone care about you, or at least appear to care about you. Maybe this is some kind of testosterone-driven competition with Drake. I don't know.

Christian smirks. "Okay, then, woman. I guess you are in charge."

"Don't you forget it," I say with a laugh.

Dang his smile is killing me.

We grow quiet again until finally Christian speaks.

"So, what was going on yesterday when you almost did some ass-kicking on those patients in the shaft? Why were you so out-of-control all of a sudden?"

Oh God, he would remember that.

"It was the whole situation—you being hurt, losing my car keys, the darkness, the eyes," I lie.

"I didn't see any eyes."

"They were there!" I answer sharply.

"Okay, okay! No need to get testy, woman." Christian pauses, then asks, "So, why were you talking about your mom then? You said something about her death. Did she pass away?"

I close my eyes and wish he didn't remember my words. After a long pause, I answer. "Yes. She's gone."

"I'm sorry. That must be hard. How old were you?"

"Fourteen."

"That sucks. Wow, sorry."

"Yeah, well I've been living with it." My mood is growing solemn.

"Do you want to talk about it? It is obviously bothering you. How did she die?"

I try to form the words to say I killed her, but instead I say, "She died in an automobile accident. She drowned."

"I bet that's been hard on you and your family. She drove into a lake or something?"

"Into a coastal marsh, actually. It was hard to see the bend in the road. She couldn't get out of her seatbelt." Tears are welling up in my eyes. I can't look at Christian at this point. I can't let him see the pain.

I can't go on. Instead, I lie down on my side.

"Jeannie, I'm sorry. Don't be sad."

I don't want to talk to him anymore. I'd rather just stare out the window and wallow in my grief. How can I tell him that her death was my fault, when I can't even fathom it at this point? I don't even know if I can really, deeply admit it to myself.

The room is silent for what feels like forever, when I hear a familiar movement in the attic. The same rusted wheels I've heard several times before, only this time, I'm comforted by them. Despite his injuries, Christian is coming over.

I turn over. He stages his cage next to mine so we are face to face.

"It's okay to be sad about it, you know. She must have been a good mom."

Tears are streaming over my nose and onto the comforter. I wipe my eyes, but I'm gushing like a fountain at this point.

Christian offers his hand through the bars. I smile and take his kind gesture. The feel of warm human skin—that is not expecting something in return—is energizing.

How did two normal people end up in this situation?

"Can you talk about it now?"

"Don't think so."

"Okay. Let's plan your escape then."

"*Our* escape," I correct.

"You are a stubborn one, Jeannie."

"What can I say? It's a family trait. So, do you have any escape ideas to add to my brilliant plan?"

"Maybe I can get Dolores to take me to the bathroom when she's back. I could whore myself out. I'll take one for the team."

"Eww, gross. Don't *ever* do that. How about if we become so unruly, they have to put us in the violent crazy ward?"

"That's not an option. It is too dangerous for you in there. I could probably handle it though."

"What, you think just because you're a detective, that you're the better choice? You think I don't have survival skills?"

"Well, I am trained in this sort of thing. I could have left here ten times already."

"Oh really? Then, why didn't you?"

"Because someone had to go and keep getting herself into trouble; spitting food at Dolores, hiding behind curtains, mouthing off to doctors."

"Oh, that? That's just minor stuff," I tease.

"Well, seriously, we need a plan."

* * * *

The next morning, Drake barrels into the attic with an arm full of newspapers and a coffee mug in hand, and heads straight for the desk. He didn't seem to notice as Christian and I quickly unlock our hands. Christian looks at me, concerned. I wonder what Drake's going to do when he notices our cages together. All I can think to do is pretend to sleep.

He slurps his coffee on occasion as he flips a newspaper page. I peek over to Christian, and he has his eyes closed too.

"So, lovebirds, how has your morning together been? Get any, Christian?"

I roll over. "Very funny, Drake. Can't you see we're in cages here?"

"That's a minor problem for you both, evidently. Lucky for

you, Dolores is on medical leave for a week or so. You'll have to deal with me now. I'm in charge." He shuffles the papers. "I guess you could say I've turned over a new leaf. No longer am I going to be your boy toy, Jeannie. I'm beyond your spells. Things are going to go my way now."

What does this mean?

"Since I'm back on the day shift, I'm going to set you both up on a strict routine. Following breakfast, you will both be taken down to the bathroom to cleanup. Then you will move on to your respective treatments: hydrotherapy for Jeannie and shock therapy for Christian. Both of these will end about the same time—one o'clock. You will then eat lunch with the rest of the patients in the main dining room, followed by game time in the pink room. After which, you will be taken to dinner and returned to your cages by seven o'clock at night. On occasions when you need to see the doctor, you will skip game time and report to dinner afterward. If you do not fight me on this or cause any trouble to other patients, we can refrain from medicating you. However, at the first sign of trouble, I will not hesitate to use the syringe and needle I always carry in my pocket."

"We're not traveling by wall shaft are we?" I ask, pretending to cringe.

"Why, yes, Jeannie, we are."

I roll back over and wink at Christian.

This couldn't get any better.

29

After a week, the daily routine has made life better on many accounts. First of all, we're out of the attic during the hottest times of the day. Second, I can search for my car keys in the shaft. Best of all, it's providing me several ideas on getting out of here.

Christian's head is another matter. Though it's not as swollen as in the past, it still causes him bouts with headaches and disproportionate swelling around the temples. It also causes other patients to stare in the dining hall. We've become the focus of crazies I'd rather not attract. Several of them just want to help, but others think it's voodoo. Today, the attraction has been so bad, the staff already brought Christian back to the attic. I had to go with him. This left me no time to sneak out to the dumbwaiter.

"I'll be back to bring you two to dinner," says Drake as he closes the attic door.

Christian is in his cage across the room and winces, breathing rapidly with pulses of pain. His hands and feet are also twitching. I haven't noticed that before.

"You going to be okay, Christian?"

"Yeah," he manages, "I just need a couple of hours."

"Okay, well just let me know when you're ready to talk about our escape."

Over and over, I run scenarios through my mind, trying to figure out the best way out of this place. I look for my car keys in the elevator shaft every day, but don't see them in the darkness, even when we open the door and the light comes in. They must be underneath the elevator platform. Day after day, I've been paying attention to routines—patient routines, attendant routines. I've watched the attendants taking care of patients and where they are stationed. The main thing I've noticed is that there's no compassion for any of the patients. Most of them are treated as if they have the plague. Attendants often wear gloves and masks. Only on occasion do I hear laughing in the game room where they play with select "calmer" patients.

The pink room is still my favorite. It reminds me of days when the place had history. The ornate mantle above the fireplaces and the white scrolled metal work along the outside porch gives away its age as being designed sometime in the 1920s or 1930s. I haven't been back to the telescope yet. It is just too painful to think of at this point, but I know I must. Only this time, I'll be using it to figure out the best path out of here, whether on foot or by roadway.

An hour or so goes by and Christian stirs, moaning.

"You there, Jeannie?"

"Yeah, I'm here."

"We need to get out of here soon. I'm not sure if I can go through much more of this treatment. It hurts just for them to place the electrodes on my head now. I've never had it every single day like this."

"I'm sorry. It must be awful."

"What are you conjuring up over there? Do you have a plan yet?"

"Yes, as a matter of fact, I do. Tomorrow, it's the normal routine, and I scope out the roads and other areas around our building with the telescope in the pink room. On the way back up in the dumbwaiter, I'm going to pretend I'm having pain or something and fall off when we're maybe five feet off the ground and find my car keys. Tomorrow night, we're out of here."

"That sounds good to me. Maybe I'll catch a lucky break and stay away from shock therapy so I'll be more coherent during our escape."

"Just pretend to be unconscious in the morning. Maybe they'll let you stay in here. I can take care of the rest. Don't worry."

"I have every faith. I just wish I could be more help."

"Keep yourself out of the fryer and that'll be help enough."

Suddenly, the attic door flies open and Drake enters with two dinner entrees, kicking the door shut behind him. He distributes them to us in silence and sits at his desk with his paper.

Christian's having difficulty opening the tray with his shaky hands.

"So, Drake? Is Dolores ever coming back?"

"Soon," he says from behind the paper. Seconds later, he folds it halfway. "Don't get any ideas about stabbing her again."

"If I had half a brain cell left, I might be able to think of those again. Being you're taking them away from me, you should have no concerns,"

Drake snickers and returns to his paper. "Good."

I wonder if I can seduce him into the wall and get this over tonight.

"How come you never come visit me anymore?" I ask.

He breaks the paper down again and looks at me. "Don't even."

"Don't even, what?"

Christian stops struggling with his tray and gives me a glare.

"Come on, I've been in here for hours. Can't we just get away for a little while?"

Christian is now alarmed. He's staring me down, as if that'll change my mind.

Drake turns to Christian and says, "What could you possibly have in mind? Maybe a blowjob? I could use one of those today. Maybe I'll take you up on that offer."

Christian pulls himself up against the bars. "Jeannie, don't!"

"I do find her attractive still, Christian, don't you?" Drake prods.

"Drake, enough of the messing with him. Take me away somewhere. I never did get those July fourth fireworks."

Drake stands up and stretches his back. He walks over to my cage and unlocks it. "Come out then."

I crawl out and ask for his help up. He obliges by pulling my arms hard enough to make me fall into him.

"Oh, wait, my dearest Jeannie. Let's not get carried away just yet," he says with a smirk in Christian's direction.

Christian starts bellowing my name, but I walk out with Drake to get my keys back.

As soon as we leave the attic, I giggle and run down the first flight of stairs to position myself near the dumbwaiter. Once there, I turn around and wait for him.

He lunges for me, kissing me passionately and pushing up against me.

"I want you so bad, Jeannie."

"Me too, but someone might see us."

"I've got an idea." He slides me away from the wall, then into it, closing the door behind him. "How's this?"

The shaft is as dark as always. It's hard to see anything.

"Let's go down some of the way in case anyone hears us and opens the door. They won't be able to see anything then," I suggest, as I'm tugging at his shirt.

He lowers us down about three quarters of the way. I can see the light from the bottom door now. I can't see him, but I can hear him wrestling with his clothing. I crawl backward from him to the edge of the platform.

"Get over here, Jeannie. I think you owe me something."

He pulls me back over to him, hard, plants his hands to the sides of my head and brings his penis to my lips. "Come on. You know what I want. Make it good."

I pull my head back. "Wait. I want to show you something first—you know, make this special."

He lets go. I back up and start pretending to wrestle with my clothes. "Hold on," I say as I try to find the edge of the platform with my toes.

Here goes nothing!

"Drake!" I scream as I fall over the side of the platform and land abruptly onto the floor.

"Jeannie!"

The fall takes my breath away, but I immediately start searching for my keys. Moaning loudly to cover the sound of my search and to make it sound like I've been badly hurt, I reach out in all directions praying for a miracle.

"I'm coming, Jeannie!" I can hear the squeak of the platform being lowered down. I have only seconds.

I crawl around the bottom of the shaft, but can't find them. Drake is inching down closer now.

Where are they? Shit! I've just blown my one great plan—for nothing.

I frantically search, but they're not here. Now, all I can do is pretend I'm hurt and hope I get another chance like this. I lie back down in an awkward position and moan Drake's name. The bottom of the platform is getting closer. I look around as a last ditch effort and that's when I see the eyes again.

I jerk back and scream.

"Oh my God, Drake!" This time, I'm not pretending. I scream out to Drake to hurry up. When I look back at the eyes, they're gone. Something makes me reach out toward them. My hands land on my keys; they were reflecting back to me the whole time. Relief floods through me and I fall backwards, inches from the bottom of the platform. It's not stopping!

"Drake, stop! You're going to kill me!"

I'm suddenly pinned beneath the platform with the weight of it—and Drake—beginning to suffocate me.

It forces me to breath out, but then, I can't breathe back in. Panicking, my arms and legs start involuntarily pounding against the platform to let Drake know I'm below him.

I've only got seconds, and he's not moving the platform up fast enough.

So this is how I die.

30

Thank God my mom's here to greet me. She's still in her white, flowing top and her eyes are open, only this time there's life in them. She reaches for me. I follow her to an open field that's filled with yesterday's breeze, reminding me of when I almost escaped from the Manor. My mom's expression is calm, soothing. It is as if she's trying to tell me that she'll protect me, but this is fleeting. Within seconds she looks concerned and grabs my arm harder, forcing me forward. I try to look behind me to see what she's pulling me away from, but I can't manage it. She's yelling at me to wake up, to wake up now.

"Jeannie! Wake up!"

I gasp for the air I couldn't take before. I frantically look around the room for my mom, eventually focusing in on the face in front of me.

Damn, it's only Drake.

I reach up for him to lift me up. He does. I heave in and out until my breathing becomes less labored, and my heart begins to slow down to normal. The weakness from the ordeal is making my body shake uncontrollably. Drake holds me until it passes, and I become quiet.

"Hold on. Let me get you out of here."

Drake opens the door and the light from the hallway is bright enough to fill the shaft floor. I clench my keys that are still in my hand, sliding them into my pocket before he notices.

"Come on," he says. "I'm taking you to the infirmary to get you checked out. I can't believe I almost crushed you. I'm so sorry! I couldn't get that stupid platform under control and it just went plummeting down."

* * * *

Before I know it, I'm on a steel table and a nurse is checking my pulse. She writes something down in the chart and takes my blood pressure.

"You're normal, perfectly normal," she says with a smile.

Wow, is it nice hearing someone actually say that to me.

"I know."

She frowns and turns to talk with some guy in a white lab coat. He glances back at me and a chill runs through my body. It's Doctor Wiggins. I look down at my pocket to make sure my keys aren't showing.

"Miss Kynde, how are you doing, my dear?"

"I've been better. I found out suffocation isn't fun."

Drake turns around at this point and walks over.

"It was an accident," he assures.

"Oh, I'm sure Drake. Of that, I have no doubt. So, Miss Kynde, do you care to join me in my office for a while? You're fine to leave now."

"I think I'd rather go back to my cage."

"Oh, come now. You'll chat a spell."

My muscles tense from the thought of it.

Doctor Wiggins turns away and says, "Drake, bring her."

Drake helps me up and guides me out of the door. I'm still somewhat unsteady and I pause every few steps to steady myself. Halfway up the hallway, a patient jumps in front of us, yelling, "Ah huh! I know you!" He then stares at me, as if he's trying to read my mind. I remember him. He's the same patient from the crazy wing that kept staring at me when I used the bathroom for the first time. A foul odor fills the air around him.

Drake pushes the patient out of the way and pulls me by my elbow.

The patient continues to yell behind us. "I've seen Miss Florence Nightingale before, yes I have! I have seen her! Long brown hair. She was on the roof!"

I quickly turn around in shock and look at the crazy man.

"Yes, yes, that's right! Florence had brown hair like hers and she was crawling on the roof! I saw it. I did!"

I turn back to Drake and say, "What's he talking about? I don't belong with these crazy people."

"I know, I know. Come on. He's harmless."

You're an idiot.

We enter Doctor Wiggin's office, and I sit down on the same patient chair I always do. At least this time I am way more coherent than I have felt any other time I've had the pleasure of his company.

"Miss Kynde, you almost had a really bad accident tonight. Why were you in the dumbwaiter shaft?"

"Drake takes me that way sometimes."

"It is pretty dark in there. Did you fall off the platform?"

"Yes."

"How did that happen?"

"I was unsteady and fell off the side. I'm lucky it wasn't too high up. Apparently, a lever got stuck and Drake almost flattened me. I saw Mom though, so that was good." I cringe as soon as I say the last part.

"You did what? You saw your mom?"

"Well, I was half dead, so I figure she was there to take me, but then Drake brought me back."

"Oh, okay. Uh huh. So, what was your mom doing?"

"She was saving me from this place, trying to get me out of here. I think she can see what you're doing to me."

Jeannie, shut up! Just shut up!

"Uh huh," he replies, writing in the chart at the same time.

"So, let me ask you a few questions for a change. Why are you going to sterilize me, and why is my dad paying for it?"

Doctor Wiggins quickly removes his glasses. "What are you talking about? There are no such plans."

"Oh, don't give me that, Doctor Wigs. I saw the chart. Look

toward the back. You know, behind all the minor stuff like my blood pressure and pulse."

Doctor Wiggins glances down at the chart, but refuses to lift even one page.

"I'm sure you're misunderstanding the handwriting. This is a prime example why no patients are allowed to review their charts. You, Miss Kynde, are in violation of hospital code, which means I obviously have not medicated you enough. I will be increasing your dosage."

I slump in the chair. "You might as well. All I do is sit in a cage."

"Miss Kynde, I've told you before. There are no cages at Deadwater Manor. That would be against state policy, and I would never allow it. Please stop spreading rumors that aren't true. I'm hearing it from the other patients now."

I slam my fist on his desk. "You've seen them yourself!"

"I did no such thing. You were apparently delirious. If you don't keep your mouth shut, I will put you in solitary, and *that's* not a very nice place. You've had it easy thus far. Drake, it's time for Miss Kynde to go back to her room."

Drake rolls in the mini cage and I squat inside.

There are no cages here. Yeah, right.

"Put her outside for a minute. I want to speak with you privately."

From outside, I can barely hear their conversation. It is something about Dolores and the medication and keeping me away from patients. Then Doctor Wiggins says slightly louder, "You and Dolores are responsible to make sure the sterilization procedure happens by the end of the year. You're a team and I expect you to follow through with my orders. Doctor Kynde wanted this pronto."

Drake doesn't reply.

"Are you having second thoughts, Mister Dymond?"

The door opens.

"No, doc."

My mind reels. I watch Drake's expressions for any signs of reaction to Doctor Wiggins' request, but he acts like it's just another day. He drops me off in the patient dining room, stating that he'll be back with Christian. I take the opportunity to view the outside through the telescope, following each road as far as I can see, examining vegetation and tree lines, calculating the distance to Deadwater River, looking for signs of people, traffic, boats. Everything and anything I can think of for a half an hour, when I hear Drake come in with Christian. He seats him at a table along the windows and I join them.

Dinner is served in silence. I sit directly across from Christian. Drake sits next to me.

I look over to Christian with concern. Drake pulls out his newspaper, so I mouth silently to Christian, "Help me!"

Christian mouths back, "What?" and glances back and forth between Drake and me.

I point in the direction of Drake behind my palm. "Doctor told him to get me sterilized soon!"

Christian mouths back, "What?"

Drake quickly folds down his paper and looks suspiciously at the both of us. We both resign to looking at the tablecloth. He returns to his reading.

"He wants me sterilized soon," I repeat.

Christian's expression is now angry. "He wants you terrorized?" he mouths.

"Sterilized!"

"What?"

I sigh in frustration.

Keep your cool, Jeannie. You need to remember he can't read lips as well as you do.

"You two are too quiet," Drake says from behind the paper. "Just talk to each other."

I cup my hands around the bridge of my nose and slide the sweat off my cheeks. Then wipe the sweat from my forehead.

"What, still no word? You know you two want to talk to each other." He looks over the paper, exposing the wicked smile on his face. Then he focuses on me. "Whoa, Jeannie. You're really sweaty today—or should I say glistening?"

I roll my eyes.

He looks me up and down. Drake is calculating his next move. I can tell from his stare.

Once he snaps out of it, he leans over toward me and asks, "Want a nice, cool bubble bath?"

Christian stiffens.

"I have some really nice bath salts that will make you silky smooth. They'll freshen you right up," Drake continues. I can sense some nervousness on Drake's part.

If I take him up on this, he gets a chance at me in the tub. If I can fight him off, I get a chance at freedom.

I know this place now. I know which doors are unlocked and when. I know where the patients and attendants will be, and I know how to sneak around, just like I used to at home.

Can I overpower Drake somehow? How will I get Christian free too?

"I think Jeannie is fine. She doesn't need a bath."

Drake scowls at Christian, but quickly returns his gaze to me. "Let's let Jeannie decide. What do you think, sweetie?"

I wish I could think faster. I'm just going to have to wing it.

"I think it sounds nice."

Drake returns a smirk to Christian. "It's settled then. While I'm helping Jeannie, you can sit in the cage outside and listen, Christian. I'm sure you'll find it very memorable."

Christian pounds his chained hands on the table and starts to get up, but Drake quickly controls him and forces him inside the cage I arrived in. He then chains my hands to the cage and leads us down the hallway to the bathroom.

"What kind of bath salts are they?" Christian asks.

Drake unchains me. "I think these are pomegranate."

He winks at Christian, making Christian spastically pull at the bars and scream for me. Drake answers with the swift stick of a needle and in seconds Christian is reduced to inconsequential babbling.

This is going to be tougher than I thought.

I get lucky and escape from Drake's grasp. I take the chance to whisper to Christian.

"Don't worry. I've got it under control."

He keeps spelling M-D-M-A over and over, whatever the heck that's supposed to mean. Drake grabs me and forces me into the bathroom. He orders me to undress and draws the water, adding a generous amount of bath salts from a glass mason jar.

I keep myself wrapped in a towel and walk over to the tub. Steam is rising from the water.

"I thought I was getting a cool bubble bath. The water looks hot and there aren't any bubbles. Also, I'm not getting in this water with you looking at me."

"That's fine. I'll wait behind the curtain until you're finished."

That's weird.

I wait until he can't see me and slide into the tub, holding the towel up to block his view on the way in, just in case. The water is hot, causing goose bumps on my arms. I sit still as I soak, not wanting to draw any attention from Drake. He is unusually quiet.

I can feel the grit of the undissolved bath salts on the bottom of the tub, so I gently move them around. The water feels soft, but the smell is not pomegranate. In fact, it's really sort of a chemical smell.

It's probably some cheap version, knowing Drake. I laugh at the thought of Drake going into a bath soap store with all the frilly decorations and smells.

Suddenly, I just can't get enough of the rubbing sensation on my legs. I've been rubbing my palms along my calves and it feels extremely good. It's kind of hard to explain, actually, but it feels like someone is gently touching my leg with a feather, almost tickling it. Then I rub my fingertips along my forearm and am surprised—even alarmed—that this too feels so wonderful. In fact, I want more and more of this feeling. It's the best I've felt in a long time.

I wonder what it would feel like if I touched my breasts.

I move my fingertips to my neck and glide them down to between my breasts, sending a surge through me that causes me to moan.

I look up, and Drake is there.

"Hi, beautiful."

"Hi, handsome," I answer, as I slowly move my fingertips up

and down my chest.

"I brought you a present," he says. The light from the window is distorting his face, almost as if he's unable to keep up with his movements. It looks like his body is lagging behind. "I think you need some music."

I'm not sure what kind of music is playing, but I know I want to dance. Besides, Drake would like that.

Drake moves closer and his ring clanks against the tub, causing another wave of excitement to pulse through me. He kisses me deeper and longer than ever. The pleasure of his touch is making me pull him into the water. He too is now moaning with my touch along his back, after he pulls his shirt off, and I'm feeling warm—very warm.

Finally, I just can't take it anymore, and I grab his hand and pull it to my breast, asking him to touch me. He obliges, sending me into even more of a pleasure state, and causing me to lift my breast up to his mouth. I just can't get enough.

After a few minutes, he pulls me from the water and says, "Dance for me, Jeannie."

I wet my lips and stumble into the curtain, wrapping myself up in it, pretending to be shy. As the music plays, I move with it, allowing a breast to fall out of the curtain here and there. Then I dance for him without the curtain or inhibitions. I've never felt so free.

Drake makes me drink some water and lets some of it drip on my chest. Then he licks my neck with his wet, cold tongue. I shiver from the temperature change. Everything he does gives me pure pleasure and all I want is more until I finally beg him to have sex with me. There's a lag in movement from him, but he follows me to the floor.

All I want is to feel good again. I *have* to feel good again.

31

Suddenly, the music stops. In fact, it sounds like the plug was ripped out of the wall.

"Drake, what the hell are you doing?"

Drake yelps and jumps up, grabbing a towel to cover his genitals.

"Can't you keep your hands off this slut?"

I laugh.

"What the hell have you done to her? Shit. Are you trying to get yourself fired—or thrown in prison?"

Dolores pulls the curtain back and looks into the tub, sniffing the air. "I know that odor."

The realization causes her eyes to pop out of her head, making me laugh all the more because she almost didn't have one eye to pop out because of me. Maybe if she had a glass eye, it would pop out and roll on the floor.

I double over in laughter and lie on the floor, curled up in a ball, still rubbing my leg. I'm completely out of control.

"Goddamn you, Drake. You've gone too far! I'm calling the police to drag your ass out of here." I pick up my hospital gown and put it on.

She's ruining my fun.

Christian also enters the bathroom with a scowl on his face. Between the two of them, you'd think we were committing adultery.

"Are you okay, Jeannie?"

Why the question? Of course, I am!

"Yes, I am. Why are you two interrupting our good time? Just leave us alone, Christian, go back to your cage where you belong, and Dolores, get the fuck away from me. Where's Drake?"

I see him across the room drying his arms, smiling.

Christian walks over in chains. "Jeannie, you've been drugged. The bath salts had ecstasy in them. I tried to warn you!"

Christian's face is distorted, but I tell him that I don't care, because I've never felt this good, and that's all thanks to Drake. I try to reach Drake, but Christian grabs me from behind and drags me out of the bathroom, with the nurse right behind us.

"Back in the cage, Christian," she demands. "The last thing I need tonight is you running free."

I feel my hands being attached to the cage, but I have my eyes closed in an attempt to maintain the ecstasy effect. Nothing has ever felt quite like it.

Dolores escorts us back to our cages and locks us in, separately. I crawl into a ball and rub my legs with my hands. The effects are wearing off, making me agitated.

Why did she have to ruin all the fun?

"Are you okay over there?" Christian asks.

"No. You ruined my fun. What were you thinking?"

"Drake wanted to rape you. Is that what you wanted? He tricked you."

I can't even comprehend this thought in my current state of mind. Frankly, I'm not sure if I care. If I had the opportunity, I'd go back to the bathroom in a heartbeat and bang his living brains out.

What business is it of Christian's, anyway? He's such a prude.

I roll over instead of responding.

* * * *

I'm jerked into consciousness by the clank of the cage door. It's Drake with breakfast and it smells grotesque. There's no way I can eat right now. I lift my head to look at him but can't manage to say anything due to my chapped lips.

How did I become dehydrated overnight?

I force myself to drink the water on the tray but eat nothing. Drake is watching me from outside of the cage.

"You don't want to come in? It is our place, right?"

"I've been forbidden. That's my punishment for last night. I'd be in jail right now if it wouldn't bring on an investigation of the whole hospital."

"I liked it! I want more!"

Christian interrupts. "You're still feeling the afterglow of the ecstasy. Try to ignore it, and him for that matter. Why the hell are you even in this room anyways, Drake? Where is Dolores?"

"I don't need to answer to you, Christian. Mind your own business over there. I'm sure Dolores will be here soon and you two can resume your relationship. In the meantime, Jeannie needs me."

He reopens the cage door and crawls in next to me, sliding his arm around my waist. "Last night was outstanding, wasn't it?"

"I've never had anyone touch me like that before, Drake. You're wonderful." I reach for his hand and snuggled into his arm.

"I'm serious," Christian warns. "You need to get away from him. Don't let him take you to that bathroom again, please. I'm begging you!"

"Shut the fuck up!" Drake shouts. "You are the poorest excuse for a man I've ever seen. This is none of your business."

I snuggle in more, feeling comfortable and safe.

Drake whispers in my good ear, "He's just jealous, Jeannie. He wants you all to himself. You made the right choice, though, because I know how to make you feel really good. Remember that. You think he'd go to those measures for you?"

I shake my head.

"You need to stay away from Christian, or he'll keep you from experiencing any of that ever again. I'm your husband and I know what's best for you. He doesn't."

"I know," I reply, feeling drowsy.

"Want to try it again later this evening? I have more bath salts left. This time, I'll lock the door so we're not interrupted. We'll go after dinner, so you can eat before we play. You need to keep up your strength, right?"

I smile and nod. He rubs my arm and it still feels a little euphoric. I kiss Drake's hand and Christian slumps down in his cage abruptly, punching the mattress on the way down.

Maybe he is jealous. Whatever. It's his problem.

* * * *

Drake wakes me up again sometime later with a kiss on my cheek. "I have to get back to work, but I'll be back so we can pick this up later. Maybe this time, we'll actually be able to finally *have* sex. I want you so bad, Jeannie; you have no idea. I'm your husband and I should be satisfied at all times. Do you understand?"

I keep my eyes shut and don't respond. I'm not feeling like going anywhere, actually. All I can think about now is how doomed I am. Am I actually going to have a life caged up in this place forever? I guess so, because I'm never getting out of here. I'm never going to see my brother again or Todd or the beach or anything that matters to me. Instead, I'll be tortured by my constant longing for the car I'll never drive away and never-ending treatments and abuse of this place. God, this sucks.

Drake leaves and I turn over so I don't have to watch him walk away, especially because I still feel a bond with him somehow. It's so sick. The cage door clanks again, but I don't hear him lock it before he leaves. I sit up to see it's unlocked. I look over to Christian, who's watching me.

"He didn't lock it," I say.

"Yeah, I know. What's up with that?"

"I don't know."

"How are you feeling?"

"Confused, tired, but mostly bummed. He wants to take me back to the bathroom tonight."

"We've got to stop him. You can get out of here. Go for it— now!"

"How am I supposed to do that?"

"You'll figure it out on the way. Just get out of here. Do you still have your keys?"

Shit. My keys. I pat my pocket.

"Well, how do you like that? I still have them." Excitement begins welling up inside me.

Could I really get out of here?

I turn to my side and feel around for the pins.

"What are you doing? Go now, before he comes back!"

"I'm not leaving you, Christian."

"Goddamnit, woman. You're going to make the same mistake as last time! If you had listened to me then, you'd be out of here already. Just go. I'll be fine."

Tears are welling up in my eyes. Where are the pins? I scurry around the mattress, digging for them.

"Jeannie!" Christian cries, in desperation.

I ignore him and keep searching. Finally, I find two of the three.

Christian's lock is a challenge. I've tried the pins every which way, but the damn thing doesn't budge. With Christian harping at me to go and the threat of Drake coming back, my hands are shaking so bad I can hardly hold onto the pins.

I can't handle another panic attack.

I stop and look past Christian toward the window. The sky is an inviting purplish blue tonight with a dusting of scattered clouds. It looks beautiful against my car windows. I check for the keys in my pocket, a talisman to give me courage.

Okay, come on. You can do this!

I return to the lock. Within a few seconds, it drops open.

Christian quickly lunges out of the cage door and throws open the attic window. It's a tight fit, but he manages to climb through the top window and waits for me to do the same. I jump up, and am halfway through the window when I hear the attic door open.

No, not now!

I peer through the window hanging upside down and see Drake heading toward my legs. I squirm faster, trying to get through before he reaches me. Christian grabs my shoulders.

Before he can pull me through, I feel hands at my feet and

legs. He almost pulls me back into the attic, but I kick hard, knocking Drake down. I manage to quickly make it out, almost sliding down the roof and bringing Christian with me. He grabs my arm and lifts me back toward him on the other side of the window from Drake, who is looking at us in disbelief. He catapults himself to the upper window, but his frame is so large, he can't fit through. He'll have to go all the way around. We need to beat him to the car.

We follow the same way I went the last time until we're in the bushes across from my car. This time, I have my keys. There's no sign of Drake, so we sprint to the car, throwing ourselves into the front seats. I put the keys into the ignition. I pray while turning the key, but the engine doesn't turn over. I try again and again, frantically.

"Are you fucking kidding me right now?"

Christian looks back and sees Drake coming.

"Come on, let's make a run for it."

We clumsily fall out of the car and run through the row of trees in the entryway as fast as we can. My legs are on fire before we're out onto Deadwater Drive, but I keep going anyway. I look back to see Drake turn around and run for the main entrance.

"Oh God," I mutter, "he's getting the dogs, I bet!"

We continue to run down Deadwater Drive until I see a vacant lot. "Christian," I yell, out of breath, "let's swim across the river!"

"Are you sure?"

"Yes!"

We run across the sandy lot that's been cleared for housing, stumbling through the uneven terrain and head down to the river. A small island of trees separates us from the bank on the other side.

"Is it low tide?" I ask.

"I have no idea, but we have no choice now. Hold onto me if you need to."

Christian throws himself into the water and hits bottom quickly. He stands up. The water is only knee deep.

"Hurry!"

I climb down to the bank and toward him.

SANDIE WILL

"Shit, the dogs! You've got to go faster. Come on!"

My legs run faster than the rest of me and I trip into the water. Christian helps me up and we run through the water toward the trees. My teeth are grinding down on each other as I follow Christian, hitting uneven river bottom hard with uneven steps. Suddenly, Christian disappears into the water.

Where is he?

I abruptly stop and look up and down the river to see if a current has undercut him, but there's no sign of him. Then, as fast as he disappeared, he bobs up, swinging his head to shake off the water. "It's the channel," he announces. I sigh in relief. I swim toward him and we head toward the trees. The deeper water is dark and cold, sending shivers through me. It's creeping me out actually, because God knows what's in this water. There could be gators, snakes, spiders, water bugs—you name it, it's in here. I can't think about that though. We must make it to the trees.

Christian maintains the lead, but I can see he's getting more and more tired. His adrenaline must be wearing out. We hear the dogs getting closer. I've never seen them, but they sound like Dobermans or pit bulls snarling and barking. I look back at the riverbank, but they're nowhere in sight. Quickly, I pass Christian and help him to the tree line.

"Come on. They shouldn't be able to smell our scent through the water, but we need to get out of their view," I say.

We quickly run onto shore and into the underbrush, falling into them to hide. The dogs are now across the bank, barking at the water. Dolores and Drake are standing with the other hospital personnel around them.

"What do we do now?" I whisper.

"Crawl," says Christian.

We crawl through to the center of the island that is only thirty feet wide or so. The trees are tall and dense, blocking the sky. We're only a few minutes away from darkness.

"I think we should swim over to the other side and make a run for it before they do," I suggest. "There's a park over there where I used to hang and it's close to my home, so I know my way around."

"After you, woman."

Halfway over, I can hear helicopters. Spotlights are paralleling the shoreline on the other side of the river. It won't be long before they're on this side.

"Come on!" I urge.

We run through the sand and up into the park shelter where my birthday party was months ago. The shelter is covered but open on the sides. We stop to assess the best route.

"We need to follow the park road to the entrance, then hit Baillie's Bluff Road to the north to my home. There's lots of trees and vegetation along the roadway we can hide in."

Christian stops. "Wait, so you want to go back home? Are you crazy?"

"You're right. What am I thinking?"

The helicopters pass overhead with spotlights falling all around us.

"Wait," Christian says as he holds my arm. "Not yet."

I scan the park but only see open areas with playgrounds and other pavilions. There isn't much coverage on the way to the park entrance.

"Stay in here for now. Don't bolt on me."

"They're going to find us."

"Not if we stay under cover. It's just the helicopter right now. If we hear dogs, it's a different story. For now, just hold on."

"Okay," I say, trying to keep the hesitation from my voice. "Once it's gone, maybe we can make it through the small line of trees through the playground. At the end of it though, there's nothing—not one tree. It's risky."

Christian looks toward the playground, but doesn't say anything. Then, I see the doublewide trailer near the park entrance. It's the residence of the park ranger, Pete Larkis. He lives there with his wife, Tammy, and little girl, Alaina. I've known them since they moved in three years ago. I wonder if he would believe this incredibly unbelievable story or if he'd turn me in. We've had numerous conversations through the years about school, the history of the area, my family roots, and his trouble with trespassers on park property after dusk. He mostly complained about teenagers, but I wasn't one of them. Maybe

Christian could talk him into providing us shelter, if I can't.

"We need to get to the ranger's home, over there to the right of the entrance. I know him, and I think he'll let us in."

"You sure? I don't want him calling the police on us just yet. I need to call my office in the morning and get things settled before we deal with that. You think he'd let us stay for the night?"

"I don't know for sure. It's definitely a risk, but I don't see what other choice we have but the woods or the shoreline, neither of which are a good option. If we could just get him to believe our story, we might have a chance."

"I don't know. He must have some officer friends. My station is south of here in Fort Myers, so it's not like I know anyone at the police station in Tarpon. If he calls them, we could be sent back to the Manor until they get it settled."

"What other option do we have?"

"Shit if I know."

The helicopter is now scanning the shoreline south of us.

"It's now or never." I look up at Christian for some kind of approval. He hesitates, so I just make a run for it. Christian reluctantly follows.

I make it to the tree line, and then run short spurts into the playground, hiding under slides to make sure the coast is clear. Finally, we reach the house and rap on the door.

Pete answers, but doesn't open the screen door.

"Pete? It's me, Jeannie Kynde. Do you remember me?" He turns on his porch light to see me better.

"Why, Jeannie, yes I do. What brings you out here this late? You know I don't like trespassers on County property after dark."

"I know, and I'm sorry, but I need help. This is Detective Christian Blaylock. We've both just been through a horrendous ordeal. Can we come in?"

"Well, I don't know. What kind of ordeal are you talking about?"

"Just hear me out, okay? You and I have known each other for a while, and this is going to sound strange. I was admitted to a psychiatric hospital against my will by my father, and I need to hide here so they don't find me."

Helicopters are making a sweep through the park again.

"Hide you? Well, I—"

"Please, Pete! They're coming back. You know I'm not crazy. I've never been trouble. You know my dad is a jerk who would do something like this." I look back toward the shoreline and see one of the helicopters heading toward the playground. "Please help us!"

"I'm a detective, and she's telling the truth. I can show you my credentials once I contact my office in the morning," Christian finally says.

I can feel the wind of the helicopter kicking up my hair.

Pete looks out at the helicopter's spotlight that is across the field just beyond the playground. He looks back at my pleading eyes.

"Oh, okay," he concedes, and opens the screen door.

"Oh, Pete! Thank you! You've just saved our lives."

32

Pete is suspicious of my story. I can tell by the distant look in his eyes that he's planning on doing some Internet research to check it out. Who could blame him? I'm not sure I'd believe such a horrific story either. Who in their right mind locks away their child and pays to have her sterilized?

Luckily, he knows about the accident with my mom and how my dad has shunned me since then. He knows Dad hates my hearing loss too and thinks I am embarrassing to the family.

I'm hoping he'll just give me one night to get myself together, so I can confront my dad tomorrow. There's no way I want to try to do that tonight. I'd rather have him scared and apprehensive over my escape, the details of which I'm sure he'll find out soon enough.

"Can we just stay one night, Pete? I'd just like to be rested before tomorrow."

Alaina peeks around the corner of the whitewashed panel hallway and smiles at me with her long locks of blonde hair. Tammy is standing near the kitchen counter looking less than thrilled.

"I could get fired for this, you know," Pete replies. "You guys are like fugitives or something, right? I don't know about this."

Christian leans forward in his chair. "Pete, I promise you. I will not let them fire you over this. Look me up on the Internet. I'm Detective Christian Blaylock with the Fort Myers Police

Department. My picture is online."

I'm not sure I want Pete to do that. Christian probably looks way different than he did back then. The swelling of his head is mostly gone, but he still has patches of hair missing near his temples and on the back of his head.

"Okay, you can stay, but only until morning."

His wife throws a spatula into the sink, disgusted with him. She storms down the hallway and slams a door.

My heart calms, and I smile at Christian.

Finally, we're getting a break.

* * * *

Pete makes up the couch and chair for us to sleep on and disappears down the hallway. It's a piece of crap couch, but it's the best piece of crap I've slept on in a long time. Christian is already asleep in the recliner with his mouth hanging open.

It didn't take him long.

I'm still on edge with the helicopter's relentless search of the area. The beat of the propellers is becoming more distant with time though, and I relax more.

I may never fully relax.

Tomorrow's eminent confrontation with my dad won't be enjoyable, that's for sure. I look forward to seeing Rick, though. I'm sure he'll be glad to see me too. Wait until he hears what Dad's been up to. It'll probably set Rick off into a rage.

"You still up?" asks Christian.

Startled, I jump with his question. "Christ, you scared me."

"Sorry. You okay?"

"Yeah. I'm just thinking how to approach my dad tomorrow."

"What do you mean?"

"He only lives down the street. I'll go to my house tomorrow and confront him."

"I don't think that's a good idea. He could have you re-committed. It'll be better once I talk to my department and get the situation under control first. Then, I'll go over there and arrest his ass."

"I can handle this myself."

"Jeannie, you can't be serious. You know what he's capable of. Besides, he knows you've escaped already."

"Exactly. I hope he worries about how I'm going to make him pay for this all night. Revenge is sweet."

"I mean it. Let me get back-up from the station and go with you, okay?"

"Goodnight, Christian," I say with a sigh. Then turn over so the conversation will end.

This is family business. There's no use arguing. I will go see Dad alone tomorrow, period.

* * * *

It was a hefty walk, but I'm finally standing in front of my house again. I never thought I'd see this day after being imprisoned against my will at the Manor.

Am I correct in thinking that my sentence began with a calculated walk down the hallway on the night of my birthday? Or had he been arranging this long before then?

Little did I know then what was coming. I could never have guessed I would be locked away for months in a cage, drugged by a nurse, seduced by an attendant, and treated for a mental illness I never had. Despite all that, I feel powerful right now. There's really nothing Dad could do or say to strip me of any dignity at this point, since I basically don't have any left. The only good thing that happened from the whole ordeal was meeting Christian, who managed to escape, too. For this, I'm grateful. Of course, I did remember my mom's death, too. It's finally out of my subconscious, and now I'll have to come to terms with it. At least I'm moving on.

I walk to the front door, which stands proud as if it's holding up the entire weight of the house. The place looks the same as always, with flowering pots on the front stoop and black shutters dressing each window. One would never know the darkness living within these walls. I'm about to expose it.

Should I knock? It's funny. Why should I even have to ask

myself this question? It is still my home—or, at least, my legal address.

My stomach sinks and every blood vessel in my body feels jittery as I slowly open the door. Who knows what my dad will do once he sees me. I know one thing, though. He won't be elated, welcoming, or compassionate.

The foyer is empty, as is the adjacent main living room. This isn't anything new though, since most of our time was spent upstairs in the loft or bedrooms since Mom died. I climb halfway up the stairs and peer into the loft, but there is no one in there either. Maybe he's in the kitchen. I know he has to be here, because I saw his black Lexus in the driveway. I round the corner to the kitchen on the main floor, but a movement catches my attention in the den.

Get ready, Jeannie. Here we go.

I take a deep breath and enter.

Dad's desk is in the same location with the same piles of papers and the same old cigarette smell. The room is dark; the world shut out by thermal curtains that flow onto the floor and are tied at the waist. There in the burgundy leather chair sits my brother. I never expected he would be here since I didn't see his car.

"Rick?" I ask, astonished.

Rick jerks his head upward, startled by my voice.

"Jeannie? Wow, is it really you?" He immediately jumps up and heads my way.

"Yes, it's me. I'm so happy to see you!" I rush over to greet him. His hug is warm and welcoming.

"I've been so worried about you! I'm so glad you're okay. Where the hell have you been all these months?"

"Dad didn't tell you that he had me locked away at Deadwater Manor?"

He stares at me, no expression on this face, as though he's trying to process this.

"He was going to try to have me sterilized. What the hell did I do so badly to deserve all of that? I had to do hydrotherapy, shock therapy, you name it."

"You're sure it was Dad?" he tests, hesitantly.

"I know it's hard to believe he would go so far, but yes, I'm sure. The doctor said he arranged it, and I saw from the receipts that he paid for it all."

Rick grabs his temples in the heels of his hands. "He could never do such a thing."

"I saw the evidence! He *did*. You don't believe me?"

"It's not that. It's just, well, he really did love you. He just couldn't show it. He wouldn't have you admitted into some psych hospital and leave you there. Come on, that doesn't make sense. Where did you run away? You took your car and drove off by yourself. Dad was here with me the day you disappeared."

I lean forward onto the desk and clamp my hands on two reams of paper. "He sent me there to see Aunt Lesley. Instead of bringing her out to see me, they drugged me and took me to an attic where they kept in a cage. I'm not joking. You, of all people, know Dad *is* capable of such a thing."

Rick backs up against Dad's chair. He looks annoyed. "Do you want some lunch, Jeannie?"

"Sure, but later. Is he here?"

"No, he's not here."

My heart drops. "Well, where the hell is he?"

"He died two months ago of a heart attack," Rick says matter-of-factly.

"What?" I grab onto the desk to steady myself. Piles of papers fall to the floor. My heart begins to palpitate, and I feel short of breath immediately. "Oh my God, are you kidding me?"

"No. They found him on the den floor. In fact, you're standing in the exact location he collapsed."

Rick turns and walks out of the room without looking at me. I jump back from "the spot" and stare at the floor.

He's gone. Wow.

I don't really know how to feel about it. Part of me is sad just because he was my dad. Another part of me is sad because I won't have the opportunity to confront him. I've heard somewhere that you should always resolve differences before someone's death, so it doesn't go to the grave and fester in your head for the rest of your life.

I guess it's going to have to fester. Wow. I can't believe it.

Still in shock, I carefully step around the floorboards that held my dad during his last breath, as if they are sacred, and pick up the papers on the floor before heading out of the room. A straggler piece of paper falls from the pile and onto the floor, landing on the sacred spot.

Are you fucking kidding me? Why can't I have any goddamn luck? Months of hidden anger rile up in me and I suddenly feel desperate.

"You mean to tell me that you hide me away for months and now you fucking die on me? Could you not have at least written in your will to let me the fuck out of there, since you wouldn't have to look at my face or be embarrassed by my hearing or hate me for Mom's death anymore?" I rail against him as if he were standing in front me. "How could you hate me that much? I was just a kid, and I loved you. I loved you so much, and I needed my dad to love me and protect me. I just wanted you to take away the years of guilt and tears instead of causing them! For this, I hate you."

How can a daughter truly hate a father though?

I sob, the tears falling down my cheeks and dotting the floor. How ironic it is that the same tears that fell onto the floors in this house for so many years out of frustration and anger, are now tears of sorrow and sadness. I pause, giving myself time to hold back my remorse.

"I've been through so much over the last few months, Dad. It was the worst time of my life, even worse than anything you did to me, but it made me strong. I escaped from there and now, without you here, I can finally move on with the life I should have had."

I bend down, feeling stronger now, and pick up the piece of paper off the floor.

A single tear falls on the paper I'm holding in my hand, and I quickly wipe it off with the back of my other hand, as if my dad is going to yell at me over it. Old habits die hard. The wetness smears some of the writing on what looks like a receipt—a Deadwater Manor receipt.

My mouth drops open as I read it. It is payment in full for this month's hospital services, including psychiatric therapy, medications, room and board, and nursing care. I examine it closer and notice the receipt is made out to my brother.

I stagger backward and look up at the empty doorway.

He knew about it? He's been paying for it? He's facilitating everything?

Tears flow freely now as I read through a pile of hospital receipts on the desk. Two months of receipts are addressed to my dad, and two months of receipts are addressed to Rick. He has been signing checks to Deadwater Manor to keep me imprisoned since my dad died. I can't even think straight right now.

"You coming, Jeannie weenie?" my brother asks from down the hall.

33

I don't answer. I can't. Wrapping my head around the fact that Rick knew where I was—much less helped to facilitate it—is unbelievable to me.

How could I have not known how little he really cared about me? All those years of protecting me from my dad meant nothing. I've got to think this through before I see him again.

Rick helped me get my driver's license months before my birthday without Dad knowing. Then Dad surprised me with a new car on my birthday. Rick was excited about it, and so was Dad, or so it seemed. Rick even said he never saw Dad so excited.

Why the change? Did Dad already know about the driver's license? Did he also know I was planning on leaving the next morning? Was Rick his confidant?

"Hey, you want lunch, or what?" Rick asks from the doorway.

"No, I've lost my appetite."

"Oh, come on. Look at you! You're a skeleton, for Christ's sake. It'll be ready in two minutes, so have a bite and then we can talk about all of your harrowing experiences. I'm sure you've got some doozies. Come on, let's eat. I'm starving," Rick says and prods me to walk with him.

"I don't think so, Rick. Why don't you tell me how you explain *this*?" I hand him one of the Deadwater Manor receipts with his signature.

Rick hesitantly enters the room and takes the receipt from my hand. When he looks back up at me, his eyes are dark and dilated.

"What, Rick? Please explain this to me! I can't believe you would play a part in my hospitalization. I thought you didn't know where I was!" My voice quivers now.

"I—I don't know how to explain this, actually. I don't know if I really need to. I had to take over the finances since Dad died, so I signed whatever was in front of me."

"You didn't know what you were signing? Really?" I ask, glancing down at the second receipt that's made out to Deadwater Manor in his handwriting also. "Looks like Deadwater Manor is written in your handwriting on the cancelled check too."

Rick paces before stopping in front of me. "I don't know how to tell you this. I mean, I am your brother and I love you. You know that. I've always been there for you, even during Dad's tirades. Over the last few months before you left, well, you were scary. I was worried about you doing something stupid to yourself. The way you looked at Dad with such hate in your eyes made me think you were better off at the hospital. I mean, I really thought you wouldn't hesitate to kill him or yourself."

"What? You can't be serious! You really thought I'd do that?"

"You were really acting weird. I didn't know what to do. Plus with Mom's death, I just thought you were going to lose it. You know how much her death bothered you. I couldn't sleep at night over it, either."

"Yeah, I know, but I really wouldn't have done anything. I just wanted to escape this place."

"I figured Deadwater was the best place for you with all that going on inside your head. Once you were cured, then you could come home."

I look down at the floor.

What can I say? He was afraid of me? I must have been in a pretty bad state. I did think of hurting Dad sometimes.

"Come on," he urges. "Let me feed you. Then we'll talk about where to go from here."

"What do you mean? I'm moving back in my room, right?"

"We'll discuss it," Rick says, patting me on the shoulder.

I follow Rick to the kitchen and sit on a bar stool at the center island covered with granite countertop. He brings over a plate of spaghetti and sprinkles Parmesan cheese on top of it. Some of the sprinkles end up on the black and white speckles. "I made one of your old favorites."

"Kind of big for lunch, don't you think?"

"No, I don't think so. Remember how we used to always eat spaghetti behind Dad's back? Maybe your memory is not so good anymore. It's okay though."

This is confusing. I don't remember ever having spaghetti or any other meal with Rick at lunchtime. Dad only allowed sandwiches. He didn't want us to use electricity.

Did the electric shock or hydrotherapy really get to me? Have I lost brain cells?

"Come on, just eat up and everything will be fine. You'll see," Rick prods.

I twist the spaghetti around my fork.

Finally, I reply, "Uh, I don't think so. I don't remember ever eating spaghetti for lunch with you."

"Well, you did lots of times. What, were you fried when you were in there or what?"

"Yes, I was, in fact. It was pretty upsetting, actually. I couldn't remember anything for hours afterwards."

Rick looks proud of himself, as if to say he told me so.

Eyeing him with a growing distrust, I continue. "That was a long time ago, though, and it was only short-term memory loss. I wouldn't forget a childhood memory. Why do you really want me to eat this?"

"Wow, sorry," he says, throwing up his hands. "I'm just trying to make you feel at home."

"What's wrong with you? You seem distant. Are you having a hard time with Dad's death? You're not feeling suicidal now, are you? I mean, I know a really good mental hospital that could help you."

"Funny, Jeannie. Listen, you know you needed to go there. You wouldn't admit to yourself or anyone else that you were driving when Mom died. You even lied to the police. I can't believe you lied to them—and me for that matter. Who could blame Dad for hating you so much? He loved her."

"I blocked it out and didn't remember until a few weeks ago. It was so traumatic. I can remember her face in the water."

"See, the place was good for you."

He can't be serious! What the fuck is he saying?

"No, it wasn't. You don't know what you're talking about." I continue to twist the spaghetti around my fork, teasing him. No way am I eating this stuff, but I do wish I knew why he's pushing me. "So, is my room any different?"

"No, it's the same."

"Maybe I'll just go upstairs and take a nap then."

"I don't know about that," Rick says, looking at his feet, fidgeting. I know the signs. He's avoiding something.

"Why not?"

"I'm not used to living with anyone anymore."

"Well, you can't just kick me out, right? By the way, do you have control of all of Dad's money now?"

"Yeah, but it's a burden more than anything else. All the bills, maintenance of the place, insurance—"

You lying fucker! Burden, my ass!

"Oh, yeah, I'm sure," I reply, exaggeratedly. "Terrible to have millions. What about my share?"

Rick sighs. "You going to eat that or what?"

"I'll eat it if you answer my question."

"What, you think I owe you something now? You think you have a right to anything of his? I'm the one that stood by him. You wished him dead."

"I wished he would stop abusing me," I correct him. "Again, where's my share?"

"He didn't leave you anything, okay? Are you happy now? You can hate him even more."

"Why don't you let me see his will, if that's the case? Why pay the hospital bills to keep me away?" I ask, trying to read his expressions. "You're lying."

"Fuck you. I'm not. You killed Mom and you wanted him dead. That's the short of it. What kind of a child does such a thing?" Rick moves around the island, looking at me in disgust. "I hate you. I've hated you since the night you killed Mom. I wish Dad were here to tell you this too. You were stupid that night and a coward for not admitting it. All these years, I've waited to get rid of you. I was happy when you were finally gone. You got what you deserved, and I'll be damned if I'll let it end."

It feels like I've just been punched in the chest. Of all people, I would have never expected this from Rick.

My breathing grows rapid.

Stay in control, Jeannie.

"I did no such thing! It was an accident with Mom, and I only wanted Dad to love me. I thought you understood that."

"Oh yeah, that's what you say now. How convenient that you suddenly remember drowning Mom. I'll never forgive you for that."

I jump up and push the stool away from me. "How dare you say that! I cherished Mom and would have never wanted anything bad to happen to her. It was an accident. She just wanted to teach me how to drive."

"Without a license?"

"Yes, without a license. I asked her, but she said it'd be okay. I was just a kid, Rick, and you know it!"

Rick smirks. "You want to kill me now, too? I'm feeling very threatened by you at this moment, as a matter of fact."

"What are you doing?"

"Being truthful."

"Truthful?" I ask, backing away from him. "You don't know what that means anymore. By the way, I'm not eating your drugged spaghetti."

"You can't be serious. I haven't drugged anything. You really are crazy."

I glance up at him to see if he's kidding.

"I guess you really did mean that all the times you said it before. I thought you were joking."

"I was, but I'm not now. Jeannie, you can't stay here, and I really think the best place for you is Deadwater. It made you come to your senses about Mom, or at least admit that you were in the car with her. It's a step in the right direction. Doctor Wiggins has worked wonders with you, but I think you still need him. It takes a while for these things to be resolved. If you go back, I bet it won't be long before you're out again."

"I'm not going back, Rick. You don't know what you're talking about. You're right about one thing, though. I won't be staying with you."

"Oh, I know exactly what I'm talking about. I saw the lap of luxury you bathed in. How relaxed you were." Rick grins when he sees that I realize what he's talking about.

In the picture it was *his* arm, not my dad's.

"You bastard!" I give him one last glare and head for the hallway that will take me to the front door and out to my freedom, just like so many months ago. This time, I'm not trying to escape my dad. I'm trying to escape the one person I thought I could always trust. Now a person like that doesn't exist anymore—anywhere.

"Yeah, run. Go ahead. We'll do the world a favor once you're captured again and sterilized."

I turn around to meet his gaze. How could he have fooled me all these years? Dad blamed me for Mom's death, and he did too. "So, why?"

"Why? Huh? Why? That's all we heard from you, Jeannie. Why would you think that we'd want a mentally ill mother to have a mentally ill child? The risk was too high, and we have a family name to uphold, you know."

"I am not mentally ill and having me put away without my consent is against the law unless it's court ordered."

Rick leans over the counter with dark eyes. "I don't really care. With you gone at some insane asylum, it's like I don't have a sister to worry about. If you're sterilized, I won't have to worry about that coming back to haunt me with some illegitimate children either."

Tears flood my eyes as all of this registers.

My brother hates me because I accidently killed our mom.

I don't want him to see me cry, so I quickly turn around and bolt for the hallway. I have to get away from him.

He comes after me, but before I get to the hallway, a dog cage flies into the kitchen and slams against a bar stool, knocking it over. Leather straps with buckles dangle back and forth inside of it from the force. My heart rate increases and breathing becomes labored.

No. He can't put me in this!

I turn back to look at Rick, but he looks as shocked as I do. What an actor. I shake my head at him and begin calculating how I'm going to escape this situation. The kitchen windows are too small, and there's no back door. I'd have to get by the cage to the side door in the den.

What am I going to do? I can't go back to the Manor. I can't!

Before I have a chance to figure it out, Christian enters the room. He's wearing his police uniform and decked out in all the gear. His shoulders are back, his posture is straight, and there's no sign of shock therapy.

"There is no way in hell I'm letting you take Jeannie anywhere. I think we'll be escorting *you* out of here instead, right Jeannie?"

Still stunned, I mechanically answer, "Right."

"So, Mister Kynde, would you like to enter the cage of your own accord, or would you like some assistance?" Christian's face is totally serious.

"What?" Rick asks, looking appalled. "I'll do no such thing!"

"What's wrong? Are you worried about what your neighbors will think? Did you know that Jeannie was transported in a contraption similar to this almost every day?"

Rick looks at me, questioningly.

"You didn't know? Well, I can confirm that, because I was there and had joy rides in this also. It's not fun, feeling like you're less than a dog, being totally controlled. It is demoralizing." Christian opens the cage door. "I'm afraid, Mister Kynde, that I must insist that you enter the cage at once, or I will make you. It's your choice, and I'll give you exactly ten seconds to decide." Christian glances at his watch to keep time.

Rick stumbles through his words and looks at the same windows I was looking at about a minute ago. Guess he's about to know how I felt at the Manor.

Good.

Rick backs up behind the bar, but Christian doesn't hesitate to move quickly forward and restrain him. Rick's arms are forced behind his back and he's moved to the side of the cage.

"Oh, you don't want to be locked in a cage like Jeannie, do you? Well, let me read you your rights, and you can tell it to a judge. Only Jeannie and I will be there to tell them all the gory details of your inexcusable behavior toward your sister. You're an ass, just like your dad."

Rick struggles with the handcuffs, looking like he wants to fight Christian. Christian smirks and says, "You wish you could have a chance at me, don't you? Well, too bad, you asshole. It's about time you felt like the caged animal your sister's been for the past few months. I can't really put you in the cage, but I can make sure you see bars from the inside of a jail cell."

Rick redirects his glare toward me and says, "Jeannie, tell this imbecile to let me go, or I'll make sure you never see the light of day again."

Christian tightens his grip on Rick and warns, "It'll be a cold day in hell before I let you anywhere near Jeannie again. You're a poor excuse for a brother. Can you imagine in that small little mind of yours how Jeannie felt knowing her own family locked her in the attic of a psych hospital, only to find out they wanted her sterilized? All this to punish her for an accident at the age of fourteen? Or was it so you didn't have to share the fortune? To think, Jeannie thought this was her dad's doing and was missing you all that time. Little did she know her cruel, selfish brother continued this disgraceful plot for months. You're a fucker, you know that?"

"Jeannie!" Rick yells as Christian begins reading him his rights and pushing him to the front door. A part of me wants to help him—sick, I know. I hold still, however, until Rick is out of the house, and then head for the front living room to watch him being led down the sidewalk. Several neighbors are gawking from their driveways, looking shocked, and whispering to each other. This is probably his worst nightmare since he's such a socialite now.

Once near the police car, Christian and his partner push him into the back and slam the door shut. The side of the car reads "Tarpon Springs Police Department."

Relief shoots through my body and for the first time, I let myself cry and mourn. I've been through hell and now my family has been completely torn apart. How could this happen?

Eventually, I walk out on the sidewalk to talk with Christian. He's filling out paperwork, but as soon as he sees me, he walks over.

"Hey, woman. Sorry, I haven't talked with you yet. I have to get him processed. Are you okay with all of this?"

"There's a whole lot of things I'm not okay with, but this is not one of them. It's sweet to see him loaded into the back of a police car and on his way to jail. Now, he'll get a little taste of what it's like to be behind bars, I hope. I know it'll be up to the judge. I wish you could have really dragged him out of there in that dog cage, though!"

"Me too. I couldn't resist when I saw the dog cage outside of the kitchen. I figured it'd distract him, so I could restrain him."

"He must have been thinking about getting a dog—or maybe he really was thinking about putting me in it if I ever showed up." I don't want to think about it. "How did you know Rick was in on this?"

"It was something Pete said after you left. He said he hadn't seen your dad in a long time but saw Rick driving his car around. It didn't take much to figure it out from there. Then I overheard the story about your mom while you were both arguing. You'll have an easy time in court, getting the rights back to your money and belongings. I'll make sure to give the good ol' Doctor Wiggins and his cronies a visit too." Christian pauses. "Oh wait! I almost forgot—"

He whistles at the driver of the squad car who turns on his vehicle and moves forward. With every foot, my Vug is revealed. Thelma never looked better.

I smile at Christian. "Are you kidding me? Is it running?"

"Yup, sure is! Just needed a new battery and a car wash. She shouldn't give you any problems now."

I rush to my car and pause to take in this moment. After all that time I spent staring at it, wishing I could slide behind the steering wheel, and regretting driving myself to that prison, here it is. I'm finally ready to drive away in my car with no fear.

"Thank you. You don't know what this means to me!" Tears well up in my eyes and I hug him.

"Oh, I think I do," Christian replies with a smile and keys in his hand. "I found these on the couch at Pete's. Take your freedom, Jeannie."

I grab the keys from him and slam the door shut as I turn on the car and roll down the windows, grinning the entire time. I can't believe this is actually happening. As I pull away, I wave at Christian and head down the road I thought I'd never see again. The breeze rushes into the car, feeling wonderful on my skin just like it always did in the evening at South Beach. How I've missed the taste of salt in the air.

Several miles down the road, my elated feeling is quickly interrupted with dread, when I pull up next to the pond that drowned my mother. I stop and stare at it. The glassy reflection reminds me of the night I saw her alive for the last time, and the night I ran away in my mind.

Only now, I think I've forgiven myself and come to terms with this.

I've healed.

I haven't felt this much in a long time. Maybe this is what normal feels like. I don't know. There's one thing I do know. I didn't drown her that night, circumstances did. I can't punish myself for the rest of my life over my reaction; my shock. I was a scared kid who escaped reality with a story. I was a kid who loved her mom so much, she couldn't bear to think of what truly happened.

"Forgive me, Mom. I hope I didn't disappoint you. I don't know what happened to me that night. I mean, I lied to everyone, even myself. I'm not sure if I'll ever be able to forgive myself for leaving you here that night, but I hope you know that I will always love you." Suddenly, a breeze kicks up from the pond and pushes against my cheek.

It is a peaceful breeze, and gentle.

"Goodbye, Mom."

I climb back into the car and slowly drive down Baillie's Bluff Road for what I know will be the last time. Cricket sounds echo in and out of the car as thousands of them chirp at me from between the bushes, seeming to cheer me on. The power plant stack looks as thin as a pencil, no longer beckoning me toward it as I drive away from years of abuse. The old oaks creak as they wave goodbye. The mangroves smile in the glow of an evening filled with all purples, yellows and blues with a scattering of sleek clouds in the sky that provided me hope for many years. Only tonight, I'm not watching the sunset from an attic window or a speeding bicycle. Tonight, I'm watching it from my rearview mirror, as I finally leave my true prison: home.

ABOUT THE AUTHOR

Sandie Will was born in Poughkeepsie, New York and moved to Florida during the 1970s. She earned her Bachelor of Science degree in Geology from the University of South Florida and Master of Science degree in Environmental Engineering Sciences from the University of Florida. She is currently working as a hydrogeologist and manager. During her career, she has written numerous technical reports and articles for various science-related publications. Now, she is adding fiction to her writing repertoire with her debut young adult psychological thriller, *The Caging at Deadwater Manor,* and has found writing fiction way more fun. Sandie currently lives in Tampa Bay, Florida, with her husband, Charlie. They have two grown sons, a lovable lab-mix and a pesky cat.

For more information on her books visit: www.sandiewill.com and www.deadwatermanor.com.

Made in the USA
Columbia, SC
08 September 2017